THE LITTLE SISTER

She wore gauntleted gloves and there was an automatic in her right hand. White bone grip. Looked like a .32.

"Turn around and put your hands behind you," she said through the towel. The voice muffled by the towel meant as little to me as the dark glasses. It was not the voice which had talked to me on the telephone. I didn't move.

"Don't ever think I'm fooling," she said. "I'll give you exactly three seconds to do what I say."

"Couldn't you make it a minute? I like looking at you."

She made a threatening gesture with the little gun. "Turn around," she snapped. "But fast."

"I like the sound of your voice too."

"All right," she said, in a tight dangerous tone. "If that's the way you want it, that's the way you want it."

"Don't forget you're a lady," I said.

THE
LITTLE SISTER

Raymond Chandler

BALLANTINE BOOKS • NEW YORK

Part of this book has appeared in *Cosmopolitan* magazine.

ISBN 0-345-32217-7

This edition published by arrangement with Houghton Mifflin Company

Manufactured in the United States of America

First Ballantine Books Edition: October 1971
Sixth Printing: November 1984

First Canadian Printing: October 1971

THE
LITTLE SISTER

1

THE PEBBLED GLASS DOOR PANEL is lettered in flaked black paint: *"Philip Marlowe . . . Investigations."* It is a reasonably shabby door at the end of a reasonably shabby corridor in the sort of building that was new about the year the all-tile bathroom became the basis of civilization. The door is locked, but next to it is another door with the same legend which is not locked. Come on in—there's nobody in here but me and a big bluebottle fly. But not if you're from Manhattan, Kansas.

It was one of those clear, bright summer mornings we get in the early spring in California before the high fog sets in. The rains are over. The hills are still green and in the valley across the Hollywood hills you can see snow on the high mountains. The fur stores are advertising their annual sales. The call houses that specialize in sixteen-year-old virgins are doing a land-office business. And in Beverly Hills the jacaranda trees are beginning to bloom.

I had been stalking the bluebottle fly for five minutes, waiting for him to sit down. He didn't want to sit down.

He just wanted to do wing-overs and sing the prologue to *Pagliacci*. I had the fly swatter poised in midair and I was all set. There was a patch of bright sunlight on the corner of the desk and I knew that sooner or later that was where he was going to light. But when he did, I didn't even see him at first. The buzzing stopped and there he was. And then the phone rang.

I reached for it inch by inch with a slow and patient left hand. I lifted the phone slowly and spoke into it softly: "Hold the line a moment, please."

I laid the phone down gently on the brown blotter. He was still there, shining and blue-green and full of sin. I took a deep breath and swung. What was left of him sailed halfway across the room and dropped to the carpet. I went over and picked him up by his good wing and dropped him into the wastebasket.

"Thanks for waiting," I said into the phone.

"Is this Mr. Marlowe, the detective?" It was a small, rather hurried, little-girlish voice. I said it was Mr. Marlowe, the detective. "How much do you charge for your services, Mr. Marlowe?"

"What was it you wanted done?"

The voice sharpened a little. "I can't very well tell you that over the phone. It's—it's very confidential. Before I'd waste time coming to your office I'd have to have some idea—"

"Forty bucks a day and expenses. Unless it's the kind of job that can be done for a flat fee."

"That's far too much," the little voice said. "Why, it might cost hundreds of dollars and I only get a small salary and—"

"Where are you now?"

"Why, I'm in a drugstore. It's right next to the building where your office is."

"You could have saved a nickel. The elevator's free."

"I—I beg your pardon?"

I said it all over again. "Come on up and let's have a look at you," I added. "If you're in my kind of trouble, I can give you a pretty good idea—"

"I have to know something about you," the small voice said very firmly. "This is a very delicate matter, very personal. I couldn't talk to just anybody."

"If it's that delicate," I said, "maybe you need a lady detective."

"Goodness, I didn't know there were any." Pause. "But I don't think a lady detective would do at all. You see, Orrin was living in a very tough neighborhood, Mr. Marlowe. At least I thought it was tough. The manager of the rooming house is a most unpleasant person. He smelled of liquor. Do you drink, Mr. Marlowe?"

"Well, now that you mention it—"

"I don't think I'd care to employ a detective that uses liquor in any form. I don't even approve of tobacco."

"Would it be all right if I peeled an orange?"

I caught the sharp intake of breath at the far end of the line. "You might at least talk like a gentleman," she said.

"Better try the University Club," I told her. "I heard they had a couple left over there, but I'm not sure they'll let you handle them." I hung up.

It was a step in the right direction, but it didn't go far enough. I ought to have locked the door and hid under the desk.

2

FIVE MINUTES LATER the buzzer sounded on the outer door of the half-office I use for a reception room. I heard the door close again. Then I didn't hear anything more. The door between me and there was half open. I listened and decided somebody had just looked in at the wrong office and left without entering. Then there was a small knocking on wood. Then the kind of cough you use for the same purpose. I got my feet off the desk, stood up and looked out. There she was. She didn't have to open her mouth for me to know who she was. And nobody ever looked less like Lady Macbeth. She was a small, neat, rather prissy-looking girl with primly smooth brown hair and rimless glasses. She was wearing a brown tailor-made and from a strap over her shoulder hung one of those awkward-looking square bags that make you think of a Sister of Mercy taking first aid to the wounded. On the smooth brown hair was a hat that had been taken from its mother too young. She had no make-up, no lipstick and no jewelry. The rimless glasses gave her that librarian's look.

4

"That's no way to talk to people over the telephone," she said sharply. "You ought to be ashamed of yourself."

"I'm just too proud to show it," I said. "Come on in." I held the door for her. Then I held the chair for her.

She sat down on about two inches of the edge. "If I talked like that to one of Dr. Zugsmith's patients," she said, "I'd lose my position. He's most particular how I speak to the patients—even the difficult ones."

"How is the old boy? I haven't seen him since that time I fell off the garage roof."

She looked surprised and quite serious. "Why surely you can't know Dr. Zugsmith." The tip of a rather anemic tongue came out between her lips and searched furtively for nothing.

"I know a Dr. George Zugsmith," I said, "in Santa Rosa."

"Oh no. This is Dr. Alfred Zugsmith, in Manhattan. Manhattan, Kansas, you know, not Manhattan, New York."

"Must be a different Dr. Zugsmith," I said. "And your name?"

"I'm not sure I'd care to tell you."

"Just window shopping, huh?"

"I suppose you could call it that. If I have to tell my family affairs to a total stranger, I at least have the right to decide whether he's the kind of person I could trust."

"Anybody ever tell you you're a cute little trick?"

The eyes behind the rimless cheaters flashed. "I should hope not."

I reached for a pipe and started to fill it. "Hope isn't exactly the word," I said. "Get rid of that hat and get yourself a pair of those slinky glasses with colored rims. You know, the ones that are all cockeyed and oriental—"

"Dr. Zugsmith wouldn't permit anything like that," she said quickly. Then, "Do you really think so?" she asked, and blushed ever so slightly.

I put a match to the pipe and puffed smoke across the desk. She winced back.

"If you hire me," I said, "I'm the guy you hire. Me. Just as I am. If you think you're going to find any lay readers in this business, you're crazy. I hung up on you, but you came up here all the same. So you need help. What's your name and trouble?"

She just stared at me.

"Look," I said. "You come from Manhattan, Kansas. The last time I memorized the *World Almanac* that was a little town not far from Topeka. Population around twelve thousand. You work for Dr. Alfred Zugsmith and you're looking for somebody named Orrin. Manhattan is a small town. It has to be. Only half a dozen places in Kansas are anything else. I already have enough information about you to find out your whole family history."

"But why should you want to?" she asked, troubled.

"Me?" I said. "I don't want to. I'm fed up with people telling me histories. I'm just sitting here because I don't have any place to go. I don't want to work. I don't want anything."

"You talk too much."

"Yes," I said, "I talk too much. Lonely men always talk too much. Either that or they don't talk at all. Shall we get down to business? You don't look like the type that goes to see private detectives, and especially private detectives you don't know."

"I know that," she said quietly. "And Orrin would be absolutely livid. Mother would be furious too. I just picked your name out of the phone book—"

"What principle?" I asked. "And with the eyes closed or open?"

She stared at me for a moment as if I were some kind of freak. "Seven and thirteen," she said quietly.

"How?"

"Marlowe has seven letters," she said, "and Philip Marlowe has thirteen. Seven together with thirteen—"

"What's *your* name?" I almost snarled.

"Orfamay Quest." She crinkled her eyes as if she could cry. She spelled the first name out for me, all one word. "I live with my mother," she went on, her voice getting rapid now as if my time is costing her. "My father died four years ago. He was a doctor. My brother Orrin was going to be a surgeon, too, but he changed into engineering after two years of medical. Then a year ago Orrin came out to work for the Cal-Western Aircraft Company in Bay City. He didn't have to. He had a good job in Wichita. I guess he just sort of wanted to come out here to California. Most everybody does."

"*Almost* everybody," I said. "If you're going to wear those rimless glasses, you might at least try to live up to them."

She giggled and drew a line along the desk with her fingertip, looking down. "Did you mean those slanting kind of glasses that make you look kind of oriental?"

"Uh-huh. Now about Orrin. We've got him to California, and we've got him to Bay City. What do we do with him?"

She thought a moment and frowned. Then she studied my face as if making up her mind. Then her words came with a burst: "It wasn't like Orrin not to write to us regularly. He only wrote twice to mother and three times to me in the last six months. And the last letter was several months ago. Mother and I got worried. So it was my vacation and I came out to see him. He'd never been away from Kansas before." She stopped. "Aren't you going to take any notes?" she asked.

I grunted.

"I thought detectives always wrote things down in little notebooks."

"I'll make the gags," I said. "You tell the story. You came out on your vacation. Then what?"

"I'd written to Orrin that I was coming but I didn't get any answer. Then I sent a wire to him from Salt Lake City but he didn't answer that either. So all I could do was go down where he lived. It's an awful long way. I went in a bus. It's in Bay City. No. 449 Idaho Street."

She stopped again, then repeated the address, and I still didn't write it down. I just sat there looking at her glasses and her smooth brown hair and the silly little hat and the fingernails with no color and her mouth with no lipstick and the tip of the little tongue that came and went between the pale lips.

"Maybe you don't know Bay City, Mr. Marlowe."

"Ha," I said. "All I know about Bay City is that every time I go there I have to buy a new head. You want me to finish your story for you?"

"Wha-a-at?" Her eyes opened so wide that the glasses made them look like something you see in the deep-sea fish tanks.

"He's moved," I said. "And you don't know where he's moved to. And you're afraid he's living a life of sin in a penthouse on top of the Regency Towers with something in a long mink coat and an interesting perfume."

"Well for goodness' sakes!"

"Or am I being coarse?" I asked.

"Please, Mr. Marlowe," she said at last, "I don't think anything of the sort about Orrin. And if Orrin heard you say that you'd be sorry. He can be awfully mean. But I know something has happened. It was just a cheap rooming house, and I didn't like the manager at all. A horrid kind of man. He said Orrin had moved away a couple of weeks before and he didn't know where to and he didn't care, and all he wanted was a good slug of gin. I don't know why Orrin would even live in a place like that."

"Did you say slug of gin?" I asked.

She blushed. "That's what the manager said. I'm just telling you."

"All right," I said. "Go on."

"Well, I called the place where he worked. The Cal-Western Company, you know. And they said he'd been laid off like a lot of others and that was all they knew. So then I went to the post office and asked if Orrin had put in a change of address to anywhere. And they said they couldn't give me any information. It was against the regulations. So I told them how it was and the man said, well if I was his sister he'd go look. So he went and looked and came back and said no. Orrin hadn't put in any change of address. So then I began to get a little frightened. He might have had an accident or something."

"Did it occur to you to ask the police about that?"

"I wouldn't dare ask the police. Orrin would never forgive me. He's difficult enough at the best of times. Our family—" She hesitated and there was something behind her eyes she tried not to have there. So she went on breathlessly: "Our family's not the kind of family—"

"Look," I said wearily, "I'm not talking about the guy lifting a wallet. I'm talking about him getting knocked down by a car and losing his memory or being too badly hurt to talk."

She gave me a level look which was not too admiring. "If it was anything like that, we'd know," she said. "Everybody has things in their pockets to tell who they are."

"Sometimes all they have left is the pockets."

"Are you trying to scare me, Mr. Marlowe?"

"If I am, I'm certainly getting nowhere fast. Just what do you think might have happened?"

She put her slim forefinger to her lips and touched it very carefully with the tip of that tongue. "I guess if I knew that I wouldn't have to come and see you. How much would you charge to find him?"

I didn't answer for a long moment, then I said: "You mean alone, without telling anybody?"

"Yes. I mean alone, without telling anybody."

"Uh-huh. Well that depends. I told you what my rates were."

She clasped her hands on the edge of the desk and squeezed them together hard. She had about the most meaningless set of gestures I had ever laid eyes on. "I thought you being a detective and all you could find him right away," she said. "I couldn't possibly afford more than twenty dollars. I've got to buy my meals here and my hotel and the train going back and you know the hotel is so terribly expensive and the food on the train—"

"Which one are you staying at?"

"I—I'd rather not tell you, if you don't mind."

"Why?"

"I'd just rather not. I'm terribly afraid of Orrin's temper. And, well I can always call you up, can't I?"

"Uh-huh. Just what is it you're scared of, besides Orrin's temper, Miss Quest?" I had let my pipe go out. I struck a match and held it to the bowl, watching her over it.

"Isn't pipe-smoking a very dirty habit?" she asked.

"Probably," I said. "But it would take more than twenty bucks to have me drop it. And don't try to side-step my questions."

"You can't talk to me like that," she flared up. "Pipe-smoking *is* a dirty habit. Mother never let father smoke in the house, even the last two years after he had his stroke. He used to sit with that empty pipe in his mouth sometimes. But she didn't like him to do that really. We owed a lot of money too and she said she couldn't afford to give him money for useless things like tobacco. The church needed it much more than he did."

"I'm beginning to get it," I said slowly. "Take a family like yours and somebody in it has to be the dark meat."

She stood up sharply and clasped the first-aid kit to her body. "I don't like you," she said. "I don't think I'm going to employ you. If you're insinuating that Orrin has done something wrong, well I can assure you that it's not Orrin who's the black sheep of our family."

I didn't move an eyelash. She swung around and marched to the door and put her hand on the knob and then she swung around again and marched back and suddenly began to cry. I reacted to that just the way a stuffed fish reacts to cut bait. She got out her little handkerchief and tickled the corners of her eyes.

"And now I suppose you'll call the p-police," she said with a catch in her voice. "And the Manhattan p-paper will hear all about it and they'll print something n-nasty about us."

"You don't suppose anything of the sort. Stop chipping at my emotions. Let's see a photo of him."

She put the handkerchief away in a hurry and dug something else out of her bag. She passed it across the desk. An envelope. Thin, but there could be a couple of snapshots in it. I didn't look inside.

"Describe him the way you see him," I said.

She concentrated. That gave her a chance to do something with her eyebrows. "He was twenty-eight years old last March. He has light brown hair, much lighter than mine, and lighter blue eyes, and he brushes his hair straight back. He's very tall, over six feet. But he only weighs about a hundred and forty pounds. He's sort of bony. He used to wear a little blond mustache but mother made him cut it off. She said—"

"Don't tell me. The minister needed it to stuff a cushion."

"You can't talk like that about my mother," she yelped, getting pale with rage.

"Oh stop being silly. There's a lot of things about you I don't know. But you can stop pretending to be an

Easter lily right now. Does Orrin have any distinguishing marks on him, like moles or scars, or a tattoo of the Twenty-Third Psalm on his chest? And don't bother to blush."

"Well you don't have to yell at me. Why don't you look at the photograph?"

"He probably has his clothes on. After all, you're his sister. You ought to know."

"No he hasn't," she said tightly. "He has a little scar on his left hand where he had a wen removed."

"What about his habits? What does he do for fun—besides not smoking or drinking or going out with girls?"

"Why—how did you know that?"

"Your mother told me."

She smiled. I was beginning to wonder if she had one in her. She had very white teeth and she didn't wave her gums. That was something. "Aren't you silly," she said. "He studies a lot and he has a very expensive camera he likes to snap people with when they don't know. Sometimes it makes them mad. But Orrin says people ought to see themselves as they really are."

"Let's hope it never happens to him," I said. "What kind of camera is it?"

"One of those little cameras with a very fine lens. You can take snaps in almost any kind of light. A Leica."

I opened the envelope and took out a couple of small prints, very clear. "These weren't taken with anything like that," I said.

"Oh no. Philip took those, Philip Anderson. A boy I was going with for a while." She paused and sighed. "And I guess that's really why I came here, Mr. Marlowe. Just because your name's Philip too."

I just said: "Uh-huh," but I felt touched in some vague sort of way. "What happened to Philip Anderson?"

"But it's about Orrin—"

"I know," I interrupted. "But what happened to Philip Anderson?"

"He's still there in Manhattan." She looked away. "Mother doesn't like him very much. I guess you know how it is."

"Yes," I said, "I know how it is. You can cry if you want to. I won't hold it against you. I'm just a big soft slob myself."

I looked at the two prints. One of them was looking down and was no good to me. The other was a fairly good shot of a tall angular bird with narrow-set eyes and a thin straight mouth and a pointed chin. He had the expression I expected to see. If you forgot to wipe the mud off your shoes, he was the boy who would tell you. I laid the photos aside and looked at Orfamay Quest, trying to find something in her face even remotely like his. I couldn't. Not the slightest trace of family resemblance, which of course meant absolutely nothing. It never has.

"All right," I said. "I'll go down there and take a look. But you ought to be able to guess what's happened. He's in a strange city. He's making good money for a while. More than he's ever made in his life, perhaps. He's meeting a kind of people he never met before. And it's not the kind of town—believe me it isn't, I know Bay City —that Manhattan, Kansas, is. So he just broke training and he doesn't want his family to know about it. He'll straighten out."

She just stared at me for a moment in silence, then she shook her head. "No. Orrin's not the type to do that, Mr. Marlowe."

"Anyone is," I said. "Especially a fellow like Orrin. The small-town sanctimonious type of guy who's lived his entire life with his mother on his neck and the minister holding his hand. Out here he's lonely. He's got dough. He'd like to buy a little sweetness and light, and not the kind that comes through the east window of a church. Not that I have anything against that. I mean he already had enough of that, didn't he?"

She nodded her head silently.

"So he starts to play," I went on, "and he doesn't know how to play. That takes experience too. He's got himself all jammed up with some floozy and a bottle of hootch and what he's done looks to him as if he'd stolen the bishop's pants. After all, the guy's going on twenty-nine years old and if he wants to roll in the gutter that's his business. He'll find somebody to blame it on after a while."

"I hate to believe you, Mr. Marlowe," she said slowly. "I'd hate for mother—"

"Something was said about twenty dollars," I cut in.

She looked shocked. "Do I have to pay you now?"

"What would be the custom in Manhattan, Kansas?"

"We don't have any private detectives in Manhattan. Just the regular police. That is, I don't think we do."

She probed in the inside of her tool kit again and dragged out a red change purse and from that she took a number of bills, all neatly folded and separate. Three fives and five ones. There didn't seem to be much left. She kind of held the purse so I could see how empty it was. Then she straightened the bills out on the desk and put one on top of the other and pushed them across. Very slowly, very sadly, as if she was drowning a favorite kitten.

"I'll give you a receipt," I said.

"I don't need a receipt, Mr. Marlowe."

"I do. You won't give me your name and address, so I want something with your name on it."

"What for?"

"To show I'm representing you." I got the receipt book out and made the receipt and held the book for her to sign the duplicate. She didn't want to. After a moment reluctantly she took the hard pencil and wrote "Orfamay

Quest" in a neat secretary's writing across the face of the duplicate.

"Still no address?" I asked.

"I'd rather not."

"Call me any time then. My home number is in the phone book, too. Bristol Apartments, Apartment 428."

"I shan't be very likely to visit you," she said coldly.

"I haven't asked you yet," I said. "Call me around four if you like. I might have something. And then again I might not."

She stood up. "I hope mother won't think I've done wrong," she said, picking at her lip now with the pale fingernail. "Coming here, I mean."

"Just don't tell me any more of the things your mother won't like," I said. "Just leave that part out."

"Well really!"

"And stop saying 'well really.' "

"I think you are a very offensive person," she said.

"No, you don't. You think I'm cute. And I think you're a fascinating little liar. You don't think I'm doing this for any twenty bucks, do you?"

She gave me a level, suddenly cool stare. "Then why?" Then when I didn't answer she added, "Because spring is in the air?"

I still didn't answer. She blushed a little. Then she giggled.

I didn't have the heart to tell her I was just plain bored with doing nothing. Perhaps it *was* the spring too. And something in her eyes that was much older than Manhattan, Kansas.

"I think you're very nice—really," she said softly. Then she turned quickly and almost ran out of the office. Her steps along the corridor outside made tiny, sharp pecky sounds, kind of like mother drumming on the edge of the dinner table when father tried to promote himself a second piece of pie. And him with no money any more.

No nothing. Just sitting in a rocker on the front porch back there in Manhattan, Kansas, with his empty pipe in his mouth. Rocking on the front porch, slow and easy, because when you've had a stroke you have to take it slow and easy. And wait for the next one. And the empty pipe in his mouth. No tobacco. Nothing to do but wait.

I put Orfamay Quest's twenty hard-earned dollars in an envelope and wrote her name on it and dropped it in the desk drawer. I didn't like the idea of running around loose with that much currency on me.

3

You could know Bay City a long time without knowing Idaho Street. And you could know a lot of Idaho Street without knowing Number 449. The block in front if it had a broken paving that had almost gone back to dirt. The warped fence of a lumberyard bordered the cracked sidewalk on the opposite side of the street. Halfway up the block the rusted rails of a spur track turned in to a pair of high, chained wooden gates that seem not to have been opened for twenty years. Little boys with chalk had been writing and drawing pictures on the gates and all along the fence.

Number 449 had a shallow, paintless front porch on which five wood and cane rockers loafed dissolutely, held together with wire and the moisture of the beach air. The green shades over the lower windows of the house were two thirds down and full of cracks. Beside the front door there was a large printed sign "No Vacancies." That had been there a long time too. It had got faded and fly-specked. The door opened on a long hall from which stairs went up a third of the way back. To the right there was a

17

narrow shelf with a chained, indelible pencil hanging beside it. There was a push button and a yellow and black sign above which read "Manager," and was held up by three thumbtacks no two of which matched. There was a pay phone on the opposite wall.

I pushed the bell. It rang somewhere near by but nothing happened. I rang it again. The same nothing happened. I prowled along to a door with a black and white metal sign on it—"Manager." I knocked on that. Then I kicked it. Nobody seemed to mind my kicking it.

I went back out of the house and down around the side where a narrow concrete walk led to the service entrance. It looked as if it was in the right place to belong to the manager's apartment. The rest of the house would be just rooms. There was a dirty garbage pail on the small porch and a wooden box full of liquor bottles. Behind the screen the back door of the house was open. It was gloomy inside. I put my face against the screen and peered in. Through the open inner door beyond the service porch I could see a straight chair with a man's coat hanging over it and in the chair a man in shirtsleeves with his hat on. He was a small man. I couldn't see what he was doing, but he seemed to be sitting at the end of the built-in breakfast table in the breakfast nook.

I banged on the screen door. The man paid no attention. I banged again, harder. This time he tilted his chair back and showed me a small pale face with a cigarette in it. "Whatcha want?" he barked.

"Manager."

"Not in, bub."

"Who are you?"

"What's it to you?"

"I want a room."

"No vacancies, bub. Can't you read large print?"

"I happen to have different information," I said.

"Yeah?" He shook ash from his cigarette by flicking

it with a nail without removing it from his small sad mouth. "Go fry your head in it."

He tilted his chair forward again and went on doing whatever it was he was doing.

I made noise getting down off the porch and none whatever coming back up on it. I felt the screen door carefully. It was hooked. With the open blade of a penknife I lifted the hook and eased it out of the eye. It made a small tinkle but louder tinkling sounds were being made beyond, in the kitchen.

I stepped into the house, crossed the service porch, went through the door into the kitchen. The little man was too busy to notice me. The kitchen had a three-burner gas stove, a few shelves of greasy dishes, a chipped icebox and the breakfast nook. The table in the breakfast nook was covered with money. Most of it was paper, but there was silver also, in all sizes up to dollars. The little man was counting and stacking it and making entries in a small book. He wetted his pencil without bothering the cigarette that lived in his face.

There must have been several hundred dollars on that table.

"Rent day?" I asked genially.

The small man turned very suddenly. For a moment he smiled and said nothing. It was the smile of a man whose mind is not smiling. He removed the stub of cigarette from his mouth, dropped it on the floor and stepped on it. He reached a fresh one out of his shirt and put it in the same hole in his face and started fumbling for a match.

"You came in nice," he said pleasantly.

Finding no match, he turned casually in his chair and reached into a pocket of his coat. Something heavy knocked against the wood of the chair. I got hold of his wrist before the heavy thing came out of the pocket. He threw his weight backwards and the pocket of the coat started to lift towards me. I yanked the chair out from under him.

He sat down hard on the floor and knocked his head against the end of the breakfast table. That didn't keep him from trying to kick me in the groin. I stepped back with his coat and took a .38 out of the pocket he had been playing with.

"Don't sit on the floor just to be chummy," I said.

He got up slowly, pretending to be groggier than he was. His hand fumbled at the back of his collar and light winked on metal as his arm swept toward me. He was a game little rooster.

I sideswiped his jaw with his own gun and he sat down on the floor again. I stepped on the hand that held the knife. His face twisted with pain but he didn't make a sound. So I kicked the knife into a corner. It was a long thin knife and it looked very sharp.

"You ought to be ashamed of yourself," I said. "Pulling guns and knives on people that are just looking for a place to live. Even for these times that's out of line."

He held his hurt hand between his knees and squeezed it and began to whistle through his teeth. The slap on the jaw didn't seem to have hurt him. "O.K.," he said, "O.K. I ain't supposed to be perfect. Take the dough and beat it. But don't ever think we won't catch up with you."

I looked at the collection of small bills and medium bills and silver on the table. "You must meet a lot of sales resistance, the weapons you carry," I told him. I walked across to the inner door and tried it. It was not locked. I turned back.

"I'll leave your gun in the mailbox," I said. "Next time ask to see the buzzer."

He was still whistling gently between his teeth and holding his hand. He gave me a narrow, thoughtful eye, then shoveled the money into a shabby briefcase and slipped its catch. He took his hat off, straightened it around, put it back jauntily on the back of his head and gave me a quiet efficient smile.

"Never mind about the heater," he said. "The town's full of old iron. But you could leave the skiv with Clausen. I've done quite a bit of work on it to get it in shape."

"And with it?" I said.

"Could be." He flicked a finger at me airily. "Maybe we meet again some day soon. When I got a friend with me."

"Tell him to wear a clean shirt," I said. "And lend you one."

"My, my," the little man said chidingly. "How tough we get how quick once we get that badge pinned on."

He went softly past me and down the wooden steps from the back porch. His footsteps tapped to the street and faded. They sounded very much like Orfamay's heels clicking along the corridor in my office building. And for some reason I had that empty feeling of having miscounted the trumps. No reason for it at all. Maybe it was the steely quality about the little man. No whimper, no bluster, just the smile, the whistling between the teeth, the light voice and the unforgetting eyes.

I went over and picked up the knife. The blade was long and round and thin, like a rattailed file that has been ground smooth. The handle and guard were lightweight plastic and seemed all one piece. I held the knife by the handle and gave it a quick flip at the table. The blade came loose and quivered in the wood.

I took a deep breath and slid the handle down over the end again and worked the blade loose from the table. A curious knife, with design and purpose in it, and neither of them agreeable.

I opened the door beyond the kitchen and went through it with the gun and knife in one hand.

It was a wall-bed living room, with the wall bed down and rumpled. There was an overstuffed chair with a hole burnt in the arm. A high oak desk with tilted doors like old-fashioned cellar doors stood against the wall by the front window. Near this there was a studio couch and on the studio couch lay a man. His feet hung over the end of the couch in knobby gray socks. His head had missed the pillow by two feet. It was nothing much to miss from the color of the slip on it. The upper part of him was contained in a colorless shirt and a threadbare gray coat-sweater. His mouth was open and his face was shining with sweat and he breathed like an old Ford with a leaky head gasket. On a table beside him was a plate full of cigarette stubs, some of which had a homemade look. On the floor a near full gin bottle and a cup that seemed to have contained coffee but not at all recently. The room was full mostly of gin and bad air, but there was also a reminiscence of marijuana smoke.

I opened a window and leaned my forehead against the screen to get a little cleaner air into my lungs and looked out into the street. Two kids were wheeling bicycles along the lumberyard fence, stopping from time to time to study the examples of rest-room art on the boarding. Nothing else moved in the neighborhood. Not even a dog. Down at the corner was dust in the air as though a car had passed that way.

I went over to the desk. Inside it was the house register, so I leafed back until I came to the name "Orrin P. Quest," written in a sharp meticulous handwriting, and the number 214 added in pencil by another hand that was by no means sharp or meticulous. I followed on through to the end of the register but found no new registration for Room 214. A party named G. W. Hicks had Room 215. I shut the register in the desk and crossed to the couch. The man stopped his snoring and bubbling and threw his right arm across his body as if he thought he was making a speech. I leaned down and gripped his nose tight between my first and second fingers and stuffed a handful of his sweater into his mouth. He stopped snoring and jerked his eyes open. They were glazed and bloodshot. He struggled against my hand. When I was sure he was fully awake I let go of him, picked the bottle full of gin off the floor and poured some into a glass that lay on its side near the bottle. I showed the glass to the man.

His hand came out to it with the beautiful anxiety of a mother welcoming a lost child.

I moved it out of his reach and said: "You the manager?"

He licked his lips stickily and said: "Gr-r-r-r."

He made a grab for the glass. I put it on the table in front of him. He grasped it carefully in both hands and poured the gin into his face. Then he laughed heartily and threw the glass at me. I managed to catch it and up-end it on the table again. The man looked me over with a studied but unsuccessful attempt at sternness.

"What gives?" he croaked in an annoyed tone.

"Manager?"

He nodded and almost fell off the couch. "Must be I'm drunky," he said. "Kind of a bit of a little bit drunky."

"You're not bad," I said. "You're still breathing."

He put his feet on the ground and pushed himself upright. He cackled with sudden amusement, took three uneven steps, went down on his hands and knees and tried to bite the leg of a chair.

I pulled him up on his feet again, set him down in the overstuffed chair with the burned arm and poured him another slug of his medicine. He drank it, shuddered violently and all at once his eyes seemed to get sane and cunning. Drunks of his type have a certain balanced moment of reality. You never know when it will come or how long it will last.

"Who the hell are you?" he growled.

"I'm looking for a man named Orrin P. Quest."

"Huh?"

I said it again. He smeared his face with his hands and said tersely: "Moved away."

"Moved away when?"

He waved his hand, almost fell out of his chair and waved it again the other way to restore his balance. "Gimme a drink," he said.

I poured another slug of the gin and held it out of his reach.

"Gimme," the man said urgently. "I'm not happy."

"All I want is the present address of Orrin P. Quest."

"Just think of that," he said wittily and made a loose pass at the glass I was holding.

I put the glass down on the floor and got one of my business cards out for him. "This might help you to concentrate," I told him.

He peered at the card closely, sneered, bent it in half and bent it again. He held it on the flat of his hand, spit on it, and tossed it over his shoulder.

I handed him the glass of gin. He drank it to my health, nodded solemnly, and threw the glass over his shoulder too. It rolled along the floor and thumped the baseboard. The man stood up with surprising ease, jerked a thumb towards the ceiling, doubled the fingers of his hand under it and made a sharp noise with his tongue and teeth.

"Beat it," he said. "I got friends." He looked at the telephone on the wall and back at me with cunning. "A couple of boys to take care of you," he sneered. I said nothing. "Don't believe me, huh?" he snarled, suddenly angry. I shook my head.

He started for the telephone, clawed the receiver off the hook, and dialed the five digits of a number. I watched him. One-three-five-seven-two.

That took all he had for the time being. He let the receiver fall and bang against the wall and he sat down on the floor beside it. He put it to his ear and growled at the wall: "Lemme talk to the Doc." I listened silently.

"Vince! The Doc!" he shouted angrily. He shook the receiver and threw it away from him. He put his hands down on the floor and started to crawl in a circle. When he saw me he looked surprised and annoyed. He got shakily to his feet again and held his hand out. "Gimme a drink."

I retrieved the fallen glass and milked the gin bottle into it. He accepted it with the dignity of an intoxicated dowager, drank it down with an airy flourish, walked calmly over to the couch and lay down, putting the glass under his head for a pillow. He went to sleep instantly.

I put the telephone receiver back on its hook, glanced out in the kitchen again, felt the man on the couch over and dug some keys out of his pocket. One of them was a passkey. The door to the hallway had a spring lock and I fixed it so that I could come in again and started up the stairs. I paused on the way to write "Doc—Vince, 13572" on an envelope. Maybe it was a clue.

The house was quite silent as I went on up.

4

THE MANAGER'S much filed passkey turned the lock of Room 214 without noise. I pushed the door open. The room was not empty. A chunky, strongly built man was bending over a suitcase on the bed, with his back to the door. Shirts and socks and underwear were laid out on the bed cover, and he was packing them leisurely and carefully, whistling between his teeth in a low monotone.

He stiffened as the door hinge creaked. His hand moved fast for the pillow on the bed.

"I beg your pardon," I said. "The manager told me this room was vacant."

He was as bald as a grapefruit. He wore dark gray flannel slacks and transparent plastic suspenders over a blue shirt. His hands came up from the pillow, went to his head, and down again. He turned and he had hair.

It looked as natural as hair ever looked, smooth, brown, not parted. He glared at me from under it.

"You can always try knocking," he said.

He had a thick voice and a broad careful face that had been around.

"Why would I? If the manager said the room was empty?"

He nodded, satisfied. The glare went out of his eyes.

I came further into the room without invitation. An open love-pulp magazine lay face down on the bed near the suitcase. A cigar smoked in a green glass ash tray. The room was careful and orderly, and, for that house, clean.

"He must have thought you had already moved out," I said, trying to look like a well-meaning party with some talent for the truth.

"Have it in half an hour," the man said.

"O.K. if I look around?"

He smiled mirthlessly. "Ain't been in town long, have you?"

"Why?"

"New around here, ain't you?"

"Why?"

"Like the house and the neighborhood?"

"Not much," I said. "The room looks all right."

He grinned, showing a porcelain jacket crown that was too white for his other teeth. "How long you been looking?"

"Just started," I said. "Why all the questions?"

"You make me laugh," the man said, not laughing. "You don't look at rooms in this town. You grab them sight unseen. This burg's so jam-packed even now that I could get ten bucks just for telling there's a vacancy here."

"That's too bad," I said. "A man named Orrin P. Quest told me about the room. So there's one sawbuck you don't get to spend."

"That so?" Not a flicker of an eye. Not a movement of a muscle. I might as well have been talking to a turtle.

"Don't get tough with me," the man said. "I'm a bad man to get tough with."

He picked his cigar out of the green glass ash tray and blew a little smoke. Through it he gave me the cold gray eye. I got a cigarette out and scratched my chin with it.

"What happens to people that get tough with you?" I asked him. "You make them hold your toupee?"

"You lay off my toupee," he said savagely.

"So sorry," I said.

"There's a 'No Vacancy' sign on the house," the man said. "So what makes you come here and find one?"

"You didn't catch the name," I said. "Orrin P. Quest." I spelled it for him. Even that didn't make him happy. There was a dead-air pause.

He turned abruptly and put a pile of handkerchiefs into his suitcase. I moved a little closer to him. When he turned back there was what might have been a watchful look on his face. But it had been a watchful face to start with.

"Friend of yours?" he asked casually.

"We grew up together," I said.

"Quiet sort of guy," the man said easily. "I used to pass the time of day with him. Works for Cal-Western, don't he?"

"He did," I said.

"Oh. He quit?"

"Let out."

We went on staring at each other. It didn't get either of us anywhere. We both had done too much of it in our lives to expect miracles.

The man put the cigar back in his face and sat down on the side of the bed beside the open suitcase. Glancing into it I saw the square butt of an automatic peeping out from under a pair of badly folded shorts.

"This Quest party's been out of here ten days," the man said thoughtfully. "So he still thinks the room is vacant, huh?"

"According to the register it *is* vacant," I said.

He made a contemptuous noise. "That rummy down-stairs probably ain't looked at the register in a month. Say—wait a minute." His eyes sharpened and his hand wandered idly over the open suitcase and gave an idle pat to something that was close to the gun. When the hand moved away, the gun was no longer visible.

"I've been kind of dreamy all morning or I'd have wised up," he said. "You're a dick."

"All right. Say I'm a dick."

"What's the beef?"

"No beef at all. I just wondered why you had the room."

"I moved from 215 across the hall. This here is a better room. That's all. Simple. Satisfied?"

"Perfectly," I said, watching the hand that could be near the gun if it wanted to.

"What kind of dick? City? Let's see the buzzer."

I didn't say anything.

"I don't believe you got no buzzer."

"If I showed it to you, you're the type of guy would say it was counterfeit. So you're Hicks."

He looked surprised.

"George W. Hicks," I said. "It's in the register. Room 215. You just got through telling me you moved from 215." I glanced around the room. "If you had a black-board here, I'd write it out for you."

"Strictly speaking, we don't have to get into no snarl-ing match," he said. "Sure I'm Hicks. Pleased to meetcha. What's yours?"

He held his hand out. I shook hands with him, but not as if I had been longing for the moment to arrive.

"My name's Marlowe," I said. "Philip Marlowe."

"You know something," Hicks said politely, "you're a Goddamn liar."

I laughed in his face.

"You ain't getting no place with that breezy manner, bub. What's your connection?"

I got my wallet out and handed him one of my business cards. He read it thoughtfully and tapped the edge against his porcelain crown.

"He coulda went somewhere without telling me," he mused.

"Your grammar," I said, "is almost as loose as your toupee."

"You lay off my toupee, if you know what's good for you," he shouted.

"I wasn't going to eat it," I said. "I'm not that hungry."

He took a step towards me, and dropped his right shoulder. A scowl of fury dropped his lip almost as far.

"Don't hit me. I'm insured," I told him.

"Oh hell. Just another screwball." He shrugged and put his lip back up on his face. "What's the lay?"

"I have to find this Orrin P. Quest," I said.

"Why?"

I didn't answer that.

After a moment he said: "O.K. I'm a careful guy myself. That's why I'm movin' out."

"Maybe you don't like the reefer smoke."

"That," he said emptily, "and other things. That's why Quest left. Respectable type. Like me. I think a couple of hard boys threw a scare into him."

"I see," I said. "That would be why he left no forwarding address. And why did they throw a scare into him?"

"You just mentioned reefer smoke, didn't you? Wouldn't he be the type to go to headquarters about that?"

"In Bay City?" I asked. "Why would he bother? Well, thanks a lot, Mr. Hicks. Going far?"

"Not far," he said. "No. Not very far. Just far enough."

"What's your racket?" I asked him.

"Racket?" He looked hurt.

"Sure. What do you shake them for? How do you make your dibs?"

"You got me wrong, brother. I'm a retired optometrist."

"That why you have the .45 gun in there?" I pointed to the suitcase.

"Nothing to get cute about," he said sourly. "It's been in the family for years." He looked down at the card again. "Private investigator, huh?" he said thoughtfully. "What kind of work do you do mostly?"

"Anything that's reasonably honest," I said.

He nodded. "Reasonably is a word you could stretch. So is honest."

I gave him a shady leer. "You're so right," I agreed. "Let's get together some quiet afternoon and stretch them." I reached out and slipped the card from between his fingers and dropped it into my pocket. "Thanks for the time," I said.

I went out and closed the door, then stood against it listening. I don't know what I expected to hear. Whatever it was I didn't hear it. I had a feeling he was standing exactly where I had left him and looking at the spot where I had made my exit. I made noise going along the hall and stood at the head of the stairs.

A car drove away from in front of the house. Somewhere a door closed. I went quietly back to Room 215 and used the passkey to enter. I closed and locked its door silently, and waited just inside.

5

NOT MORE THAN two minutes passed before Mr. George W. Hicks was on his way. He came out so quietly that I wouldn't have heard him if I hadn't been listening for precisely that kind of movement. I heard the slight metallic sound of the doorknob turning. Then slow steps. Then very gently the door was closed. The steps moved off. The faint distant creak of the stairs. Then nothing. I waited for the sound of the front door. It didn't come. I opened the door of 215 and moved along the hall to the stairhead again. Below there was the careful sound of a door being tried. I looked down to see Hicks going into the manager's apartment. The door closed behind him. I waited for the sound of voices. No voices.

I shrugged and went back to 215.

The room showed signs of occupancy. There was a small radio on a night table, an unmade bed with shoes under it, and an old bathrobe hung over the cracked, pull-down green shade to keep the glare out.

I looked at all this as if it meant something, then stepped back into the hall and relocked the door. Then I made another pilgrimage into Room 214. Its door was now unlocked. I searched the room with care and patience and found nothing that connected it in any way with Orrin P. Quest. I didn't expect to. There was no reason why I should. But you always have to look.

I went downstairs, listened outside the manager's door, heard nothing, went in and crossed to put the keys on the desk. Lester B. Clausen lay on his side on the couch with his face to the wall, dead to the world. I went through the desk, found an old account book that seemed to be concerned with rent taken in and expenses paid out and nothing else. I looked at the register again. It wasn't up to date but the party on the couch seemed enough explanation for that. Orrin P. Quest had moved away. Somebody had taken over his room. Somebody else had the room registered to Hicks. The little man counting money in the kitchen went nicely with the neighborhood. The fact that he carried a gun and a knife was a social eccentricity that would cause no comment at all on Idaho Street.

I reached the small Bay City telephone book off the hook beside the desk. I didn't think it would be much of a job to sift out the party that went by the name of "Doc" or "Vince" and the phone number one-three-five-seven-two. First of all I leafed back through the register. Something which I ought to have done first. The page with Orrin Quest's registration had been torn out. A careful man, Mr. George W. Hicks. Very careful.

I closed the register, glanced over at Lester B. Clausen again, wrinkled my nose at the stale air and the sickly sweetish smell of gin and of something else, and started back to the entrance door. As I reached it, something for the first time penetrated my mind. A drunk like Clausen ought to be snoring very loudly. He ought to be snoring his head off with a nice assortment of checks and gurgles and snorts. He wasn't making any sound at all.

A brown army blanket was pulled up around his shoulders and the lower part of his head. He looked very comfortable, very calm. I stood over him and looked down. Something which was not an accidental fold held the army blanket away from the back of his neck. I moved it. A square yellow wooden handle was attached to the back of Lester B. Clausen's neck. On the side of the yellow handle were printed the words "Compliments of the Crumsen Hardware Company." The position of the handle was just below the occipital bulge.

It was the handle of an ice pick. . . .

I did a nice quiet thirty-five getting away from the neighborhood. On the edge of the city, a frog's jump from the line, I shut myself in an outdoor telephone booth and called the Police Department.

"Bay City Police. Moot talking," a furry voice said.

I said: "Number 449 Idaho Street. In the apartment of the manager. His name's Clausen."

"Yeah?" The voice said. "What do we do?"

"I don't know," I said. "It's a bit of a puzzle to me. But the man's name is Lester B. Clausen. Got that?"

"What makes it important?" the furry voice said without suspicion.

"The coroner will want to know," I said, and hung up.

6

I DROVE BACK to Hollywood and locked myself in the
office with the Bay City telephone book. It took me a
quarter-hour to find out that the party who went with
the telephone number one-three-five-seven-two in Bay
City was a Dr. Vincent Lagardie, who called himself a
neurologist, had his home and offices on Wyoming Street,
which according to my map was not quite in the best
residential neighborhood and not quite out of it. I locked
the Bay City telephone book up in my desk and went
down to the corner drugstore for a sandwich and a cup
of coffee and used a pay booth to call Dr. Vincent Lagardie. A woman answered and I had some trouble getting
through to Dr. Lagardie himself. When I did his voice was
impatient. He was very busy, in the middle of an examination he said. I never knew a doctor who wasn't. Did
he know Lester B. Clausen? He never heard of him. What
was the purpose of my inquiry?

"Mr. Clausen tried to telephone you this morning," I
said. "He was too drunk to talk properly."

"But I don't know Mr. Clausen," the doctor's cool

voice answered. He didn't seem to be in quite such a hurry now.

"Well that's all right then," I said. "Just wanted to make sure. Somebody stuck an ice pick into the back of his neck."

There was a quiet pause. Dr. Lagardie's voice was now almost unctuously polite. "Has this been reported to the police?"

"Naturally," I said. "But it shouldn't bother you—unless of course it was your ice pick."

He passed that one up. "And who is this speaking?" he inquired suavely.

"The name is Hicks," I said. "George W. Hicks. I just moved out of there. I don't want to get mixed up with that sort of thing. I just figured when Clausen tried to call you—this was before he was dead you understand—that you might be interested."

"I'm sorry, Mr. Hicks," Dr. Lagardie's voice said, "but I don't *know* Mr. Clausen. I have never *heard* of Mr. Clausen or had any contact with him whatsoever. And I have an excellent memory for names."

"Well, that's fine," I said. "And you won't meet him now. But somebody *may* want to know why he tried to telephone you—unless I forget to pass the information along."

There was a dead pause. Dr. Lagardie said: "I can't think of any comment to make on that."

I said: "Neither can I. I may call you again. Don't get me wrong, Dr. Lagardie. This isn't any kind of a shake. I'm just a mixed-up little man who needs a friend. I kind of felt that a doctor—like a clergyman—"

"I'm at your entire disposal," Dr. Lagardie said. "Please feel free to consult me."

"Thank you, doctor," I said fervently. "Thank you very very much."

I hung up. If Dr. Vincent Lagardie was on the level,

he would now telephone the Bay City Police Department and tell them the story. If he didn't telephone the police, he wasn't on the level. Which might or might not be useful to know.

7

THE PHONE on my desk rang at four o'clock sharp.

"Did you find Orrin yet, Mr. Marlowe?"

"Not yet. Where are you?"

"Why I'm in the drugstore next to—"

"Come on up and stop acting like Mata Hari," I said.

"Aren't you ever polite to anybody?" she snapped.

I hung up and fed myself a slug of Old Forester to brace my nerves for the interview. As I was inhaling it I heard her steps tripping along the corridor. I moved across and opened the door.

"Come in this way and miss the crowd," I said.

She seated herself demurely and waited.

"All I could find out," I told her, "is that the dump on Idaho Street is peddling reefers. That's marijuana cigarettes."

"Why, how disgusting," she said.

"We have to take the bad with the good in this life," I said. "Orrin must have got wise and threatened to report it to the police."

"You mean," she said in her little-girl manner, "that they might hurt him for doing that?"

"Well, most likely they'd just throw a scare into him first."

"Oh, they couldn't scare Orrin, Mr. Marlowe," she said decisively. "He just gets mean when people try to run him."

"Yeah," I said. "But we're not talking about the same things. You can scare anybody—with the right technique."

She set her mouth stubbornly. "No, Mr. Marlowe. They couldn't scare Orrin."

"Okay," I said. "So they didn't scare him. Say they just cut off one of his legs and beat him over the head with it. What would he do then—write to the Better Business Bureau?"

"You're making fun of me," she said politely. Her voice was as cool as boarding-house soup. "Is that all you did all day? Just find Orrin had moved and it was a bad neighborhood? Why I found that out for myself, Mr. Marlowe. I thought you being a detective and all—" She trailed off, leaving the rest of it in the air.

"I did a little more than that," I said. "I gave the landlord a little gin and went through the register and talked to a man named Hicks. George W. Hicks. He wears a toupee. I guess maybe you didn't meet him. He has, or had, Orrin's room. So I thought maybe—" It was my turn to do a little trailing in the air.

She fixed me with her pale blue eyes enlarged by the glasses. Her mouth was small and firm and tight, her hands clasped on the desk in front of her over her large square bag, her whole body stiff and erect and formal and disapproving.

"I paid you twenty dollars, Mr. Marlowe," she said coldly. "I understood that was in payment of a day's work. It doesn't seem to me that you've done a day's work."

"No," I said. "That's true. But the day isn't over yet. And don't bother about the twenty bucks. You can have it back if you like. I didn't even bruise it."

I opened the desk drawer and got out her money. I pushed it across the desk. She looked at it but didn't touch it. Her eyes came up slowly to meet mine.

"I didn't mean it like that. I know you're doing the best you can, Mr. Marlowe."

"With the facts I have."

"But I've told you all I know."

"I don't think so," I said.

"Well I'm sure I can't help what you think," she said tartly. "After all, if I knew what I wanted to know already, I wouldn't have come here and asked you to find it out, would I?"

"I'm not saying you know all you want to know," I answered. "The point is I don't know all I want to know in order to do a job for you. And what you tell me doesn't add up."

"What doesn't add up? I've told you the truth. I'm Orrin's sister. I guess I know what kind of person he is."

"How long did he work for Cal-Western?"

"I've told you that. He came out to California just about a year ago. He got work right away because he practically had the job before he left."

"He wrote home how often? Before he stopped writing."

"Every week. Sometimes oftener. He'd take turns writing to mother and me. Of course the letters were for both of us."

"About what?"

"You mean what did he write about?"

"What did you think I meant?"

"Well, you don't have to snap at me. He wrote about his work and the plant and the people there and sometimes about a show he'd been to. Or it was about California. He'd write about church too."

"Nothing about girls?"

"I don't think Orrin cared much for girls."

"And lived at the same address all this time?"

She nodded, looking puzzled.

"And he stopped writing how long ago?"

That took thought. She pressed her lips and pushed a fingertip around the middle of the lower one. "About three or four months," she said at last.

"What was the date of his last letter?"

"I—I'm afraid I can't tell you exactly the date. But it was like I said, three or four—"

I waved a hand at her. "Anything out of the ordinary in it? Anything unusual said or anything unusual unsaid?"

"Why no. It seemed just like all the rest."

"Don't you have any friends or relatives in this part of the country?"

She gave me a funny stare, started to say something, then shook her head sharply. "No."

"Okay. Now I'll tell you what's wrong. I'll skip over your not telling me where you're staying, because it might be just that you're afraid I'll show up with a quart of hooch under my arm and make a pass at you."

"That's not a very nice way to talk," she said.

"Nothing I say is nice. I'm not nice. By your standards nobody with less than three prayerbooks could be nice. But I *am* inquisitive. What's wrong with this picture is that you're not scared. Neither you personally nor your mother. And you ought to be scared as hell."

She clutched her bag to her bosom with tight little fingers. "You mean something has happened to him?" Her voice faded off into a sort of sad whisper, like a mortician asking for a down payment.

"I don't know that anything has. But in your position, knowing the kind of guy Orrin was, the way his letters came through and then didn't, I can't see myself waiting for my summer vacation to come around before I start asking questions. I can't see myself by-passing the police who have an organization for finding people. And going to a lone-wolf operator you never heard of, asking him to root around for you in the rubble. And I can't see your dear old mother just sitting there in Manhattan, Kansas, week after week darning the minister's winter underwear. No letter from Orrin. No news. And all she does about it is take a long breath and mend up another pair of pants."

She came to her feet with a lunge. "You're a horrid, disgusting person," she said angrily. "I think you're vile. Don't you dare say mother and I weren't worried. Just don't you dare."

I pushed the twenty dollars' worth of currency a little closer to the other side of the desk. "You were worried twenty dollars' worth, honey," I said. "But about what I wouldn't know. I guess I don't really want to know. Just put this hunk of the folding back in your saddlebag and forget you ever met me. You might want to lend it to another detective tomorrow."

She snapped her bag shut viciously on the money. "I'm not very likely to forget your rudeness," she said between her teeth. "Nobody in the world's ever talked to me the way you have."

I stood up and wandered around the end of the desk. "Don't think about it too much. You might get to like it."

I reached up and twitched her glasses off. She took half a step back, almost stumbled, and I reached an arm around her by pure instinct. Her eyes widened and she put her hands against my chest and pushed. I've been pushed harder by a kitten.

"Without the cheaters those eyes are really something," I said in an awed voice.

She relaxed and let her head go back and her lips open

a little. "I suppose you do this to all the clients," she said softly. Her hands now had dropped to her sides. The bag whacked against my leg. She leaned her weight on my arm. If she wanted me to let go of her, she had her signals mixed.

"I just didn't want you to lose your balance," I said.

"I knew you were the thoughtful type." She relaxed still more. Her head went back now. Her upper lids drooped, fluttered a bit and her lips came open a little farther. On them appeared the faint provocative smile that nobody ever has to teach them. "I suppose you thought I did it on purpose," she said.

"Did what on purpose?"

"Stumbled, sort of."

"Wel-l-l-l."

She reached a quick arm around my neck and started to pull. So I kissed her. It was either that or slug her. She pushed her mouth hard at me for a long moment, then quietly and very comfortably wriggled around in my arms and nestled. She let out a long easy sigh.

"In Manhattan, Kansas, you could be arrested for this," she said.

"If there was any justice, I could be arrested just for being there," I said.

She giggled and poked the end of my nose with a fingertip. "I suppose you really prefer fast girls," she said, looking up at me sideways. "At least you won't have to wipe off any lip rouge. Maybe I'll wear some next time."

"Maybe we'd better sit down on the floor," I said. "My arm's getting tired."

She giggled again and disengaged herself gracefully. "I guess you think I've been kissed lots of times," she said.

"What girl hasn't?"

She nodded, gave me the up-from-under look that made her eyelashes cut across the iris. "Even at the church socials they play kissing games," she said.

"Or there wouldn't be any church socials," I said.

We looked at each other with no particular expression.

"Well-l-l—" she began at last. I handed her back her glasses. She put them on. She opened her bag, looked at herself in a small mirror, rooted around in her bag and came out with her hand clenched.

"I'm sorry I was mean," she said, and pushed something under the blotter of my desk. She gave me another little frail smile and marched to the door and opened it.

"I'll call you," she said intimately. And out she went, tap, tap, tap down the hall.

I went over and lifted the blotter and smoothed out the crumpled currency that lay under it. It hadn't been much of a kiss, but it looked like I had another chance at the twenty dollars.

The phone rang before I had quite started to worry about Mr. Lester B. Clausen. I reached for it absently. The voice I heard was an abrupt voice, but thick and clogged, as if it was being strained through a curtain or somebody's long white beard.

"You Marlowe?" it said.

"Speaking."

"You got a safe-deposit box, Marlowe?"

I had enough of being polite for one afternoon. "Stop asking and start telling," I said.

"I asked you a question, Marlowe."

"I didn't answer it," I said. "Like this." I reached over and pressed down the riser on the phone. Held it that way while I fumbled around for a cigarette. I knew he would call right back. They always do when they think they're tough. They haven't used their exit line. When it rang again I started right in.

"If you have a proposition, state it. And I get called 'mister' until you give me some money."

"Don't let that temper ride you so hard, friend. I'm in a jam. I need help. I need something kept in a safe place.

For a few days. Not longer. And for that you make a little quick money."

"How little?" I asked. "And how quick?"

"A *C* note. Right here and waiting. I'm warming it for you."

"I can hear it purr," I said. "Right where and waiting?" I was listening to the voice twice, once when I heard it and once when it echoed in my mind.

"Room 332, Van Nuys Hotel. Knock two quick ones and two slow ones. Not too loud. I got to have live action. How fast can you—"

"What is it you want me to keep?"

"That'll wait till you get here. I said I was in a hurry."

"What's your name?"

"Just Room 332."

"Thanks for the time," I said. "Goodbye."

"Hey. Wait a minute, dope. It's nothing hot like you think. No ice. No emerald pendants. It just happens to be worth a lot of money to me—and nothing at all to anybody else."

"The hotel has a safe."

"Do you want to die poor, Marlowe?"

"Why not? Rockefeller did. Goodbye again."

The voice changed. The furriness went out of it. It said sharply and swiftly: "How's every little thing in Bay City?"

I didn't speak. Just waited. There was a dim chuckle over the wire. "Thought that might interest you, Marlowe. Room 332 it is. Tramp on it friend. Make speed."

The phone clicked in my ear. I hung up. For no reason a pencil rolled off the desk and broke its point on the glass doohickey under one of the desk legs. I picked it up and slowly and carefully sharpened it in the Boston sharpener screwed to the edge of the window frame, turning the pencil around to get it nice and even. I laid it down in the tray on the desk and dusted off my hands.

I had all the time in the world. I looked out of the window. I didn't see anything. I didn't hear anything.

And then, for even less reason, I saw Orfamay Quest's face without the glasses, and polished and painted and with blonde hair piled up high on the forehead with a braid around the middle of it. And bedroom eyes. They all have to have bedroom eyes. I tried to imagine this face in a vast close-up being gnawed by some virile character from the wide-open spaces of Romanoff's bar.

It took me twenty-nine minutes to get to the Van Nuys Hotel.

8

ONCE, LONG AGO, it must have had a certain elegance. But no more. The memories of old cigars clung to its lobby like the dirty gilt on its ceiling and the sagging springs of its leather lounging chairs. The marble of the desk had turned a yellowish brown with age. But the floor carpet was new and had a hard look, like the room clerk. I passed him up and strolled over to the cigar counter in the corner and put down a quarter for a package of Camels. The girl behind the counter was a straw blonde with a long neck and tired eyes. She put the cigarettes in front of me, added a packet of matches, dropped my change into a slotted box marked "The Community Chest Thanks You."

"You'd want me to do that, wouldn't you," she said, smiling patiently. "You'd want to give your change to the poor little underprivileged kids with bent legs and stuff, wouldn't you?"

"Suppose I didn't," I said.

"I dig up seven cents," the girl said, "and it would be

very painful." She had a low lingering voice with a sort of moist caress in it like a damp bath towel. I put a quarter after the seven cents. She gave me her big smile then. It showed more of her tonsils.

"You're nice," she said. "I can see you're nice. A lot of fellows would have come in here and made a pass at a girl. Just think. Over seven cents. A pass."

"Who's the house peeper here now?" I asked her, without taking up the option.

"There's two of them." She did something slow and elegant to the back of her head, exhibiting what seemed like more than one handful of blood-red fingernails in the process. "Mr. Hady is on nights and Mr. Flack is on days. It's day now so it would be Mr. Flack would be on."

"Where could I find him?"

She leaned over the counter and let me smell her hair, pointing with a half-inch fingernail toward the elevator bank. "It's down along that corridor there, next to the porter's room. You can't miss the porter's room on account of it has a half-door and says PORTER on the upper part in gold letters. Only that half is folded back like, so I guess maybe you can't see it."

"I'll see it," I said. "Even if I have to get a hinge screwed to my neck. What does this Flack look like?"

"Well," she said, "he's a little squatty number, with a bit of a mustache. A sort of chunky type. Thick-set like, only not tall." Her fingers moved languidly along the counter to where I could have touched them without jumping. "He's not interesting," she said. "Why bother?"

"Business," I said, and made off before she threw a half-nelson on me.

I looked back at her from the elevators. She was staring after me with an expression she probably would have said was thoughtful.

The porter's room was halfway down the corridor to

the Spring Street entrance. The door beyond it was half open. I looked around its edge, then went in and closed it behind me.

A man was sitting at a small desk which had dust on it, a very large ash tray and very little else. He was short and thick-set. He had something dark and bristly under his nose about an inch long. I sat down across from him and put a card on the desk.

He reached for the card without excitement, read it, turned it over and read the back with as much care as the front. There was nothing on the back to read. He picked half of a cigar out of his ash tray and burned his nose lighting it.

"What's the gripe?" he growled at me.

"No gripe. You Flack?"

He didn't bother to answer. He gave me a steady look which may or may not have concealed his thoughts, depending on whether he had any to conceal.

"Like to get a line on one of the customers," I said.

"What name?" Flack asked, with no enthusiasm.

"I don't know what name he's using here. He's in Room 332."

"What name was he using before he came here?" Flack asked.

"I don't know that either."

"Well, what did he look like?" Flack was suspicious now. He reread my card but it added nothing to his knowledge.

"I never saw him, so far as I know."

Flack said: "I must be overworked. I don't get it."

"I had a call from him," I said. "He wanted to see me."

"Am I stopping you?"

"Look, Flack. A man in my business makes enemies at times. You ought to know that. This party wants something done. Tells me to come on over, forgets to give his name, and hangs up. I figured I'd do a little checking before I went up there."

Flack took the cigar out of his mouth and said patiently: "I'm in terrible shape. I still don't get it. Nothing makes sense to me any more."

I leaned over the desk and spoke to him slowly and distinctly: "The whole thing could be a nice way to get me into a hotel room and knock me off and then quietly check out. You wouldn't want anything like that to happen in your hotel, would you, Flack?"

"Supposing I cared," he said, "you figure you're that important?"

"Do you smoke that piece of rope because you like it or because you think it makes you look tough?"

"For forty-five bucks a week," Flack said, "would I smoke anything better?" He eyed me steadily.

"No expense account yet," I told him. "No deal yet."

He made a sad sound and got up wearily and went out of the room. I lit one of my cigarettes and waited. He came back in a short time and dropped a registration card on the desk. *Dr. G. W. Hambleton, El Centro, California* was written on it in a firm round hand in ink. The clerk had written other things on it, including the room number and daily rate. Flack pointed a finger that needed a manicure or failing that a nailbrush.

"Came in at 2.47 P.M.," he said. "Just today, that is. Nothing on his bill. One day's rent. No phone calls. No nothing. That what you want?"

"What does he look like?" I asked.

"I didn't see him. You think I stand out there by the desk and take pictures of them while they register?"

"Thanks," I said. "Dr. G. W. Hambleton, El Centro. Much obliged." I handed him back the registration card.

"Anything I ought to know," Flack said as I went

out, "don't forget where I   live. That is, if you call it living."

I nodded and went out. There are days like that. Everybody you meet is a dope. You begin to look at yourself in the glass and wonder.

9

Room 332 was at the back of the building near the door to the fire escape. The corridor which led to it had a smell of old carpet and furniture oil and the drab anonymity of a thousand shabby lives. The sand bucket under the racked fire hose was full of cigarette and cigar stubs, an accumulation of several days. A radio pounded brassy music through an open transom. Through another transom people were laughing fit to kill themselves. Down at the end by Room 332 it was quieter.

I knocked the two longs and two shorts as instructed. Nothing happened. I felt jaded and old. I felt as if I had spent my life knocking at doors in cheap hotels that nobody bothered to open. I tried again. Then turned the knob and walked in. A key with a red fiber tab hung in the inside keyhole.

There was a short hall with a bathroom on the right. Beyond the hall the upper half of a bed was in view and a man lay on it in shirt and pants.

I said: "Dr. Hambleton?"

The man didn't answer. I went past the bathroom door

towards him. A whiff of perfume reached me and I started to turn, but not quickly enough. A woman who had been in the bathroom was standing there holding a towel in front of the lower part of her face. Dark glasses showed above the towel. And then the brim of a wide-brimmed straw hat in a sort of dusty delphinium blue. Under that was fluffed-out pale blond hair. Blue earbuttons lurked somewhere back in the shadows. The sunglasses were in white frames with broad flat sidebows. Her dress matched her hat. An embroidered silk or rayon coat was open over the dress. She wore gauntleted gloves and there was an automatic in her right hand. White bone grip. Looked like a .32.

"Turn around and put your hands behind you," she said through the towel. The voice muffled by the towel meant as little to me as the dark glasses. It was not the voice which had talked to me on the telephone. I didn't move.

"Don't ever think I'm fooling," she said. "I'll give you exactly three seconds to do what I say."

"Couldn't you make it a minute? I like looking at you."

She made a threatening gesture with the little gun. "Turn around," she snapped. "But fast."

"I like the sound of your voice too."

"All right," she said, in a tight dangerous tone. "If that's the way you want it, that's the way you want it."

"Don't forget you're a lady," I said, and turned around and put my hands up to my shoulders. A gun muzzle poked into the back of my neck. Breath almost tickled my skin. The perfume was an elegant something or other, not strong, not decisive. The gun against my neck went away and a white flame burned for an instant behind my eyes. I grunted and fell forward on my hands and knees and reached back quickly. My hand touched a leg in a nylon stocking but slipped off, which seemed a pity. It felt like a nice leg. The jar of another blow on the head took the pleasure out of this and I made the hoarse sound of a man in desperate shape. I collapsed on the floor. The door opened. A key rattled. The door closed. The key turned. Silence.

I climbed up to my feet and went into the bathroom. I bathed my head with a towel from the rack soaked with cold water. It felt as if the heel of a shoe had hit me. Certainly it was not a gun butt. There was a little blood, not much. I rinsed the towel out and stood there patting the bruise and wondering why I didn't run after her screaming. But what I was doing was staring into the open medicine cabinet over the basin. The upper part of a can of talcum had been pried off the shoulder. There was talcum all over the shelf. A toothpaste tube had been cut open. Someone had been looking for something.

I went back to the little hallway and tried the room door. Locked from the outside. I bent down and looked through the keyhole. But it was an up-and-down lock, with the outer and inner keyholes on different levels. The girl in the dark glasses with the white rims didn't know much about hotels. I twisted the night latch, which opened the outside lock, opened the door, looked along the empty corridor, and closed the door again.

Then I went towards the man on the bed. He had not moved during all this time, for a somewhat obvious reason.

Beyond the little hallway the room widened towards a pair of windows through which the evening sun slanted in a shaft that reached almost across the bed and came to a stop under the neck of the man that lay there. What it stopped on was blue and white and shining and round. He lay quite comfortably half on his face with his hands down at his sides and his shoes off. The side of his face was on the pillow and he seemed relaxed. He was wearing a toupee. The last time I had talked to him his name had been George W. Hicks. Now it was Dr. G. W. Hamble-

ton. Same initials. Not that it mattered any more. I wasn't
going to be talking to him again. There was no blood. None
at all, which is one of the few nice things about an expert
ice-pick job.

I touched his neck. It was still warm. While I was
doing it the shaft of sunlight moved away from the knob
of the ice pick towards his left ear. I turned away and
looked the room over. The telephone bell box had been
opened and left open. The Gideon Bible was thrown in
the corner. The desk had been searched. I went to a
closet and looked into that. There were clothes in it and
a suitcase I had seen before. I found nothing that seemed
important. I picked a snap-brim hat off the floor and
put it on the desk and went back to the bathroom. The
point of interest now was whether the people who had ice-
picked Dr. Hambleton had found what they came for.
They had had very little time.

I searched the bathroom carefully. I moved the top of
the toilet tank and drained it. There was nothing in it.
I peered down the overflow pipe. No thread hung there
with a small object at the end of it. I searched the bureau.
It was empty except for an old envelope. I unhooked the
window screens and felt under the sills outside. I picked
the Gideon Bible off the floor and leafed through it again.
I examined the backs of three pictures and studied the
edge of the carpet. It was tacked close to the wall and
there were little pockets of dust in the depressions made
by the tacks. I got down on the floor and examined the
part under the bed. Just the same. I stood on a chair,
looked into the bowl of the light fixture. It contained dust
and dead moths. I looked the bed over. It had been made
up by a professional and not touched since. I felt the
pillow under the dead man's head, then got the extra
pillow out of the closet and examined its edges. Nothing.

Dr. Hambleton's coat hung over a chair back. I went

through that, knowing it was the least likely place to find anything. Somebody with a knife had worked on the lining and the shoulder padding. There were matches, a couple of cigars, a pair of dark glasses, a cheap handkerchief not used, a Bay City movie theater ticket stub, a small comb, an unopened package of cigarettes. I looked at it in the light. It showed no sign of having been disturbed. I disturbed it. I tore off the cover, went through it, found nothing but cigarettes.

That left Dr. Hambleton himself. I eased him over and got into his trouser pockets. Loose change, another handkerchief, a small tube of dental floss, more matches, a bunch of keys, a folder of bus schedules. In a pigskin wallet was a book of stamps, a second comb (here was a man who really took care of his toupee), three flat packages of white powder, seven printed cards reading *Dr. G. W. Hambleton, O. D. Tustin Building, El Centro, California, Hours 9–12 and 2–4, and by Appointment. Telephone El Centro 50406*. There was no driver's license, no social-security card, no insurance cards, no real identification at all. There was $164 in currency in the wallet. I put the wallet back where I found it.

I lifted Dr. Hambleton's hat off the desk and examined the sweatband and the ribbon. The ribbon bow had been picked loose with a knife point, leaving hanging threads. There was nothing hidden inside the bow. No evidence of any previous ripping and restitching.

This was the take. If the killers knew what they were looking for, it was something that could be hidden in a book, a telephone box, a tube of toothpaste, or a hatband. I went back into the bathroom and looked at my head again. It was still oozing a tiny trickle of blood. I gave it more cold water and dried the cut with toilet paper and flushed that down the bowl. I went back and stood a moment looking down on Dr. Hambleton, wondering what his mistake had been. He had seemed a fairly wise bird. The sunlight had moved over to the far edge of the room now, off the bed and down into a sad dusty corner.

I grinned suddenly, bent over and quickly and with the grin still on my face, out of place as it was, pulled off Dr. Hambleton's toupee and turned it inside out. As simple as all that. To the lining of the toupee a piece of orange-colored paper was fastened by Scotch tape, protected by a square of cellophane. I pulled it loose, turned it over, and saw that it was a numbered claim check belonging to the Bay City Camera Shop. I put it in my wallet and put the toupee carefully back on the dead egg-bald head.

I left the room unlocked because I had no way to lock it.

Down the hall the radio still blared through the transom and the exaggerated alcoholic laughter accompanied it from across the corridor.

10

OVER THE TELEPHONE the Bay City Camera Shop man said: "Yes, Mr. Hicks. We have them for you. Six enlarged prints on glossy from your negative."

"What time do you close?" I asked.

"Oh in about five minutes. We open at nine in the morning."

"I'll pick them up in the morning. Thanks."

I hung up, reached mechanically into the slot and found somebody else's nickel. I walked over to the lunch counter and bought myself a cup of coffee with it, and sat there sipping and listening to the auto horns complaining on the street outside. It was time to go home. Whistles blew. Motors raced. Old brake linings squeaked. There was a dull steady mutter of feet on the sidewalk outside. It was just after five-thirty. I finished the coffee, stuffed a pipe, and strolled a half-block back to the Van Nuys Hotel. In the writing room I folded the orange camera-shop check into a sheet of hotel stationery and addressed an envelope to myself. I put a special-delivery stamp on it and dropped

it in the mail chute by the elevator bank. Then I went
along to Flack's office again.

Again I closed his door and sat down across from him.
Flack didn't seem to have moved an inch. He was chewing morosely on the same cigar butt and his eyes were
still full of nothing. I relit my pipe by striking a match
on the side of his desk. He frowned.

"Dr. Hambleton doesn't answer his door," I said.

"Huh?" Flack looked at me vacantly.

"Party in 332. Remember? He doesn't answer his
door."

"What should I do—bust my girdle?" Flack asked.

"I knocked several times," I said. "No answer. Thought
he might be taking a bath or something, although I couldn't
hear anything. Went away for a while, then tried again.
Same no answer again."

Flack looked at a turnip watch he got from his vest.
"I'm off at seven," he said. "Jesus. A whole hour to go,
and more. Boy, am I hungry."

"Working the way you do," I said, "you must be. You
have to keep your strength up. Do I interest you at all
in Room 332?"

"You said he wasn't in," Flack said irritably. "So what?
He wasn't in."

"I didn't say he wasn't in. I said he didn't answer his
door."

Flack leaned forward. Very slowly he removed the
débris of the cigar from his mouth and put it in the glass
tray. "Go on. Make me like it," he said, carefully.

"Maybe you'd like to run up and look," I said. "Maybe
you didn't see a first-class ice-pick job lately."

Flack put his hands on the arms of his chair and
squeezed the wood hard. "Aw," he said painfully, "aw."
He got to his feet and opened the desk drawer. He took
out a large black gun, flicked the gate open, studied the
cartridges, squinted down the barrel, snapped the cylinder

back into place. He unbuttoned his vest and tucked the gun down inside his waistband. In an emergency he could probably have got to it in less than a minute. He put his hat on firmly and jerked a thumb at the door.

We went up to the third floor in silence. We went down the corridor. Nothing had changed. No sound had increased or diminished. Flack hurried along to 332 and knocked from force of habit. Then tried the door. He looked back at me with a twisted mouth.

"You said the door wasn't locked," he complained.

"I didn't exactly say that. It *was* unlocked, though."

"It ain't now," Flack said, and unshipped a key on a long chain. He unlocked the door and glanced up and down the hall. He twisted the knob slowly without sound and eased the door a couple of inches. He listened. No sounds came from within. Flack stepped back, took the black gun out of his waistband. He removed the key from the door, kicked it wide open, and brought the gun up hard and straight, like the wicked foreman of the Lazy Q. "Let's go," he said out of the corner of his mouth.

Over his shoulder I could see that Dr. Hambleton lay exactly as before, but the ice-pick handle didn't show from the entrance. Flack leaned forward and edged cautiously into the room. He reached the bathroom door and put his eye to the crack, then pushed the door open until it bounced against the tub. He went in and came out, stepped down into the room, a tense and wary man who was taking no chances.

He tried the closet door, leveled his gun and jerked it wide open. No suspects in the closet.

"Look under the bed," I said.

Flack bent swiftly and looked under the bed.

"Look under the carpet," I said.

"You kidding me?" Flack asked nastily.

"I just like to watch you work."

He bent over the dead man and studied the ice pick.

"Somebody locked that door," he sneered. "Unless you're lying about its being unlocked."

I said nothing.

"Well I guess it's the cops," he said slowly. "No chance to cover up on this one."

"It's not your fault," I told him. "It happens even in good hotels."

11

THE REDHEADED INTERN filled out a DOA form and clipped his stylus to the outside pocket of his white jacket. He snapped the book shut with a faint grin on his face.

"Punctured spinal cord just below the occipital bulge, I'd say," he said carelessly. "A very vulnerable spot. If you know how to find it. And I suppose you do."

Detective Lieutenant Christy French growled. "Think it's the first time I've seen one?"

"No, I guess not," the intern said. He gave a last quick look at the dead man, turned and walked out of the room. "I'll call the coroner," he said over his shoulder. The door closed behind him.

"What a stiff means to those birds is what a plate of warmed-up cabbage means to me," Christy French said sourly to the closed door. His partner, a cop named Fred Beifus, was down on one knee by the telephone box. He had dusted it for fingerprints and blown off the loose powder. He was looking at the smudge through a small magnifying glass. He shook his head, then picked something off the screw with which the box had been fastened shut.

"Gray cotton undertaker's gloves," he said disgustedly. "Cost about four cents a pair wholesale. Fat lot of good printing this joint. They were looking for something in the telephone box, huh?"

"Evidently something that could be there," French said. "I didn't expect prints. These ice-pick jobs are a specialty. We'll get the experts after a while. This is just a quick-over."

He was stripping the dead man's pockets and laying what had been in them out on the bed beside the quiet and already waxy corpse. Flack was sitting in a chair by the window, looking out morosely. The assistant manager had been up, said nothing with a worried expression, and gone away. I was leaning against the bathroom wall and sorting out my fingers.

Flack said suddenly: "I figure an ice-pick job's a dame's work. You can buy them anywhere. Ten cents. If you want one fast, you can slip it down inside a garter and let it hang there."

Christy French gave him a brief glance which had a kind of wonder in it. Beifus said: "What kind of dames you been running around with, honey? The way stockings cost nowadays a dame would as soon stick a saw down her sock."

"I never thought of that," Flack said.

Beifus said: "Leave us do the thinking sweetheart. It takes equipment."

"No need to get tough," Flack said.

Beifus took his hat off and bowed. "You mustn't deny us our little pleasures, Mr. Flack."

Christy French said: "Besides, a woman would keep on jabbing. She wouldn't even know how much was enough. Lots of the punks don't. Whoever did this one was a per-former. He got the spinal cord the first try. And another thing—you have to have the guy quiet to do it. That means more than one guy, unless he was doped, or the killer was a friend of his."

I said: "I don't see how he could have been doped, if he's the party that called me on the phone."

French and Beifus both looked at me with the same expression of patient boredom. "If," French said, "and since you didn't know the guy—according to you—there's always the faint possibility that you wouldn't know his voice. Or am I being too subtle?"

"I don't know," I said. "I haven't read your fan mail."

French grinned.

"Don't waste it on him," Beifus told French. "Save it for when you talk to the Friday Morning Club. Some of them old ladies in the shiny-nose league go big for the nicer angles of murder."

French rolled himself a cigarette and lit it with a kitchen match he struck on the back of a chair. He sighed.

"They worked the technique out in Brooklyn," he explained. "Sunny Moe Stein's boys specialized in it, but they run it into the ground. It got so you couldn't walk across a vacant lot without finding some of their work. Then they came out here, what was left of them. I wonder why did they do that."

"Maybe we just got more vacant lots," Beifus said.

"Funny thing, though," French said, almost dreamily. "When Weepy Moyer had the chill put on Sunny Moe Stein over on Franklin Avenue last February, the killer used a gun. Moe wouldn't have liked that at all."

"I betcha that was why his face had that disappointed look, after they washed the blood off," Beifus remarked.

"Who's Weepy Moyer?" Flack asked.

"He was next to Moe in the organization," French told him. "This could easily be his work. Not that he'd have done it personal."

"Why not?" Flack asked sourly.

"Don't you guys ever read a paper? Moyer's a gentleman now. He knows the nicest people. Even has another name. And as for the Sunny Moe Stein job, it just happened we had him in jail on a gambling rap. We didn't get anywhere. But we did make him a very sweet alibi. Anyhow he's a gentleman like I said, and gentlemen don't go around sticking ice picks into people. They hire it done."

"Did you ever have anything on Moyer?" I asked.

French looked at me sharply. "Why?"

"I just had an idea. But it's very fragile," I said.

French eyed me slowly. "Just between us girls in the powder room," he said, "we never even proved the guy we had *was* Moyer. But don't broadcast it. Nobody's supposed to know but him and his lawyer and the D.A. and the police beat and the city hall and maybe two or three hundred other people."

He slapped the dead man's empty wallet against his thigh and sat down on the bed. He leaned casually against the corpse's leg, lit a cigarette and pointed with it.

"That's enough time on the vaudeville circuit. Here's what we got, Fred. First off, the customer here was not too bright. He was going by the name of Dr. G. W. Hambleton and had the cards printed with an El Centro address and a phone number. It took just two minutes to find out there ain't any such address or any such phone number. A bright boy doesn't lay open that easy. Next, the guy is definitely not in the chips. He has fourteen smackeroos folding in here and about two bucks loose change. On his key ring he don't have any car key or any safe-deposit key or any house key. All he's got is a suitcase key and seven filed Yale master keys. Filed fairly recently at that. I figure he was planning to sneak the hotel a little. Do you think these keys would work in your dump, Flack?"

Flack went over and stared at the keys. "Two of

them are the right size," he said. "I couldn't tell if they'd work by just looking. If I want a master key I have to get it from the office. All I carry is a passkey. I can only use that if the guest is out." He took a key out of his pocket, a key on a long chain, and compared it. He shook his head. "They're no good without more work," he said. "Far too much metal on them."

French flicked ash into the palm of his hand and blew it off as dust. Flack went back to his chair by the window.

"Next point," Christy French announced. "He don't have a driver's license or any identification. None of his outside clothes were bought in El Centro. He had some kind of a grift, but he don't have the looks or personality to bounce checks."

"You didn't really see him at his best," Beifus put in.

"And this hotel is the wrong dump for that anyway," French went on. "It's got a crummy reputation."

"Now wait a minute!" Flack began.

French cut him short with a gesture. "I know every hotel in the metropolitan district, Flack. It's my business to know. For fifty bucks I could organize a double-strip act with French trimmings inside of an hour in any room in this hotel. Don't kid me. You earn your living and I'll earn mine. Just don't kid me. All right. The customer had something he was afraid to keep around. That means he knew somebody was after him and getting close. So he offers Marlowe a hundred bucks to keep it for him. But he doesn't have that much money on him. So what he must have been planning on was getting Marlowe to gamble with him. It couldn't have been hot jewelry then. It had to be something semi-legitimate. That right, Marlowe?"

"You could leave out the semi," I said.

French grinned faintly. "So what he had was something that could be kept flat or rolled up—in a phone box, a hatband, a Bible, a can of talcum. We don't know whether it was found or not. But we do know there was very little time. Not much more than half an hour."

"If Dr. Hambleton did the phoning," I said. "You opened that can of beans yourself."

"It's kind of pointless any other way. The killers wouldn't be in a hurry to have him found. Why should they ask anybody to come over to his room?" He turned to Flack. "Any chance to check his visitors?"

Flack shook his head gloomily. "You don't even have to pass the desk to get to the elevators."

Beifus said: "Maybe that was one reason he came here. That, and the homey atmosphere."

"All right," French said. "Whoever knocked him off could come and go without any questions asked. All he had to know was his room number. And that's about all we know. Okay, Fred?"

Beifus nodded.

I said: "Not quite all. It's a nice toupee, but it's still a toupee."

French and Beifus both swung around quickly. French reached, carefully removed the dead man's hair, and whistled. "I wondered what that damn intern was grinning at," he said. "The bastard didn't even mention it. See what I see, Fred?"

"All I see is a guy without no hair," Beifus answered.

"Maybe you never knew him at that. Mileaway Marston. Used to be a runner for Ace Devore."

"Why sure enough," Beifus chuckled. He leaned over and patted the dead bald head gently. "How you been all this time, Mileaway? I didn't see you in so long I forgot. But you know me, pal. Once a softy always a softy."

The man on the bed looked old and hard and shrunken without his toupee. The yellow mask of death was beginning to set his face into rigid lines.

French said calmly: "Well, that takes a load off my

mind. This punk ain't going to be no twenty-four-hour-a-day job. The hell with him." He replaced the toupee over one eye and stood up off the bed. "That's all for you two," he said to Flack and me.

Flack stood up.

"Thanks for the murder, honey," Beifus told him. "You get any more in your nice hotel, don't forget our service. Even when it ain't good, it's quick."

Flack went down the short hall and yanked the door open. I followed him out. On the way to the elevator we didn't speak. Nor on the way down. I walked with him along to his little office, followed him in and shut the door. He seemed surprised.

He sat down at his desk and reached for his telephone. "I got to make a report to the Assistant Manager," he said. "Something you want?"

I rolled a cigarette around on my fingers, put a match to it and blew smoke softly across the desk. "One hundred and fifty dollars," I said.

Flack's small, intent eyes became round holes in a face washed clean of expression. "Don't get funny in the wrong place," he said.

"After those two comedians upstairs, you could hardly blame me if I did. But I'm not being funny." I beat a tattoo on the edge of the desk and waited.

Tiny beads of sweat showed on Flack's lip above his little mustache. "I got business to attend to," he said, more throatily this time. "Beat it and keep going."

"Such a tough little man," I said. "Dr. Hambleton had $164 currency in his wallet when I searched him. He promised me a hundred as retainer, remember? Now, in the same wallet, he has fourteen dollars. And I *did* leave the door of his room unlocked. And somebody else locked it. You locked it, Flack."

Flack took hold of the arms of his chair and squeezed.

His voice came from the bottom of a well saying: "You can't prove a damn thing."

"Do I have to try?"

He took the gun out of his waistband and laid it on the desk in front of him. He stared down at it. It didn't have any message for him. He looked up at me again. "Fifty-fifty, huh?" he said brokenly.

There was a moment of silence between us. He got his old shabby wallet out and rooted in it. He came up with a handful of currency and spread bills out on the desk, sorted them into two piles and pushed one pile my way.

I said: "I want the whole hundred and fifty."

He hunched down in his chair and stared at a corner of the desk. After a long time, he sighed. He put the two piles together and pushed them over—to my side of the desk.

"It wasn't doing him any good," Flack said. "Take the dough and breeze. I'll remember you, buddy. All you guys make me sick to my stomach. How do I know you didn't take half a grand off him."

"I'd take it all. So would the killer. Why leave fourteen dollars?"

"So why did I leave fourteen dollars?" Flack asked, in a tired voice, making vague movements along the desk edge with his fingers. I picked up the money, counted it and threw it back at him.

"Because you're in the business and could size him up. You knew he'd at least have room rent, and a few dollars for loose change. The cops would expect the same thing. Here, I don't want the money. I want something else."

He stared at me with his mouth open.

"Put that dough out of sight," I said.

He reached for it and crammed it back in his wallet. "What something else?" His eyes were small and thoughtful. His tongue pushed out his lower lip. "It don't seem to me *you're* in a very hot trading position either."

"You could be a little wrong about that. If I have to go back up there and tell Christy French and Beifus I was up there before and searched the body, I'd get a tongue-lashing all right. But he'd understand that I haven't been holding out just to be smart. He'd know that somewhere in the background I had a client I was trying to protect. I'd get tough talk and bluster. But that's not what *you'd* get." I stopped and watched the faint glisten of moisture forming on his forehead now. He swallowed hard. His eyes were sick.

"Cut out the wise talk and lay your deal on the deck," he said. He grinned suddenly, rather wolfishly. "Got here a little late to protect her, didn't you?" The fat sneer he lived with was coming home again, but slowly, but gladly.

I killed my cigarette and got another one out and went through all the slow futile face-saving motions of lighting it, getting rid of the match, blowing smoke off to one side, inhaling deeply as though that scrubby little office was a hilltop overlooking the bouncing ocean—all the tired clichéd mannerisms of my trade.

"All right," I said. "I'll admit it was a woman. I'll admit she must have been up there while he was dead, if that makes you happy. I guess it was just shock that made her run away."

"Oh sure," Flack said nastily. The fat sneer was all the way home now. "Or maybe she hadn't ice-picked a guy in a month. Kind of lost touch."

"But why would she take his key?" I said, talking to myself. "And why leave it at the desk? Why not just walk away and leave the whole thing? What if she did think she had to lock the door? Why not drop the key in a sand jar and cover it up? Or take it away with her and lose it? Why do anything with that key that would connect her with that room?" I brought my eyes down and gave Flack a thick leaden stare. "Unless of course she was seen to leave the room—with the key in her hand—and followed out of the hotel."

"What for would anybody do that?" Flack asked.

"Because whoever saw her could have got into that room at once. He had a passkey."

Flack's eyes flicked up at me and dropped all in one motion.

"So he must have followed her," I said. "He must have seen her dump the key at the desk and stroll out of the hotel and he must have followed her a little further than that."

Flack said derisively: "What makes you so wonderful?"

I leaned down and pulled the telephone towards me. "I'd better call Christy and get this over with," I said. "The more I think about it the scareder I get. Maybe she did kill him. I can't cover up for a murderer."

I took the receiver off the hook. Flack slammed his moist paw down hard on top of my hand. The phone jumped on the desk. "Lay off." His voice was almost a sob. "I followed her to a car parked down the street. Got the number. Christ sake, pal, give me some kind of a break." He was fumbling wildly in his pockets. "Know what I make on this job? Cigarette and cigar money and hardly a dime more. Wait a minute now. I think—" He looked down and played solitaire with some dirty envelopes, finally selected one and tossed it over to me. "License number," he said wearily, "and if it's any satisfaction to you, I can't even remember what it was."

I looked down at the envelope. There was a scrawled license number on it all right. Ill-written and faint and oblique, the way it would be written hastily on a paper held in a man's hand on the street. 6N333. California 1947.

"Satisfied?" This was Flack's voice. Or it came out of

his mouth. I tore the number off and tossed the envelope back to him.

"4P 327," I said, watching his eyes. Nothing flicked in them. No trace of derision or concealment. "But how do I know this isn't just some license number you had already?"

"You just got to take my word for it."

"Describe the car," I said.

"Caddy convertible, not new, top up. About 1942 model. Sort of dusty blue color."

"Describe the woman."

"Want a lot for your dough, don't you, peeper?"

"Dr. Hambleton's dough."

He winced. "All right. Blonde. White coat with some colored stitching on it. Wide blue straw hat. Dark glasses. Height about five two. Built like a Conover model."

"Would you know her again—without the glasses?" I asked carefully.

He pretended to think. Then shook his head, no.

"What was that license number again, Flackie?" I caught him off guard.

"Which one?" he said.

I leaned across the desk and dropped some cigarette ash on his gun. I did some more staring into his eyes. But I knew he was licked now. He seemed to know too. He reached for his gun, blew off the ash and put it back in the drawer of his desk.

"Go on. Beat it," he said between his teeth. "Tell the cops I frisked the stiff. So what? Maybe I lose a job. Maybe I get tossed in the fishbowl. So what? When I come out I'm solid. Little Flackie don't have to worry about coffee and crullers. Don't think for a minute those dark cheaters fool little Flackie. I've seen too many movies to miss that lovely puss. And if you ask me that babe'll be around for a long time. She's a comer—and who knows—" he leered at me triumphantly—"she'd need a bodyguard one of these days. A guy to have around, watch things, keep her out of jams. Somebody that knows the ropes and ain't unreasonable about dough. . . . What's the matter?"

I had put my head on one side and was leaning forward. I was listening. "I thought I heard a church bell," I said.

"There ain't any church around here," he said contemptuously. "It's that platinum brain of yours getting cracks in it."

"Just one bell," I said. "Very slow. Tolling is the word, I believe."

Flack listened with me. "I don't hear anything," he said sharply.

"Oh you wouldn't hear it," I said. "You'd be the one guy in the whole world who wouldn't hear it."

He just sat there and stared at me with his nasty little eyes half closed and his nasty little mustache shining. One of his hands twitched on the desk, an aimless movement.

I left him to his thoughts, which were probably as small, ugly and frightened as the man himself.

12

THE APARTMENT HOUSE was over on Doheny Drive, just down the hill from the Strip. It was really two buildings, one behind the other, loosely connected by a floored patio with a fountain, and a room built over the arch. There were mailboxes and bells in the imitation marble foyer. Three out of the sixteen had no names over them. The names that I read meant nothing to me. The job needed a little more work. I tried the front door, found it unlocked, and the job still needed more work.

Outside stood two Cadillacs, a Lincoln Continental and a Packard Clipper. Neither of the Cadillacs had the right color or license. Across the way a guy in riding breeches was sprawled with his legs over the door of a low-cut Lancia. He was smoking and looking up at the pale stars which know enough to keep their distance from Hollywood. I walked up the steep hill to the boulevard and a block east and smothered myself in an outdoor sweat-box phone booth. I dialed a man named Peoria Smith, who was so-called because he stuttered—another little mystery I hadn't had time to work out.

"Mavis Weld," I said. "Phone number. This is Marlowe."

"S-s-s-ure," he said. "M-M-Mavis Weld huh? You want h-h-her ph-ph-phone number?"

"How much?"

"Be-b-b-be ten b-b-b-bucks," he said.

"Just forget I called," I said.

"W-W-Wait a minute! I ain't supposed to give out with them b-b-babes' phone numbers. An assistant prop man is taking a hell of a chance."

I waited and breathed back my own breath.

"The address goes with it naturally," Peoria whined, forgetting to stutter.

"Five bucks," I said. "I've got the address already. And don't haggle. If you think you're the only studio grifter in the business of selling unlisted telephone numbers—"

"Hold it," he said wearily, and went to get his little red book. A left-handed stutterer. He only stuttered when he wasn't excited. He came back and gave it to me. A Crestview number of course. If you don't have a Crestview number in Hollywood you're a bum.

I opened up the steel-and-glass cell to let in some air while I dialed again. After two rings a drawling sexy voice answered. I pulled the door shut.

"Ye-e-e-s," the voice cooed.

"Miss Weld, please."

"And who is calling Miss Weld if you please?"

"I have some stills Whitey wants me to deliver tonight."

"Whitey? And who is Whitey, amigo?"

"The head still-photographer at the studio," I said. "Don't you know that much? I'll come up if you'll tell me which apartment. I'm only a couple of blocks away."

"Miss Weld is taking a bath." She laughed. I guess it was a silvery tinkle where she was. It sounded like somebody putting away saucepans where I was. "But of course bring up the photographs. I am sure she is dying to see them. The apartment number is fourteen."

"Will you be there too?"

"But of course. But naturally. Why do you ask that?"

I hung up and staggered out into the fresh air. I went down the hill. The guy in the riding breeches was still hanging out of the Lancia but one of the Cadillacs was gone and two Buick convertibles had joined the cars in front. I pushed the bell to number fourteen, went on through the patio where scarlet Chinese honeysuckle was lit by a peanut spotlight. Another light glowed down on the big ornamental pool full of fat goldfish and silent lily pads, the lilies folded tight for the night. There were a couple of stone seats and a lawn swing. The place didn't look very expensive except that every place was expensive that year. The apartment was on the second floor, one of two doors facing across a wide landing.

The bell chimed and a tall dark girl in jodhpurs opened the door. Sexy was very faint praise for her. The jodhpurs, like her hair, were coal black. She wore a white silk shirt with a scarlet scarf loose around her throat. It was not as vivid as her mouth. She held a long brown cigarette in a pair of tiny golden tweezers. The fingers holding it were more than adequately jeweled. Her black hair was parted in the middle and a line of scalp as white as snow went over the top of her head and dropped out of sight behind. Two thick braids of her shining black hair lay one on each side of her slim brown neck. Each was tied with a small scarlet bow. But it was a long time since she was a little girl.

She looked sharply down at my empty hands. Studio stills are usually a little too big to put in your pocket.

I said: "Miss Weld please."

"You can give me the stills." The voice was cool, drawling and insolent, but the eyes were something else. She looked almost as hard to get as a haircut.

"For Miss Weld personally. Sorry."

"I told you she was taking a bath."

"I'll wait."

"Are you quite sure you have the stills, amigo?"

"As sure as I'll ever be. Why?"

"Your name?" Her voice froze on the second word, like a feather taking off in a sudden draft. Then it cooed and hovered and soared and eddied and the silent invitation of a smile picked delicately at the corners of her lips, very slowly, like a child trying to pick up a snowflake.

"Your last picture was wonderful, Miss Gonzales."

The smile flashed like lightning and changed her whole face. The body came erect and vibrant with delight. "But it was stinking," she glowed. "Positively God-damned stinking, you sweet lovely man. You know but positively God-damn well it was stinking."

"Nothing with you in it stinks for me, Miss Gonzales."

She stood away from the door and waved me in. "We will have a drink," she said. "The God-damnest drink we will have. I adore flattery, however dishonest."

I went in. A gun in the kidney wouldn't have surprised me a bit. She stood so that I had to practically push her mammaries out of the way to get through the door. She smelled the way the Taj Mahal looks by moonlight. She closed the door and danced over to a small portable bar.

"Scotch? Or would you prefer a mixed drink? I mix a perfectly loathsome Martini," she said.

"Scotch is fine, thanks."

She made a couple of drinks in a couple of glasses you could almost have stood umbrellas in. I sat down in a chintz chair and looked around. The place was old-fashioned. It had a false fireplace with gas logs and a marble mantel, cracks in the plaster, a couple of vigorously colored daubs on the walls that looked lousy enough to have cost money, an old black chipped Steinway and for once no Spanish shawl on it. There were a lot of new-looking books in bright jackets scattered around and a double-barreled shotgun with a handsomely carved stock stood in the corner with a white satin bow tied around the barrels. Hollywood wit.

The dark lady in the jodhpurs handed me a glass and perched on the arm of my chair. "You may call me Dolores if you wish," she said, taking a hearty swig out of her own tumbler.

"Thanks."

"And what may I call you?"

I grinned.

"Of course," she said, "I am most fully aware that you are a God-damn liar and that you have no stills in your pockets. Not that I wish to inquire into your no doubt very private business."

"Yeah?" I inhaled a couple of inches of my liquor. "Just what kind of bath is Miss Weld taking? An old-fashioned soap or something with Arabian spices in it?"

She waved the remains of the brown cigarette in the small gold clasp. "Perhaps you would like to help her. The bathroom is over there—through the arch and to the right. Most probably the door is not locked."

"Not if it's that easy," I said.

"Oh," she gave me the brilliant smile again. "You like to do the difficult things in life. I must remember to be less approachable, must I not?" She removed herself elegantly from the arm of my chair and ditched her cigarette, bending over enough so that I could trace the outline of her hips.

"Don't bother, Miss Gonzales. I'm just a guy who came here on business. I don't have any idea of raping anybody."

"No?" The smile became soft, lazy and, if you can't think of a better word, provocative.

"But I'm sure as hell working up to it," I said.

"You are an amusing son-of-a-bitch," she said with a shrug and went off through the arch, carrying her half-quart of Scotch and water with her. I heard a gentle tapping on a door and her voice: "Darling, there's a man here who says he has some stills from the studio. He says. Muy simpático. Muy guapo también. Con cojones."

A voice I had heard before said sharply: "Shut up, you little bitch. I'll be out in a second."

The Gonzales came back through the archway humming. Her glass was empty. She went to the bar again. "But you are not drinking," she cried, looking at my glass.

"I ate dinner. I only have a two-quart stomach anyway. I understand a little Spanish."

She tossed her head. "You are shocked?" Her eyes rolled. Her shoulders did a fan dance.

"I'm pretty hard to shock."

"But you heard what I said? Madre de Dios. I'm so terribly sorry."

"I'll bet," I said.

She finished making herself another highball.

"Yes. I am so sorry," she sighed. "That is, I think I am. Sometimes I am not sure. Sometimes I do not give a good goddamn. It is so confusing. All my friends tell me I am far too outspoken. I do shock you, don't I?" She was on the arm of my chair again.

"No. But if I wanted to be shocked I'd know right where to come." She reached her glass behind her indolently and leaned towards me.

"But I do not live here," she said. "I live at the Chateau Bercy."

"Alone?"

She slapped me delicately across the tip of my nose.

The next thing I knew I had her in my lap and she was trying to bite a piece off my tongue. "You are a very sweet son-of-a-bitch," she said. Her mouth was as hot as ever a mouth was. Her lips burned like dry ice. Her tongue was driving hard against my teeth. Her eyes looked enormous and black and the whites showed under them.

"I am so tired," she whispered into my mouth. "I am so worn, so incredibly tired."

I felt her hand in my breast pocket. I shoved her off hard, but she had my wallet. She danced away with it laughing, flicked it open and went through it with fingers that darted like little snakes.

"So glad you two got acquainted," a voice off to one side said coolly. Mavis Weld stood in the archway.

Her hair was fluffed out carelessly and she hadn't bothered with make-up. She wore a hostess gown and very little else. Her legs ended in little green and silver slippers. Her eyes were empty, her lips contemptuous. But she was the same girl all right, dark glasses on or off.

The Gonzales gave her a quick darting glance, closed my wallet and tossed it. I caught it and put it away. She strolled to a table and picked up a black bag with a long strap, hooked it over her shoulder and moved towards the door.

Mavis Weld didn't move, didn't look at her. She looked at me. But there was no emotion of any kind in her face. The Gonzales opened the door and glanced outside and almost closed it and turned.

"The name is Philip Marlowe," she said to Mavis Weld. "Nice don't you think?"

"I didn't know you bothered to ask them their names," Mavis Weld said. "You so seldom know them long enough."

"I see," the Gonzales answered gently. She turned and smiled at me faintly. "Such a charming way to call a girl a whore, don't you think?"

Mavis Weld said nothing. Her face had no expression.

"At least," the Gonzales said smoothly as she pulled the door open again, "I haven't been sleeping with any gunmen lately."

"Are you sure you can remember?" Mavis Weld asked her in exactly the same tone. "Open the door, honey. This is the day we put the garbage out."

The Gonzales looked back at her slowly, levelly, and with a knife in her eyes. Then she made a faint sound with her lips and teeth and yanked the door wide. It closed behind her with a jarring smash. The noise didn't even flicker the steady dark-blue glare in Mavis Weld's eyes.

"Now suppose you do the same—but more quietly," she said.

I got out a handkerchief and scrubbed the lipstick over my face. It looked exactly the color of blood, fresh blood. "That could happen to anybody," I said. "I wasn't petting her. She was petting me."

She marched to the door and heaved it open. "On your way, dreamboat. Make with the feet."

"I came here on business, Miss Weld."

"Yes. I can imagine. Out. I don't know you. I don't want to know you. And if I did, this wouldn't be either the day or the hour."

"Never the time and place and the loved one all together," I said.

"What's that?" She tried to throw me out with the point of her chin, but even she wasn't that good.

"Browning. The poet, not the automatic. I feel sure you'd prefer the automatic."

"Look little man, do I have to call the manager to bounce you downstairs like a basketball?"

I went over and pushed the door shut. She held on to the last moment. She didn't quite kick me, but it cost her an effort not to. I tried to ease her away from the door without appearing to. She didn't ease worth a darn. She stood her ground, one hand still reaching for the doorknob, her eyes full of dark-blue rage.

"If you're going to stand that close to me," I said, "maybe you'd better put some clothes on."

She took her hand back and swung it hard. The slap sounded like Miss Gonzales slamming the door, but it stung. And it reminded me of the sore place on the back of my head.

"Did I hurt you?" she said softly.

I nodded.

"That's fine." She hauled off and slapped me again, harder if anything. "I think you'd better kiss me," she breathed. Her eyes were clear and limpid and melting. I glanced down casually. Her right hand was balled into a very businesslike fist. It wasn't too small to work with, either.

"Believe me," I said. "There's only one reason I don't. Even if you had your little black gun with you. Or the brass knuckles you probably keep on your night table."

She smiled politely.

"I might just happen to be working for you," I said. "And I don't go whoring around after every pair of legs I see." I looked down at hers. I could see them all right and the flag that marked the goal line was no larger than it had to be. She pulled the hostess gown together and turned and walked over to the little bar shaking her head.

"I'm free, white and twenty-one," she said. "I've seen all the approaches there are. I think I have. If I can't scare you, lick you, or seduce you, what the hell can I buy you with?"

"Well—"

"Don't tell me," she interrupted sharply and turned with a glass in her hand. She drank and tossed the loose hair around and smiled a thin little smile. "Money, of course. How damned stupid of me to overlook that."

"Money would help," I said.

Her mouth twisted in wry disgust but the voice was almost affectionate. "How much money?"

"Oh a hundred bucks would do to start with."

"You're cheap. It's a cheap little bastard, isn't it? A hundred bucks it says. Is a hundred bucks money in your circle, darling?"

"Make it two hundred then. I could retire on that."

"Still cheap. Every week of course. In a nice clean envelope?"

"You could skip the envelope. I'd only get it dirty."

"And just what would I get for this money, my charming little gum-shoe? I'm quite sure of what you are, of course."

"You'd get a receipt. Who told you I was a gum-shoe?"

She stared out of her own eyes for a brief instant before the act dropped over her again. "It must have been the smell." She sipped her drink and stared at me over it with a faint smile of contempt.

"I'm beginning to think you write your own dialogue," I said. "I've been wondering just what was the matter with it."

I ducked. A few drops splattered me. The glass splintered on the wall behind me. The broken pieces fell soundlessly.

"And with that," she said, completely calm, "I believe I must have used up my entire stock of girlish charm."

I went over and picked up my hat. "I never thought *you* killed him," I said. "But it would help to have some sort of reason for not telling you were there. It's a help to have enough money for a retainer just to establish myself. And enough information to justify my accepting the retainer."

She picked a cigarette out of a box, tossed it in the air, caught it between her lips effortlessly and lit it with a match that came from nowhere.

"My goodness. Am I supposed to have killed somebody?" she asked. I was still holding the hat. It made me feel foolish. I don't know why. I put it on and started for the door.

"I trust you have carfare home," the contemptuous voice said behind me.

I didn't answer. I just kept going. When I had the door ready to open she said: "I also trust Miss Gonzales gave you her address and phone number. You should be able to get almost anything out of her—including, I am told, money."

I let go of the doorknob and went back across the room fast. She stood her ground and the smile on her lips didn't slip a millimeter.

"Look," I said. "You're going to find this hard to believe. But I came over here with the quaint idea that you might be a girl who needed some help—and would find it rather hard to get anyone you could bank on. I figured you went to that hotel room to make some kind of a pay-off. And the fact that you went by yourself and took chances on being recognized—and *were* recognized by a house dick whose standard of ethics would take about as much strain as a very tired old cobweb—all this made me think you might be in one of those Hollywood jams that really mean curtains. But you're not in any jam. You're right up front under the baby spot pulling every tired ham gesture you ever used in the most tired B-picture you ever acted in—if acting is the word—"

"Shut up," she said, between teeth so tight they grated. "Shut up, you slimy, blackmailing keyhole peeper."

"You don't need me," I said. "You don't need anybody. You're so God-damn smart you could talk your way out of a safe-deposit box. Okay. Go ahead and talk your way out. I won't stop you. Just don't make me listen to it. I'd burst out crying to think a mere slip of an innocent little girl like you should be so clever. You do things to me, honey. Just like Margaret O'Brien."

She didn't move or breathe when I reached the door, nor when I opened it. I don't know why. The stuff wasn't *that* good.

I went down the stairs and across the court and out of the front door, almost bumping into a slim dark-eyed man who was standing there lighting a cigarette.

"Excuse me," he said quietly, "I'm afraid I'm in your way."

I started to go around him, then I noticed that his lifted right hand held a key. I reached out and snapped it out of his hand for no reason at all. I looked at the number stamped on it. No. 14. Mavis Weld's apartment. I threw it off behind some bushes.

"You don't need that," I said. "The door isn't locked."

"Of course," he said. There was a peculiar smile on his face. "How stupid of me."

"Yeah," I said. "We're both stupid. Anybody's stupid that bothers with that tramp."

"I wouldn't quite say that," he answered quietly, his small sad eyes watching me without any particular expression.

"You don't have to," I said. "I just said it for you. I beg your pardon. I'll get your key." I went over behind the bushes, picked it up and handed it to him.

"Thank you very much," he said. "And by the way—" He stopped. I stopped. "I hope I don't interrupt an interesting quarrel," he said. "I should hate to do that. No?" He smiled. "Well, since Miss Weld is a friend in common, may I introduce myself. My name is Steelgrave. Haven't I seen you somewhere?"

"No you haven't seen me anywhere, Mr. Steelgrave," I said. "My name's Marlowe, Philip Marlowe. It's extremely unlikely that we've met. And strange to relate I never heard of you, Mr. Steelgrave. And I wouldn't give a damn, even if your name was Weepy Moyer." I never knew quite why I said that. There was nothing to make me say it, except that the name had been mentioned. A peculiar stillness came over his face. A peculiar fixed look in his silent black eyes. He took the cigarette out of his mouth, looked at the tip, flicked a little ash off it, although there was no ash to flick off, looking down as he said: "Weepy Moyer? Peculiar name. I don't think I ever heard that. Is he somebody I should know?"

"Not unless you're unusually fond of ice picks," I said, and left him. I went on down the steps, crossed to my car, looked back before I got in. He was standing there looking down at me, the cigarette between his lips. From that distance I couldn't see whether there was any expression on his face. He didn't move or make any kind of gesture when I looked back at him. He didn't even turn away. He just stood there. I got in and drove off.

13

I DROVE EAST on Sunset but I didn't go home. At La Brea I turned north and swung over to Highland, out over Cahuenga Pass and down on to Ventura Boulevard, past Studio City and Sherman Oaks and Encino. There was nothing lonely about the trip. There never is on that road. Fast boys in stripped-down Fords shot in and out of the traffic streams, missing fenders by a sixteenth of an inch, but somehow always missing them. Tired men in dusty coupés and sedans winced and tightened their grip on the wheel and ploughed on north and west towards home and dinner, an evening with the sports page, the blatting of the radio, the whining of their spoiled children and the gabble of their silly wives. I drove on past the gaudy neons and the false fronts behind them, the sleazy hamburger joints that look like palaces under the colors, the circular drive-ins as gay as circuses with the chipper hard-eyed car-hops, the brilliant counters, and the sweaty greasy kitchens that would have poisoned a toad. Great double trucks rumbled down over Sepulveda from Wilmington and San Pedro and crossed towards the Ridge Route, starting up in low-low from the traffic lights with a growl of lions in the zoo.

Behind Encino an occasional light winked from the hills through thick trees. The homes of screen stars. Screen stars, phooey. The veterans of a thousand beds. Hold it, Marlowe, you're not human tonight.

The air got cooler. The highway narrowed. The cars were so few now that the headlights hurt. The grade rose against chalk walls and at the top a breeze, unbroken from the ocean, danced casually across the night.

I ate dinner at a place near Thousand Oaks. Bad but quick. Feed 'em and throw 'em out. Lots of business. We can't bother with you sitting over your second cup of coffee, mister. You're using money space. See those people over there behind the rope? They want to eat. Anyway they think they have to. God knows why they want to eat here. They could do better home out of a can. They're just restless. Like you. They have to get the car out and go somewhere. Sucker-bait for the racketeers that have taken over the restaurants. Here we go again. You're not human tonight, Marlowe.

I paid off and stopped in a bar to drop a brandy on top of the New York cut. Why New York, I thought. It was Detroit where they made machine tools. I stepped out into the night air that nobody had yet found out how to option. But a lot of people were probably trying. They'd get around to it.

I drove on to the Oxnard cut-off and turned back along the ocean. The big eight-wheelers and sixteen-wheelers were streaming north, all hung over with orange lights. On the right the great fat solid Pacific trudging into shore like a scrubwoman going home. No moon, no fuss, hardly a sound of the surf. No smell. None of the harsh wild smell of the sea. A California ocean. California, the department-store state. The most of everything and the best of nothing. Here we go again. You're not human tonight, Marlowe.

All right. Why would I be? I'm sitting in that office, playing with a dead fly and in pops this dowdy little item from Manhattan, Kansas, and chisels me down to a shopworn twenty to find her brother. He sounds like a creep but she wants to find him. So with this fortune clasped to my chest, I trundle down to Bay City and the routine I go through is so tired I'm half asleep on my feet. I meet nice people, with and without ice picks in their necks. I leave, and I leave myself wide-open too. Then she comes in and takes the twenty away from me and gives me a kiss and gives it back to me because I didn't do a full day's work.

So I go see Dr. Hambleton, retired (and how) optometrist from El Centro, and meet again the new style in neckwear. And I don't tell the cops. I just frisk the customer's toupee and put on an act. Why? Who am I cutting my throat for this time? A blonde with sexy eyes and too many door keys? A girl from Manhattan, Kansas? I don't know. All I know is that something isn't what it seems and the old tired but always reliable hunch tells me that if the hand is played the way it is dealt the wrong person is going to lose the pot. Is that my business? Well, what is my business? Do I know? Did I ever know? Let's not go into that. You're not human tonight, Marlowe. Maybe I never was or ever will be. Maybe I'm an ectoplasm with a private license. Maybe we all get like this in the cold half-lit world where always the wrong thing happens and never the right.

Malibu. More movie stars. More pink and blue bathtubs. More tufted beds. More Chanel No. 5. More Lincoln Continentals and Cadillacs. More wind-blown hair and sunglasses and attitudes and pseudo-refined voices and waterfront morals. Now, wait a minute. Lots of nice peo-

ple work in pictures. You've got the wrong attitude, Marlowe. You're not human tonight.

I smelled Los Angeles before I got to it. It smelled
stale and old like a living room that had been closed too
long. But the colored lights fooled you. The lights were
wonderful. There ought to be a monument to the man
who invented neon lights. Fifteen stories high, solid marble. There's a boy who really made something out of
nothing.

So I went to a picture show and it had to have Mavis
Weld in it. One of those glass-and-chromium deals where
everybody smiled too much and talked too much and
knew it. The women were always going up a long curving
staircase to change their clothes. The men were always
taking monogrammed cigarettes out of expensive cases and
snapping expensive lighters at each other. And the help
was round-shouldered from carrying trays with drinks
across the terrace to a swimming pool about the size of
Lake Huron but a lot neater.

The leading man was an amiable ham with a lot of
charm, some of it turning a little yellow at the edges. The
star was a bad-tempered brunette with contemptuous eyes
and a couple of bad close-ups that showed her pushing
forty-five backwards almost hard enough to break a wrist.
Mavis Weld played second lead and she played it with
wraps on. She was good, but she could have been ten
times better. But if she had been ten times better half her
scenes would have been yanked out to protect the star.
It was as neat a bit of tightrope walking as I ever saw.
Well it wouldn't be a tightrope she'd be walking from
now on. It would be a piano wire. It would be very high.
And there wouldn't be any net under it.

14

I HAD A REASON for going back to the office. A special-delivery letter with an orange claim check ought to have arrived there by now. Most of the windows were dark in the building, but not all. People work nights in other businesses than mine. The elevator man said "Howdy" from the depths of his throat and trundled me up. The corridor had lighted open doors where the scrubwomen were still cleaning up the débris of the wasted hours. I turned a corner past the slobbery hum of a vacuum cleaner, let myself into my dark office and opened the windows. I sat there at the desk doing nothing, not even thinking. No special-delivery letter. All the noise of the building, except the vacuum cleaner, seemed to have flowed out into the street and lost itself among the turning wheels of innumerable cars. Then somewhere along the hall outside a man started whistling "Lili Marlene" with elegance and virtuosity. I knew who that was. The night man checking office doors. I switched the desk lamp on and he passed without trying mine. His steps went away, then came back with a different sound, more of a shuffle. The buzzer sounded in the other office which was still unlocked. That would be special delivery. I went out to get it, only it wasn't.

A fat man in sky-blue pants was closing the door with that beautiful leisure only fat men ever achieve. He wasn't alone, but I looked at him first. He was a large man and wide. Not young nor handsome, but he looked durable. Above the sky-blue gabardine slacks he wore a two-tone leisure jacket which would have been revolting on a ze-bra. The neck of his canary-yellow shirt was open wide, which it had to be if his neck was going to get out. He was hatless and his large head was decorated with a rea-sonable amount of pale salmon-colored hair. His nose had been broken but well set and it hadn't been a col-lector's item in the first place.

The creature with him was a weedy number with red eyes and sniffles. Age about twenty, five feet nine, thin as a broom straw. His nose twitched and his mouth twitched and his hands twitched and he looked very un-happy.

The big man smiled genially. "Mr. Marlowe, no doubt?"

I said: "Who else?"

"It's a little late for a business call," the big man said and hid half the office by spreading out his hands. "I hope you don't mind. Or do you already have all the busi-ness you can handle?"

"Don't kid me. My nerves are frayed," I said. "Who's the junky?"

"Come along, Alfred," the big man said to his com-panion. "And stop acting girlish."

"In a pig's valise," Alfred told him.

The big man turned to me placidly. "Why do all these punks keep saying that? It isn't funny. It isn't witty. It doesn't mean anything. Quite a problem, this Alfred. I got him off the stuff, you know, temporarily at least. Say 'how do you do' to Mr. Marlowe, Alfred."

"Screw him," Alfred said.

The big man sighed. "My name's Toad," he said. "Joseph P. Toad."

I didn't say anything.

"Go ahead and laugh," the big man said. "I'm used to it. Had the name all my life." He came towards me with his hand out. I took it. The big man smiled pleasantly into my eyes. "O.K. Alfred," he said without looking back.

Alfred made what seemed to be a very slight and unimportant movement at the end of which a heavy automatic was pointing at me.

"Careful, Alfred," the big man said, holding my hand with a grip that would have bent a girder. "Not yet."

"In a pig's valise," Alfred said. The gun pointed at my chest. His finger tightened around the trigger. I watched it tighten. I knew at precisely what moment that tightening would release the hammer. It didn't seem to make any difference. This was happening somewhere else in a cheesy program picture. It wasn't happening to me.

The hammer of the automatic clicked dryly on nothing. Alfred lowered the gun with a grunt of annoyance and it disappeared whence it had come. He started to twitch again. There was nothing nervous about his movements with the gun. I wondered just what junk he was off of.

The big man let go of my hand, the genial smile still over his large healthy face.

He patted a pocket. "I got the magazine," he said. "Alfred ain't reliable lately. The little bastard might have shot you."

Alfred sat down in a chair and tilted it against the wall and breathed through his mouth.

I let my heels down on the floor again.

"I bet he scared you," Joseph P. Toad said.

I tasted salt on my tongue.

"You ain't so tough," Toad said, poking me in the stomach with a fat finger.

I stepped away from the finger and watched his eyes.

"What does it cost?" he asked almost gently.

"Let's go into my parlor," I said.

I turned my back on him and walked through the door into the other office. It was hard work but I made it. I sweated all the way. I went around behind the desk and stood there waiting. Mr. Toad followed me in placidly. The junky came twitching in behind him.

"You don't have a comic book around, do you?" Toad asked. "Keeps him quiet."

"Sit down," I said. "I'll look."

He reached for the chair arms. I jerked a drawer open and got my hand around the butt of a Luger. I brought it up slowly, looking at Alfred. Alfred didn't even look at me. He was studying the corner of the ceiling and trying to keep his mouth out of his eye.

"This is as comic as I get," I said.

"You won't need that," the big man said, genially.

"That's fine," I said, like somebody else talking, far away behind a wall. I could just barely hear the words. "But if I do, here it is. And this one's loaded. Want me to prove it to you?"

The big man looked as near worried as he would ever look. "I'm sorry you take it like that," he said. "I'm so used to Alfred I hardly notice him. Maybe you're right. Maybe I ought to do something about him."

"Yeah," I said. "Do it this afternoon before you come up here. It's too late now."

"Now wait a minute, Mr. Marlowe." He put his hand out. I slashed at it with the Luger. He was fast, but not fast enough. I cut the back of his hand open with the sight on the gun. He grabbed at it and sucked at the cut. "Hey, please! Alfred's my nephew. My sister's kid. I kind of look after him. He wouldn't hurt a fly, really."

"Next time you come up I'll have one for him not to hurt," I said.

"Now don't be like that, mister. Please don't be like that. I've got quite a nice little proposition—"

"Shut up," I said. I sat down very slowly. My face burned. I had difficulty speaking clearly at all. I felt a little drunk. I said, slowly and thickly: "A friend of mine told me about a fellow that had something like this pulled on him. He was at a desk the way I am. He had a gun, just the way I have. There were two men on the other side of the desk, like you and Alfred. The man on my side began to get mad. He couldn't help himself. He began to shake. He couldn't speak a word. He just had this gun in his hand. So without a word he shot twice under the desk, right where your belly is."

The big man turned a sallow green color and started to get up. But he changed his mind. He got a violent-looking handkerchief out of his pocket and mopped his face. "You seen that in a picture," he said.

"That's right," I said. "But the man who made the picture told me where he got the idea. *That* wasn't in any picture." I put the Luger down on the desk in front of me and said in a more natural voice: "You've got to be careful about firearms, Mr. Toad. You never know but what it may upset a man to have an Army .45 snapped in his face—especially when he doesn't know it's not loaded. It made me kind of nervous for a minute. I haven't had a shot of morphine since lunch time."

Toad studied me carefully with narrow eyes. The junky got up and went to another chair and kicked it around and sat down and tilted his greasy head against the wall. But his nose and hands kept on twitching.

"I heard you were kind of hard-boiled," Toad said slowly, his eyes cool and watchful.

"You heard wrong. I'm a very sensitive guy. I go all to pieces over nothing."

"Yeah. I understand." He stared at me a long time without speaking. "Maybe we played this wrong. Mind if I put my hand in my pocket? I don't wear a gun."

"Go ahead," I said. "It would give me the greatest possible pleasure to see you try to pull a gun."

He frowned, then very slowly got out a flat pigskin wallet and drew out a crisp new one-hundred-dollar bill. He laid it on the edge of the glass top, drew out another just like it, then one by one three more. He laid them carefully in a row along the desk, end to end. Alfred let his chair settle to the floor and stared at the money with his mouth quivering.

"Five C's," the big man said. He folded his wallet and put it away. I watched every movement he made. "For nothing at all but keeping the nose clean. Check?"

I just looked at him.

"You ain't looking for nobody," the big man said. "You couldn't find nobody. You don't have time to work for nobody. You didn't hear a thing or see a thing. You're clean. Five C's clean. Okay?"

There was no sound in the office but Alfred's sniffling. The big man half turned his head. "Quiet Alfred. I'll give you a shot when we leave," the big man told him. "Try to act nice." He sucked again at the cut on the back of his hand.

"With you for a model that ought to be easy," I said.

"Screw you," Alfred said.

"Limited vocabulary," the big man told me. "Very limited. Get the idea, chum?" He indicated the money. I fingered the butt of the Luger. He leaned forward a little. "Relax, can't you. It's simple. This is a retainer. You don't do a thing for it. Nothing is what you do. If you keep on doing nothing for a reasonable length of time you get the same amount later on. That's simple, isn't it?"

"And who am I doing this nothing for?" I asked.

"Me. Joseph P. Toad."

"What's your racket?"

"Business representative, you might call me."

"What else could I call you? Besides what I could think up myself?"

"You could call me a guy that wants to help out a guy that don't want to make trouble for a guy."

"And what could I call that lovable character?" I asked.

Joseph P. Toad gathered the five hundred-dollar bills together, lined up the edges neatly and pushed the packet across the desk. "You can call him a guy that would rather spill money than blood," he said. "But he don't mind spilling blood if it looks like that's what he's got to do."

"How is he with an ice pick?" I asked. "I can see how lousy he is with a .45."

The big man chewed his lower lip, then pulled it out with a blunt forefinger and thumb and nibbled on the inside of it softly, like a milch cow chewing her cud. "We're not talking about ice picks," he said at length. "All we're talking about is how you might get off on the wrong foot and do yourself a lot of harm. Whereas if you don't get off on no foot at all, you're sitting pretty and money coming in."

"Who is the blonde?" I asked.

He thought about that and nodded. "Maybe you're into this too far already," he sighed. "Maybe it's too late to do business."

After a moment he leaned forward and said gently: "Okay. I'll check back with my principal and see how far out he wants to come. Maybe we can still do business. Everything stands as it is until you hear from me. Check?"

I let him have that one. He put his hands on the desk and very slowly stood up, watching the gun I was pushing around on the blotter.

"You can keep the dough," he said. "Come on, Alfred." He turned and walked solidly out of the office.

Alfred's eyes crawled sideways watching him, then jerked to the money on the desk. The big automatic appeared with the same magic in his thin right hand. Dartingly as an eel he moved over to the desk. He kept the gun on me and reached for the money with his left hand. It disappeared into his pocket. He gave me a smooth cool empty grin, nodded and moved away, apparently not realizing for a moment that I was holding a gun too.

"Come on, Alfred," the big man called sharply from outside the door. Alfred slipped through the door and was gone.

The outer door opened and closed. Steps went along the hall. Then silence. I sat there thinking back over it, trying to make up my mind whether it was pure idiocy or just a new way to toss a scare.

Five minutes later the telephone rang.

A thick pleasant voice said: "Oh by the way, Mr. Marlowe, I guess you know Sherry Ballou, don't you?"

"Nope."

"Sheridan Ballou, Incorporated. The big agent? You ought to look him up sometime."

I held the phone silently for a moment. Then I said: "Is he her agent?"

"He might be," Joseph P. Toad said, and paused a moment. "I suppose you realize we're just a couple of bit players, Mr. Marlowe. That's all. Just a couple of bit players. Somebody wanted to find out a little something about you. It seemed the simplest way to do it. Now, I'm not so sure."

I didn't answer. He hung up. Almost at once the phone rang again.

A seductive voice said: "You do not like me so well, do you, amigo?"

"Sure I do. Just don't keep biting me."

"I am at home at the Chateau Bercy. I am lonely."

"Call an escort bureau."

"But please. That is no way to talk. This is business of a great importance."

"I bet. But not the business I'm in."

"That slut—What does she say about me?" she hissed.

"Nothing. Oh, she might have called you a Tijuana hooker in riding pants. Would you mind?"

That amused her. The silvery giggle went on for a little while. "Always the wisecrack with you. Is it not so? But you see I did not then know you were a detective. That makes a very big difference."

I could have told her how wrong she was. I just said: "Miss Gonzales, you said something about business. What kind of business, if you're not kidding me?"

"Would you like to make a great deal of money? A very great deal of money?"

"You mean without getting shot?" I asked.

Her incaught breath came over the wire. "Sí," she said thoughtfully. "There is also that to consider. But you are so brave, so big, so—"

"I'll be at my office at nine in the morning, Miss Gonzales. I'll be a lot braver then. Now if you'll excuse me—"

"You have a date? Is she beautiful? More beautiful than I am?"

"For Christ's sake," I said. "Don't you ever think of anything but one thing?"

"The hell with you, darling," she said and hung up in my face.

I turned the lights out and left. Halfway down the hall I met a man looking at numbers. He had a special delivery in his hand. So I had to go back to the office and put it in the safe. And the phone rang again while I was doing this.

I let it ring. I had had enough for one day. I just didn't care. It could have been the Queen of Sheba with her cellophane pajamas on—or off—I was too tired to bother. My brain felt like a bucket of wet sand.

It was still ringing as I reached the door. No use. I had to go back. Instinct was stronger than weariness. I lifted the receiver.

Orfamay Quest's twittery little voice said: "Oh Mr. Marlowe I've been trying to get you for just the longest time. I'm so supset. I'm—"

"In the morning," I said. "The office is closed."

"Please, Mr. Marlowe—just because I lost my temper for a moment—"

"In the morning."

"But I tell you I have to see you." The voice didn't quite rise to a yell. "It's terribly important."

"Unhuh."

She sniffled. "You—you kissed me."

"I've kissed better since," I said. To hell with her. To hell with all women.

"I've heard from Orrin," she said.

That stopped me for a moment, then I laughed. "You're a nice little liar," I said. "Goodbye."

"But really I have. He called me. On the telephone. Right here where I'm staying."

"Fine," I said. "Then you don't need a detective at all. And if you did, you've got a better one than I am right in the family. I couldn't even find out where you were staying."

There was a little pause. She still had me talking to her anyway. She'd kept me from hanging up. I had to give her that much.

"I wrote to him where I'd be staying," she said at last.

"Unhuh. Only he didn't get the letter because he had moved and he didn't leave any forwarding address. Remember? Try again some time when I'm not so tired. Goodnight, Miss Quest. And you don't have to tell me where you are staying now. I'm not working for you."

"Very well, Mr. Marlowe. I'm ready to call the police

now. But I don't think you'll like it. I don't think you'll like it at all."

"Why?"

"Because there's murder in it, Mr. Marlowe, and murder is a very nasty word—don't you think?"

"Come on up," I said. "I'll wait."

I hung up. I got the bottle of Old Forester out. There was nothing slow about the way I poured myself a drink and dropped it down my throat.

15

SHE CAME IN briskly enough this time. Her motions were small and quick and determined. There was one of those thin little, bright little smiles on her face. She put her bag down firmly, settled herself in the customer's chair and went on smiling.

"It's nice of you to wait for me," she said. "I bet you haven't had your dinner yet, either."

"Wrong," I said. "I have had my dinner. I am now drinking whiskey. You don't approve of whiskey-drinking do you?"

"I certainly do not."

"That's just dandy," I said. "I hoped you hadn't changed your mind." I put the bottle up on the desk and poured myself another slug. I drank a little of it and gave her a leer above the glass.

"If you keep on with that you won't be in any condition to listen to what I have to say," she snapped.

"About this murder," I said. "Anybody I know? I can see you're not murdered—yet."

"Please don't be unnecessarily horrid. It's not my fault.

You doubted me over the telephone so I had to convince you. Orrin did call me up. But he wouldn't tell me where he was or what he was doing. I don't know why."

"He wanted you to find out for yourself," I said. "He's building your character."

"That's not funny. It's not even smart."

"But you've got to admit it's nasty," I said. "Who was murdered? Or is that a secret too?"

She fiddled a little with her bag, not enough to overcome her embarrassment, because she wasn't embarrassed. But enough to needle me into taking another drink.

"That horrid man in the rooming house was murdered. Mr.—Mr.—I forget his name."

"Let's both forget it," I said. "Let's do something together for once." I dropped the whiskey bottle into the desk drawer and stood up. "Look, Orfamay, I'm not asking you how you know all this. Or rather how Orrin knows it all. Or if he *does* know it. You've found him. That's what you wanted me to do. Or he's found you, which comes to the same thing."

"It's not the same thing," she cried. "I haven't really found him. He wouldn't tell me where he was living."

"Well if it is anything like the last place, I don't blame him."

She set her lips in a firm line of distaste. "He wouldn't tell me anything really."

"Just about murders," I said. "Trifles like that."

She laughed bubblingly. "I just said that to scare you. I don't really mean anybody was murdered, Mr. Marlowe. You sounded so cold and distant. I thought you wouldn't help me any more. And—well, I just made it up."

I took a couple of deep breaths and looked down at my hands. I straightened out the fingers slowly. Then I stood up. I didn't say anything.

"Are you mad at me?" she asked timidly, making a little circle on the desk with the point of a finger.

"I ought to slap your face off," I said. "And quit acting innocent. Or it mightn't be your face I'd slap."

Her breath caught with a jerk. "Why, how dare you!"

"You used that line," I said. "You used it too often. Shut up and get the hell out of here. Do you think I enjoy being scared to death? Oh—there's this." I yanked a drawer open, got out her twenty dollars and threw them down in front of her. "Take this money away. Endow a hospital or a research laboratory with it. It makes me nervous having it around."

Her hand reached automatically for the money. Her eyes behind the cheaters were round and wondering. "Goodness," she said, assembling her handbag with a nice dignity. "I'm sure I didn't know you scared that easy. I thought you were tough."

"That's just an act," I growled, moving around the desk. She leaned back in her chair away from me. "I'm only tough with little girls like you that don't let their fingernails grow too long. I'm all mush inside." I took hold of her arm and yanked her to her feet. Her head went back. Her lips parted. I was hell with the women that day.

"But you will find Orrin for me, won't you?" she whispered. "It was all a lie. Everything I've told you was a lie. He didn't call me up. I—I don't know anything."

"Perfume," I said sniffing. "Why, you little darling. You put perfume behind your ears—and all for me!"

She nodded her little chin half an inch. Her eyes were melting. "Take my glasses off," she whispered, "Philip. I don't mind if you take a little whiskey once in a while. Really I don't."

Our faces were about six inches apart. I was afraid to take her glasses off. I might have socked her on the nose.

"Yes," I said in a voice that sounded like Orson Welles with his mouth full of crackers. "I'll find him for you, honey, if he's still alive. And for free. Not a dime of expense involved. I only ask one thing."

"What, Philip?" she asked softly and opened her lips a little wider.

"Who was the black sheep in your family?"

She jerked away from me like a startled fawn might, if I had a startled fawn and it jerked away from me. She stared at me stony-faced.

"You said Orrin wasn't the black sheep in your family. Remember? With a very peculiar emphasis. And when you mentioned your sister Leila, you sort of passed on quickly as if the subject was distasteful."

"I—I don't remember saying anything like that," she said very slowly.

"So I was wondering," I said. "What name does your sister Leila use in pictures?"

"Pictures?" she sounded vague. "Oh you mean motion pictures? Why I never said she was in pictures. I never said anything about her like that."

I gave her my big homely lopsided grin. She suddenly flew into a rage.

"Mind your own business about my sister Leila," she spit at me. "You leave my sister Leila out of your dirty remarks."

"What dirty remarks?" I asked. "Or should I try to guess?"

"All you think about is liquor and women," she screamed. "I hate you!" She rushed to the door and yanked it open and went out. She practically ran down the hall.

I went back around my desk and slumped into the chair. A very strange little girl. Very strange indeed. After a while the phone started ringing again, as it would. On the fourth ring I leaned my head on my hand and groped for it, fumbled it to my face.

"Utter McKinley Funeral Parlors," I said.

A female voice said: "Wha-a-t?" and went off into a shriek of laughter. That one was a riot at the police smoker in 1921. What a wit. Like a hummingbird's beak. I put the lights out and went home.

16

EIGHT-FORTY-FIVE the next morning found me parked a couple of doors from the Bay City Camera Shop, breakfasted and peaceful and reading the local paper through a pair of sunglasses. I had already chewed my way through the Los Angeles paper, which contained no item about ice picks in the Van Nuys or any other hotel. Not even MYSTERIOUS DEATH IN DOWNTOWN HOTEL, with no names or weapons specified. The Bay City *News* wasn't too busy to write up a murder. They put it on the first page, right next to the price of meat.

LOCAL MAN FOUND STABBED
IN IDAHO STREET ROOMING HOUSE

An anonymous telephone call late yesterday sent police speeding to an address on Idaho Street opposite the Seamans and Jansing Company's lumber yard. Entering the unlocked door of his apartment, officers found Lester B. Clausen, 45, manager of the rooming house, dead on the couch. Clausen had been stabbed in the neck with an ice pick which was still in his body. After a preliminary examination, Coroner Frank L. Crowdy announced that Clausen had been drinking heavily and may have been unconscious at the time of his death. No signs of struggle were observed by the police.

Detective Lieutenant Moses Maglashan immediately took charge and questioned tenants of the rooming house on their return from work, but no light has so far been thrown on the circumstances of the crime. Interviewed by this reporter, Coroner Crowdy stated that Clausen's death might have been suicide but that the position of the wound made this unlikely. Examination of the rooming-house register disclosed that a page had recently been torn out. Lieutenant Maglashan, after questioning the tenants at length, stated that a thick-set middle-aged man with brown hair and heavy features had been noticed in the hallway of the rooming house on several occasions, but that none of the tenants knew his name or occupation. After carefully checking all rooms, Maglashan further gave it as his opinion that one of the roomers had left recently and in some haste. The mutilation of the register, however, the character of the neighborhood, the lack of an accurate description of the missing man, made the job of tracing him extremely difficult.

"I have no idea at present why Clausen was murdered," Maglashan announced at a late hour last night. *"But I have had my eye on this man for some time. Many of his associates are known to me. It's a tough case, but we'll crack it."*

It was a nice piece and only mentioned Maglashan's name twelve times in the text and twice more in picture captions. There was a photo of him on page three holding an ice pick and looking at it with profound thought wrinkling his brows. There was a photo of 449 Idaho

Street which did it more than justice, and a photo of something with a sheet over it on a couch and Lieutenant Maglashan pointing at it sternly. There was also a close-up of the mayor looking as executive as hell behind his official desk and an interview with him on the subject of post-war crime. He said just what you would expect a mayor to say—a watered-down shot of J. Edgar Hoover with some extra bad grammar thrown in.

At three minutes to nine the door of the Bay City Camera Shop opened and an elderly Negro began to sweep dirt across the sidewalk into the gutter. At nine A.M. a neat-appearing young guy in glasses fixed the lock on the door and I went in there with the black-and-orange check Dr. G. W. Hambleton had pasted to the inside of his toupee.

The neat-appearing young man gave me a searching glance as I exchanged the check and some money for an envelope containing a tiny negative and half a dozen shiny prints blown up to eight times the size of the negative. He didn't say anything, but the way he looked at me gave me the impression that he remembered I was not the man who had left the negative.

I went out and sat in my car and looked over the catch. The prints showed a man and a blond girl sitting in a rounded booth in a restaurant with food in front of them. They were looking up as though their attention had suddenly been attracted and they had only just had time to react before the camera had clicked. It was clear from the lighting that no flashbulb had been used.

The girl was Mavis Weld. The man was rather small, rather dark, rather expressionless. I didn't recognize him. There was no reason why I should. The padded leather seat was covered with tiny figures of dancing couples. That made the restaurant THE DANCERS. This added to the confusion. Any amateur camera hound that tried to flash a lens in there without getting an okay from the management would have been thrown out so hard that he would have bounced all the way down to Hollywood and Vine. I figured it must have been the hidden-camera trick, the way they took Ruth Snyder in the electric chair. He would have the little camera up hanging by a strap under his coat collar, the lens just peeping out from his open jacket, and he would have rigged a bulb release that he could hold in his pocket. It wasn't too hard for me to guess who had taken the picture. Mr. Orrin P. Quest must have moved fast and smooth to get out of there with his face still in front of his head.

I put the pictures in my vest pocket and my fingers touched a crumpled piece of paper. I got it out and read: "Doctor Vincent Lagardie, 965 Wyoming Street, Bay City." That was the Vince I had talked to on the phone, the one Lester B. Clausen might have been trying to call.

An elderly flatfoot was strolling down the line of parked cars, marking tires with yellow chalk. He told me where Wyoming Street was. I drove out there. It was a cross-town street well out beyond the business district, parallel with two numbered streets. Number 965, a gray-white frame house, was on a corner. On its door a brass plate said *Vincent Lagardie, M.D., Hours 10.00 to 12.00 and 2.30 to 4.00.*

The house looked quiet and decent. A woman with an unwilling small boy was going up the steps. She read the plate, looked at a watch pinned to her lapel and chewed irresolutely on her lip. The small boy looked around carefully, then kicked her on the ankle. She winced but her voice was patient. "Now, Johnny, you mustn't do that to Aunty Fern," she said mildly.

She opened the door and dragged the little ape in with her. Diagonally across the intersection was a big white colonial mansion with a portico which was roofed and much too small for the house. Floodlight reflectors were set into the front lawn. The walk was bordered by tree roses in bloom. A large black and silver sign over the portico said: *"The Garland Home of Peace."* I wondered how Dr. Lagardie liked looking out of his front windows at a funeral parlor. Maybe it made him careful.

I turned around at the intersection and drove back to Los Angeles, and went up to the office to look at my mail and lock my catch from the Bay City Camera Shop up in the battered green safe—all but one print. I sat down at the desk and studied this through a magnifying glass. Even with that and the camera shop blow-up the detail was still clear. There was an evening paper, a *News-Chronicle,* lying on the table in front of the dark thin expressionless man who sat beside Mavis Weld. I could just read the headline. *LIGHT HEAVYWEIGHT CONTENDER SUCCUMBS TO RING INJURIES.* Only a noon or late sports edition would use a headline like that. I pulled the phone towards me. It rang just as I got my hand on it.

"Marlowe? This is Christy French downtown. Any ideas this morning?"

"Not if your teletype's working. I've seen a Bay City paper."

"Yeah, we got that," he said casually. "Sounds like the same guy, don't it? Same initials, same description, same method of murder, and the time element seems to check. I hope to Christ this doesn't mean Sunny Moe Stein's mob have started in business again."

"If they have, they've changed their technique," I said. "I was reading up on it last night. The Stein mob used to jab their victims full of holes. One of them had over a hundred stab wounds in him."

"They could learn better," French said a little evasively, as if he didn't want to talk about it. "What I called you about was Flack. Seen anything of him since yesterday afternoon?"

"No."

"He skipped out. Didn't come to work. Hotel called his landlady. Packed up and left last night. Destination unknown."

"I haven't seen him or heard from him," I said.

"Didn't it strike you as kind of funny our stiff only had fourteen bucks in his kick?"

"It did a little. You answered that yourself."

"I was just talking. I don't buy that any more. Flack's either scared out or come into money. Either he saw something he didn't tell and got paid to breeze, or else he lifted the customer's case dough, leaving the fourteen bucks to make it look better."

I said: "I'll buy either one. Or both at the same time. Whoever searched that room so thoroughly wasn't looking for money."

"Why not?"

"Because when this Dr. Hambleton called me up I suggested the hotel safe to him. He wasn't interested."

"A type like that wouldn't have hired you to hold his dough anyway," French said. "He wouldn't have hired you to keep anything for him. He wanted protection or he wanted a sidekick—or maybe just a messenger."

"Sorry," I said. "He told me just what I told you."

"And seeing he was dead when you got over there," French said with a too casual drawl, "you couldn't hardly have given him one of your business cards."

I held the phone too tight and thought back rapidly over my talk with Hicks in the Idaho Street rooming house. I saw him holding my card between his fingers, looking down at it. And then I saw myself taking it out of his hand quickly, before he froze to it. I took a deep breath and let it out slowly.

"Hardly," I said. "And stop trying to scare me to death."

"He had one, chum. Folded twice across in his pants watch pocket. We missed it the first time."

"I gave Flack a card," I said, stiff-lipped.

There was silence. I could hear voices in the background and the clack of a typewriter. Finally French said dryly: "Fair enough. See you later." He hung up abruptly.

I put the phone down very slowly in its cradle and flexed my cramped fingers. I stared down at the photo lying on the desk in front of me. All it told me was that two people, one of whom I knew, were having lunch at The Dancers. The paper on the table told me the date, or would.

I dialed the *News-Chronicle* and asked for the sports section. Four minutes later I wrote on a pad: "Ritchy Belleau, popular young light heavyweight contender, died in the Sisters Hospital just before midnight February 19 as a result of ring injuries sustained the previous evening in the main event at the Hollywood Legion Stadium. The *News-Chronicle* Noon Sports Edition for February 20 carried the headlines."

I dialed the same number again and asked for Kenny Haste in the City Room. He was an ex-crime reporter I had known for years. We chatted around for a minute and then I said:

"Who covered the Sunny Moe Stein killing for you?"

"Tod Barrow. He's on the *Post-Despatch* now. Why?"

"I'd like the details, if any."

He said he would send to the morgue for the file and call me, which he did ten minutes later. "He was shot twice in the head, in his car, about two blocks from the Chateau Bercy on Franklin. Time, about 11.15 P.M."

"Date, February 20," I said, "or was it?"

"Check, it was. No witnesses, no arrests except the usual police stock company of book-handlers, out-of-work fight managers and other professional suspects. What's in it?"

"Wasn't a pal of his supposed to be in town about that time?"

"Nothing here says so. What name?"

"Weepy Moyer. A cop friend of mine said something about a Hollywood money man being held on suspicion and then released for lack of evidence."

Kenny said: "Wait a minute. Something's coming back to me—yeah. Fellow named Steelgrave, owns The Dancers, supposed to be a gambler and so on. Nice guy. I've met him. That was a bust."

"How do you mean, a bust?"

"Some smart monkey tipped the cops he was Weepy Moyer and they held him for ten days on an open charge for Cleveland. Cleveland brushed it off. That didn't have anything to do with the Stein killing. Steelgrave was under glass all that week. No connection at all. Your cop friend has been reading pulp magazines."

"They all do," I said. "That's why they talk so tough. Thanks, Kenny."

We said goodbye and hung up and I sat leaning back in my chair and looking at my photograph. After a while I took scissors and cut out the piece that contained the folded newspaper with the headline. I put the two pieces in separate envelopes and put them in my pocket with the sheet from the pad.

I dialed Miss Mavis Weld's Crestview number. A woman's voice answered after several rings. It was a remote and formal voice that I might or might not have heard before. All it said was, "Hello?"

"This is Philip Marlowe. Is Miss Weld in?"

"Miss Weld will not be in until late this evening. Do you care to leave a message?"

"Very important. Where could I reach her?"

"I'm sorry. I have no information."

"Would her agent know?"

"Possibly."

"You're quite sure *you're* not Miss Weld?"

"Miss Weld is not in." She hung up.

I sat there and listened to the voice. At first I thought yes, then I thought no. The longer I thought the less I knew. I went down to the parking lot and got my car out.

17

ON THE TERRACE at The Dancers a few early birds were getting ready to drink their lunch. The glass-fronted upstairs room had the awning let down in front of it. I drove on past the curve that goes down into the Strip and stopped across the street from a square building of two stories of rose-red brick with small white leaded bay windows and a Greek porch over the front door and what looked, from across the street, like an antique pewter doorknob. Over the door was a fanlight and the name Sheridan Ballou, Inc., in black wooden letters severely stylized. I locked my car and crossed to the front door. It was white and tall and wide and had a keyhole big enough for a mouse to crawl through. Inside this keyhole was the real lock. I went for the knocker, but they had thought of that too. It was all in one piece and didn't knock.

So I patted one of the slim fluted white pillars and opened the door and walked directly into the reception room which filled the entire front of the building. It was furnished in dark antique-looking furniture and many chairs and settees of quilted chintz-like material. There were lace curtains at the windows and chintz boxes around them that matched the chintz of the furniture. There was a flowered carpet and a lot of people waiting to see Mr. Sheridan Ballou.

Some of them were bright and cheerful and full of hope. Some looked as if they had been there for days. One small dark girl was sniffling into her handkerchief in the corner. Nobody paid any attention to her. I got a couple of profiles at nice angles before the company decided I wasn't buying anything and didn't work there.

A dangerous-looking redhead sat languidly at an Adam desk talking into a pure-white telephone. I went over there and she put a couple of cold blue bullets into me with her eyes and then stared at the cornice that ran around the room.

"No," she said into the phone. "No. So sorry. I'm afraid it's no use. Far, far too busy." She hung up and ticked off something on a list and gave me some more of her steely glance.

"Good morning. I'd like to see Mr. Ballou," I said. I put my plain card on her desk. She lifted it by one corner, smiled at it amusedly.

"Today?" she inquired amiably. "This week?"

"How long does it usually take?"

"It *has* taken six months," she said cheerfully. "Can't somebody else help you?"

"No."

"So sorry. Not a chance. Drop in again won't you? Somewhere about Thanksgiving." She was wearing a white wool skirt, a burgundy silk blouse and a black velvet over-jacket with short sleeves. Her hair was a hot sunset. She wore a golden topaz bracelet and topaz earrings and a topaz dinner ring in the shape of a shield. Her fingernails matched her blouse exactly. She looked as if it would take a couple of weeks to get her dressed.

"I've got to see him," I said.

She read my card again. She smiled beautifully. "Everyone has," she said. "Why—er—Mr. Marlowe. Look at all these lovely people. Every one of them has been here since the office opened two hours ago."

"This is important."

"No doubt. In what way if I may ask?"

"I want to peddle a little dirt."

She picked a cigarette out of a crystal box and lit it with a crystal lighter. "Peddle? You mean for money—in Hollywood?"

"Could be."

"What kind of dirt? Don't be afraid to shock me."

"It's a bit obscene, Miss—Miss—" I screwed my head around to read the plaque on her desk.

"Helen Grady," she said. "Well, a little well-bred obscenity never did any harm, did it?"

"I didn't say it was well-bred."

She leaned back carefully and puffed smoke in my face.

"Blackmail in short." She sighed. "Why the hell don't you lam out of here, bud? Before I throw a handful of fat coppers in your lap?"

I sat on the corner of her desk, grabbed a double handful of her cigarette smoke and blew it into her hair. She dodged angrily. "Beat it, lug," she said in a voice that could have been used for paint remover.

"Oh oh. What happened to the Bryn Mawr accent?"

Without turning her head she said sharply: "Miss Vane."

A tall slim elegant dark girl with supercilious eyebrows looked up. She had just come through an inner door camouflaged as a stained-glass window. The dark girl came over. Miss Grady handed her my card: "Spink."

Miss Vane went back through the stained-glass window with the card.

"Sit down and rest your ankles, big stuff," Miss Grady informed me. "You may be here all week."

I sat down in a chintz winged chair, the back of which came eight inches above my head. It made me feel shrunken. Miss Grady gave me her smile again, the one with the hand-honed edge, and bent to the telephone once more.

I looked around. The little girl in the corner had stopped crying and was making up her face with calm unconcern. A very tall distinguished-looking party swung up a graceful arm to stare at his elegant wrist watch and oozed gently to his feet. He set a pearl-gray homburg at a rakish angle on the side of his head, checked his yellow chamois gloves and his silver-knobbed cane, and strolled languidly over to the red-headed receptionist.

"I have been waiting two hours to see Mr. Ballou," he said icily in a rich sweet voice that had been modulated by a lot of training. "I'm not accustomed to waiting two hours to see anybody."

"So sorry, Mr. Fortescue. Mr. Ballou is just too busy for words this A.M."

"I'm sorry I cannot leave him a check," the elegant tall party remarked with a weary contempt. "Probably the only thing that would interest him. But in default of that—"

"Just a minute, kid." The redhead picked up a phone and said into it: "Yes? . . . Who says so besides Goldwyn? Can't you reach somebody that's not crazy? . . . Well try again." She slammed the telephone down. The tall party had not moved.

"In default of that," he resumed as if he had never stopped speaking, "I should like to leave a short personal message."

"Please do," Miss Grady told him. "I'll get it to him somehow."

"Tell him with my love that he is a dirty polecat."

"Make it skunk, darling," she said. "He doesn't know any English words."

"Make it skunk and double skunk," Fortescue told her. "With a slight added nuance of sulphurated hydrogen and a very cheap grade of whore-house perfume." He adjusted his hat and gave his profile the once over in a mirror. "I now bid you good morning and to hell with Sheridan Ballou, Incorporated."

The tall actor stalked out elegantly, using his cane to open the door.

"What's the matter with him?" I asked.

She looked at me pityingly. "Billy Fortescue? Nothing's the matter with him. He isn't getting any parts so he comes in every day and goes through that routine. He figures somebody might see him and like it."

I shut my mouth slowly. You can live a long time in Hollywood and never see the part they use in pictures.

Miss Vane appeared through the inner door and made a chin-jerk at me. I went in past her. "This way. Second on the right." She watched me while I went down the corridor to the second door which was open. I went in and closed the door.

A plump white-haired Jew sat at the desk smiling at me tenderly. "Greetings," he said. "I'm Moss Spink. What's on the thinker, pal? Park the body. Cigarette?" He opened a thing that looked like a trunk and presented me with a cigarette which was not more than a foot long. It was in an individual glass tube.

"No thanks," I said. "I smoke tobacco."

He sighed. "All right. Give. Let's see. Your name's Marlowe. Huh? Marlowe. Marlowe. Have I ever heard of anybody named Marlowe?"

"Probably not," I said. "I never heard of anybody named Spink. I asked to see a man named Ballou. Does that sound like Spink? I'm not looking for anybody named

Spink. And just between you and me, the hell with people – named Spink."

"Anti-Semitic huh?" Spink said. He waved a generous hand on which a canary-yellow diamond looked like an amber traffic light. "Don't be like that," he said. "Sit down and dust off the brains. You don't know me. You don't want to know me. O.K. I ain't offended. In a business like this you got to have somebody around that don't get offended."

"Ballou," I said.

"Now be reasonable, pal. Sherry Ballou's a very busy guy. He works twenty hours a day and even then he's way behind schedule. Sit down and talk it out with little Spinky."

"You're what around here?" I asked him.

"I'm his protection, pal. I gotta protect him. A guy like Sherry can't see everybody. I see people for him. I'm the same as him——up to a point you understand."

"Could be I'm past the point you're up to," I said.

"Could be," Spink agreed pleasantly. He peeled a thick tape off an aluminum individual cigar container, reached the cigar out tenderly and looked it over for birthmarks. "I don't say not. Why not demonstrate a little? Then we'll know. Up to now all you're doing is throwing a line. We get so much of that in here it don't mean a thing to us."

I watched him clip and light the expensive-looking cigar. "How do I know you wouldn't double-cross him?" I asked cunningly.

Spink's small tight eyes blinked and I wasn't sure but that there were tears in them. "Me cross Sherry Ballou?" he asked brokenly in a hushed voice, like a six-hundred-dollar funeral. "Me? I'd sooner double-cross my own mother."

"That doesn't mean anything to me either," I said. "I never met your mother."

Spink laid his cigar aside in an ash tray the size of a

bird bath. He waved both his arms. Sorrow was eating into him. "Oh pal. What a way to talk," he wailed. "I love Sherry Ballou like he was my own father. Better. My father—well, skip it. Come on, pal. Be human. Give with a little of the old trust and friendliness. Spill the dirt to little Spinky, huh?"

I drew an envelope from my pocket and tossed it across the desk to him. He pulled the single photograph from it and stared at it solemnly. He laid it down on the desk. He looked up at me, down at the photo, up at me. "Well," he said woodenly, in a voice suddenly empty of the old trust and friendliness he had been talking about. "What's it got that's so wonderful?"

"Do I have to tell you who the girl is?"

"Who's the guy?" Spink snapped.

I said nothing.

"I said who's the guy?" Spink almost yelled at me. "Cough up, mug. Cough up."

I still didn't say anything. Spink reached slowly for his telephone, keeping his hard bright eyes on my face.

"Go on. Call them," I said. "Call downtown and ask for Lieutenant Christy French in the homicide bureau. There's another boy that's hard to convince."

Spink took his hand off the phone. He got up slowly and went out with the photograph. I waited. Outside on Sunset Boulevard traffic went by distantly, monotonously. The minutes dropped silently down a well. The smoke of Spink's freshly lit cigar played in the air for a moment, then was sucked through the vent of the air-conditioning apparatus. I looked at the innumerable inscribed photos on the walls, all inscribed to Sherry Ballou with somebody's eternal love. I figured they were back numbers if they were in Spink's office.

18

AFTER A WHILE Spink came back and gestured to me. I followed him along the corridor through double doors into an anteroom with two secretaries. Past them towards more double doors of heavy black glass with silver peacocks etched into the panels. As we neared the doors they opened of themselves.

We went down three carpeted steps into an office that had everything in it but a swimming pool. It was two stories high, surrounded by a balcony loaded with book shelves. There was a concert grand Steinway in the corner and a lot of glass and bleached-wood furniture and a desk about the size of a badminton court and chairs and couches and tables and a man lying on one of the couches with his coat off and his shirt open over a Charvet scarf you could have found in the dark by listening to it purr. A white cloth was over his eyes and forehead and a lissome blond girl was wringing out another in a silver bowl of ice water at a table beside him.

The man was a big shapely guy with wavy dark hair and a strong brown face below the white cloth. An arm dropped to the carpet and a cigarette hung between fingers, wisping a tiny thread of smoke.

The blond girl changed the cloth deftly. The man on the couch groaned. Spink said: "This is the boy, Sherry. Name of Marlowe."

The man on the couch groaned. "What does he want?"

Spink said: "Won't spill."

The man on the couch said: "What did you bring him in for then? I'm tired."

Spink said: "Well you know how it is, Sherry. Sometimes you kind of got to."

The man on the couch said: "What did you say his beautiful name was?"

Spink turned to me. "You can tell us what you want now. And make it snappy, Marlowe."

I said nothing.

After a moment the man on the couch slowly raised the arm with the cigarette at the end of it. He got the cigarette wearily into his mouth and drew on it with the infinite languor of a decadent aristocrat moldering in a ruined château.

"I'm talking to you, pal," Spink said harshly. The blonde changed the cloth again, looking at nobody. The silence hung in the room as acrid as the smoke of the cigarette. "Come on, lug. Snap it up."

I got one of my Camels out and lit it and picked out a chair and sat down. I stretched my hand out and looked at it. The thumb twitched up and down slowly every few seconds.

Spink's voice cut into this furiously: "Sherry don't have all day, you."

"What would he do with the rest of the day?" I heard myself asking. "Sit on a white satin couch and have his toenails gilded?"

The blonde turned suddenly and stared at me. Spink's mouth fell open. He blinked. The man on the couch lifted a slow hand to the corner of the towel over his eyes. He removed enough so that one seal-brown eye looked at me. The towel fell softly back into place.

"You can't talk like that in here," Spink said in a tough voice.

I stood up. I said: "I forgot to bring my prayer book. This is the first time I knew God worked on commission."

Nobody said anything for a minute. The blonde changed the towel again.

From under it the man on the couch said calmly: "Get the Jesus out of here, darlings. All but the new chum."

Spink gave me a narrow glare of hate. The blonde left silently.

Spink said: "Why don't I just toss him out on his can?"

The tired voice under the towel said: "I've been wondering about that so long I've lost interest in the problem. Beat it."

"Okay, boss," Spink said. He withdrew reluctantly. He paused at the door, gave me one more silent snarl and disappeared.

The man on the couch listened to the door close and then said: "How much?"

"You don't want to buy anything."

He pushed the towel off his head, tossed it to one side and sat up slowly. He put his bench-made pebble-grain brogues on the carpet and passed a hand across his forehead. He looked tired but not dissipated. He fumbled another cigarette from somewhere, lit it and stared morosely through the smoke at the floor.

"Go on," he said.

"I don't know why you wasted all the build-up on me," I said. "But I credit you with enough brains to know you couldn't buy anything, and know it would stay bought."

Ballou picked up the photo that Spink had put down near him on a long low table. He reached out a languid hand. "The piece that's cut out would be the punch line, no doubt," he said.

I got the envelope out of my pocket and gave him the cut out corner, watched him fit the two pieces together.

"With a glass you can read the headline," I said.

"There's one on my desk. Please."

I went over and got the magnifying glass off his desk. "You're used to a lot of service, aren't you, Mr. Ballou?"

"I pay for it." He studied the photograph through the glass and sighed. "Seems to me I saw that fight. They ought to take more care of these boys."

"Like you do of your clients," I said.

He laid down the magnifying glass and leaned back to stare at me with cool untroubled eyes.

"That's the chap that owns The Dancers. Name's Steelgrave. The girl is a client of mine, of course." He made a vague gesture towards a chair. I sat down in it. "What were you thinking of asking, Mr. Marlowe?"

"For what?"

"All the prints and the negative. The works."

"Ten grand," I said, and watched his mouth. The mouth smiled, rather pleasantly.

"It needs a little more explanation, doesn't it? All I see is two people having lunch in a public place. Hardly disastrous to the reputation of my client. I assume that was what you had in mind."

I grinned. "You can't buy anything, Mr. Ballou. I could have had a positive made from the negative and another negative from the positive. If that snap is evidence of something, you could never know you had suppressed it."

"Not much of a sales talk for a blackmailer," he said, still smiling.

"I always wonder why people pay blackmailers. They can't buy anything. Yet they do pay them, sometimes over and over and over again. And in the end are just where they started."

"The fear of today," he said, "always overrides the fear of tomorrow. It's a basic fact of the dramatic emotions that the part is greater than the whole. If you see a glamour star on the screen in a position of great danger, you fear for her with one part of your mind, the emotional part. Notwithstanding that your reasoning mind knows that she is the star of the picture and nothing very bad is going to happen to her. If suspense and menace didn't defeat reason, there would be very little drama."

I said: "Very true, I guess," and puffed some of my Camel smoke around.

His eyes narrowed a little. "As to really being able to buy anything, if I paid you a substantial price and didn't get what I bought, I'd have you taken care of. Beaten to a pulp. And when you got out of the hospital, if you felt aggressive enough, you could try to get me arrested."

"It's happened to me," I said. "I'm a private eye. I know what you mean. Why are you talking to me?"

He laughed. He had a deep pleasant effortless laugh. "I'm an agent, sonny. I always tend to think traders have a little something in reserve. But we won't talk about any ten grand. She hasn't got it. She only makes a grand a week so far. I admit she's very close to the big money, though."

"That would . stop her cold," I said, pointing to the photo. "No big money, no swimming pool with underwater lights, no platinum mink, no name in neons, no nothing. All blown away like dust."

He laughed contemptuously.

"Okay if I show this to the johns down town, then?" I said.

He stopped laughing. His eyes narrowed. Very quietly he asked:

"Why would they be interested?"

I stood up. "I don't think we're going to do any business, Mr. Ballou. And you're a busy man. I'll take myself off."

He got up off the couch and stretched, all six feet two of him. He was a very fine hunk of man. He came over and stood close to me. His seal-brown eyes had little gold flecks in them. "Let's see who you are, sonny."

He put his hand out. I dropped my open wallet into it. He read the photostat of my license, poked a few more things out of the wallet and glanced at them. He handed it back.

"What would happen, if you did show your little picture to the cops?"

"I'd first of all have to connect it up with something they're working on—something that happened in the Van Nuys Hotel yesterday afternoon. I'd connect it up through the girl—who won't talk to me—that's why I'm talking to you."

"She told me about it last night," he sighed.

"Told you how much?" I asked.

"That a private detective named Marlowe had tried to force her to hire him, on the ground that she was seen in a downtown hotel inconveniently close to where a murder was committed."

"How close?" I asked.

"She didn't say."

"Nuts she didn't."

He walked away from me to a tall cylindrical jar in the corner. From this he took one of a number of short thin malacca canes. He began to walk up and down the carpet, swinging the cane deftly past his right shoe.

I sat down again and killed my cigarette and took a deep breath. "It could only happen in Hollywood," I grunted.

He made a neat about turn and glanced at me. "I beg your pardon."

"That an apparently sane man could walk up and down

inside the house with a Piccadilly stroll and a monkey stick in his hand."

He nodded. "I caught the disease from a producer at MGM. Charming fellow. Or so I've been told." He stopped and pointed the cane at me. "You amuse the hell out of me, Marlowe. Really you do. You're so transparent. You're trying to use me for a shovel to dig yourself out of a jam."

"There's some truth in that. But the jam I'm in is nothing to the jam your client would be in if I hadn't done the thing that put me in the jam."

He stood quite still for a moment. Then he threw the cane away from him and walked over to a liquor cabinet and swung the two halves of it open. He poured something into a couple of pot-bellied glasses. He carried one of them over to me. Then went back and got his own. He sat down with it on the couch.

"Armagnac," he said. "If you knew me, you'd appreciate the compliment. This stuff is pretty scarce. The Krauts cleaned most of it out. Our brass got the rest. Here's to you."

He lifted the glass, sniffed and sipped a tiny sip. I put mine down in a lump. It tasted like good French brandy.

Ballou looked shocked. "My God, you sip that stuff, you don't swallow it whole."

"I swallow it whole," I said. "Sorry. She also told you that if somebody didn't shut my mouth, she would be in a lot of trouble."

He nodded.

"Did she suggest how to go about shutting my mouth?"

"I got the impression she was in favor of doing it with some kind of heavy blunt instrument. So I tried out a mixture of threat and bribery. We have an outfit down the street that specializes in protecting picture people. Apparently they didn't scare you and the bribe wasn't big enough."

"They scared me plenty," I said. "I damn near fanned a Luger at them. That junky with the .45 puts on a terrific act. And as for the money not being big enough, it's all a question of how it's offered to me."

He sipped a little more of his Armagnac. He pointed at the photograph lying in front of him with the two pieces fitted together.

"We got to where you were taking that to the cops. What then?"

"I don't think we got that far. We got to why she took this up with you instead of with her boy friend. He arrived just as I left. He has his own key."

"Apparently she just didn't." He frowned and looked down into his Armagnac.

"I like that fine," I said. "I'd like it still better if the guy didn't have her doorkey."

He looked up rather sadly. "So would I. So would we all. But show business has always been like that—any kind of show business. If these people didn't live intense and rather disordered lives, if their emotions didn't ride them too hard—well, they wouldn't be able to catch those emotions in flight and imprint them on a few feet of celluloid or project them across the footlights."

"I'm not talking about her love life," I said. "She doesn't have to shack up with a redhot."

"There's no proof of that, Marlowe."

I pointed to the photograph. "The man that took that is missing and can't be found. He's probably dead. Two other men who lived at the same address are dead. One of them was trying to peddle those pictures just before he got dead. She went to his hotel in person to take delivery. So did whoever killed him. She didn't get delivery and neither did the killer. They didn't know where to look."

"And you did?"

"I was lucky. I'd seen him without his toupee. None of this is what I call proof, maybe. You could build an argument against it. Why bother? Two men have been killed, perhaps three. She took an awful chance. Why? She wanted that picture. Getting it was worth an awful chance. Why, again? It's just two people having lunch on a certain day. The day Moe Stein was shot to death on Franklin Avenue. The day a character named Steelgrave was in jail because the cops got a tip he was a Cleveland redhot named Weepy Moyer. That's what the record shows. But the photo says he was out of jail. And by saying that about him on that particular day it says who is he. And she knows it. And he still has her doorkey."

I paused and we eyed each other solidly for a while. I said:

"You don't really want the cops to have that picture, do you? Win, lose or draw, they'd crucify her. And when it was all over it wouldn't make a damn bit of difference whether Steelgrave was Moyer or whether Moyer killed Stein or had him killed or just happened to be out on a jail pass the day he was killed. If he got away with it, there'd always be enough people to think it was a fix. She wouldn't get away with anything. She's a gangster's girl in the public mind. And as far as your business is concerned, she's definitely and completely through."

Ballou was silent for a moment, staring at me without expression. "And where are you all this time?" he asked softly.

"That depends a good deal on you, Mr. Ballou."

"What do you really want?" His voice was thin and bitter now.

"What I wanted from her and couldn't get. Something that gives me a colorable right to act in her interests up to the point where I decided I can't go any farther."

"By suppressing evidence?" he asked tightly.

"If it *is* evidence. The cops couldn't find out without smearing Miss Weld. Maybe I can. They wouldn't be bothered to try; they don't care enough. I do."

"Why?"

"Let's say it's the way I earn my living. I might have other motives, but that one's enough."

"What's your price?"

"You sent it to me last night. I wouldn't take it then. I'll take it now. With a signed letter employing my services to investigate an attempt to blackmail one of your clients."

I got up with my empty glass and went over and put it down on the desk. As I bent down I heard a soft whirring noise. I went around behind the desk and yanked upon a drawer. A wire recorder slid out on a hinged shelf. The motor was running and the fine steel wire was moving steadily from one spool to the other. I looked across at Ballou.

"You can shut it off and take the record with you," he said. "You can't blame me for using it."

I moved the switch over to rewind and the wire reversed direction and picked up speed until the wire was winding so fast I couldn't see it. It made a sort of high keening noise, like a couple of pansies fighting for a piece of silk. The wire came loose and the machine stopped. I took the spool off and dropped it into my pocket.

"You might have another one," I said. "I'll have to chance that."

"Pretty sure of yourself, aren't you, Marlowe?"

"I only wish I was."

"Press that button on the end of the desk, will you?"

I pressed it. The black glass doors opened and a dark girl came in with a stenographer's notebook.

Without looking at her Ballou began to dictate. "Letter to Mr. Philip Marlowe, with his address. Dear Mr. Marlowe: This agency herewith employs you to investigate an attempt to blackmail one of its clients, particulars of which have been given to you verbally. Your fee is to be one hundred dollars a day with a retainer of five hundred dollars, receipt of which you acknowledge on the copy of this letter. Blah, blah, blah. That's all, Eileen. Right away please."

I gave the girl my address and she went out.

I took the wire spool out of my pocket and put it back in the drawer.

Ballou crossed his knees and danced the shiny tip of his shoe up and down staring at it. He ran his hand through crisp dark hair.

"One of these days," he said, "I'm going to make the mistake which a man in my business dreads above all other mistakes. I'm going to find myself doing business with a man I can trust and I'm going to be just too god-damn smart to trust him. Here you'd better keep this." He held out the two pieces of the photograph.

Five minutes later I left. The glass doors opened when I was three feet from them. I went past the two secretaries and down the corridor past the open door of Spink's office. There was no sound in there, but I could smell his cigar smoke. In the reception room exactly the same people seemed to be sitting around in the chintzy chairs. Miss Helen Grady gave me her Saturday-night smile. Miss Vane beamed at me.

I had been forty minutes with the boss. That made me as gaudy as a chiropractor's chart.

19

THE STUDIO COP at the semicircular glassed-in desk put down his telephone and scribbled on a pad. He tore off the sheet and pushed in through the narrow slit not more than three quarters of an inch wide where the glass did not quite meet the top of his desk. His voice coming through the speaking device set into the glass panel had a metallic ring.

"Straight through to the end of the corridor," he said, "you'll find a drinking fountain in the middle of the patio. George Wilson will pick up there."

I said: "Thanks. Is this bullet-proof glass?"

"Sure. Why?"

"I just wondered," I said. "I never heard of anybody shooting his way into the picture business."

Behind me somebody snickered. I turned to look at a girl in slacks with a red carnation behind her ear. She was grinning.

"Oh brother, if a gun was all it took."

I went over to an olive-green door that didn't have any handle. It made a buzzing sound and let me push it open.

Beyond was an olive-green corridor with bare walls and a door at the far end. A rat trap. If you got into that and something was wrong, they could still stop you. The far door made the same buzz and click. I wondered how the cop knew I was at it. So I looked up and found his eyes staring at me in a tilted mirror. As I touched the door the mirror went blank. They thought of everything.

Outside in the hot midday sun flowers rioted in a small patio with tiled walks and a pool in the middle and a marble seat. The drinking fountain was beside the marble seat. An elderly and beautifully dressed man was lounging on the marble seat watching three tan-colored boxers root up some tea-rose begonias. There was an expression of intense but quiet satisfaction on his face. He didn't glance at me as I came up. One of the boxers, the biggest one, came over and made a wet on the marble seat beside his pants leg. He leaned down and patted the dog's hard short-haired head.

"You Mr. Wilson?" I asked.

He looked up at me vaguely. The middle-sized boxer trotted up and sniffed and wet after the first one.

"Wilson?" He had a lazy voice with a touch of drawl to it. "Oh no. My name's not Wilson. Should it be?"

"Sorry." I went over to the drinking fountain and hit myself in the face with a stream of water. While I was wiping it off with a handkerchief the smallest boxer did his duty on the marble bench.

The man whose name was not Wilson said lovingly, "Always do it in the exact same order. Fascinates me."

"Do what?" I asked.

"Pee," he said. "Question of seniority it seems. Very orderly. First Maisie. She's the mother. Then Mac. Year older than Jock, the baby. Always the same. Even in my office."

"In your office?" I said, and nobody ever looked stupider saying anything.

He lifted his whitish eyebrows at me, took a plain brown cigar out of his mouth, bit the end off and spit it into the pool.

"That won't do the fish any good," I said.

He gave me an up-from-under look. "I raise boxers. The hell with fish."

I figured it was just Hollywood. I lit a cigarette and sat down on the bench. "In your office," I said. "Well, every day has its new idea, hasn't it."

"Up against the corner of the desk. Do it all the time. Drives my secretaries crazy. Gets into the carpet, they say. What's the matter with women nowadays? Never bothers me. Rather like it. You get fond of dogs, you even like to watch them pee."

One of the dogs heaved a full-blown begonia plant into the middle of the tiled walk at his feet. He picked it up and threw it into the pool.

"Bothers the gardeners, I suppose," he remarked as he sat down again. "Oh well, if they're not satisfied, they can always—" He stopped dead and watched a slim mail girl in yellow slacks deliberately detour in order to pass through the patio. She gave him a quick side glance and went off making music with her hips.

"You know what's the matter with this business?" he asked me.

"Nobody does," I said.

"Too much sex," he said. "All right in its proper time and place. But we get it in carload lots. Wade through it. Stand up to our necks in it. Gets to be like flypaper." He stood up. "We have too many flies too. Nice to have met you, Mister—"

"Marlowe," I said. "I'm afraid you don't know me."

"Don't know anybody," he said. "Memory's going. Meet too many people. Name's Oppenheimer."

"Jules Oppenheimer?"

He nodded. "Right. Have a cigar." He held one out to

me. I showed my cigarette. He threw the cigar into the pool, then frowned. "Memory's going," he said sadly. "Wasted fifty cents. Oughtn't to do that."

"You run this studio," I said.

He nodded absently. "Ought to have saved that cigar. Save fifty cents and what have you got?"

"Fifty cents," I said, wondering what the hell he was talking about.

"Not in this business. Save fifty cents in this business and all you have is five dollars worth of bookkeeping." He paused and made a motion to the three boxers. They stopped whatever they were rooting at and watched him. "Just run the financial end," he said. "That's easy. Come on children, back to the brothel." He sighed. "Fifteen hundred theaters," he added.

I must have been wearing my stupid expression again. He waved a hand around the patio. "Fifteen hundred theaters is all you need. A damn sight easier than raising purebred boxers. The motion-picture business is the only business in the world in which you can make all the mistakes there are and still make money."

"Must be the only business in the world where you can have three dogs pee up against your office desk," I said.

"You have to have the fifteen hundred theaters."

"That makes it a little harder to get a start," I said.

He looked pleased. "Yes. That *is* the hard part." He looked across the green clipped lawn at a four-story building which made one side of the open square. "All offices over there," he said. "I never go there. Always redecorating. Makes me sick to look at the stuff some of these people put in their suites. Most expensive talent in the world. Give them anything they like, all the money they want. Why? No reason at all. Just habit. Doesn't matter a damn what they do or how they do it. Just give me fifteen hundred theaters."

"You wouldn't want to be quoted on that, Mr. Oppenheimer?"

"You a newspaper man?"

"No."

"Too bad. Just for the hell of it I'd like to see somebody try to get that simple elementary fact of life into the papers." He paused and snorted. "Nobody'd print it. Afraid to. Come on, children!"

The big one, Maisie, came over and stood beside him. The middle-sized one paused to ruin another begonia and then trotted up beside Maisie. The little one, Jock, lined up in order, then with a sudden inspiration, lifted a hind leg at the cuff of Oppenheimer's pants. Maisie blocked him off casually.

"See that?" Oppenheimer beamed. "Jock tried to get out of turn. Maisie wouldn't stand for it." He leaned down and patted Maisie's head. She looked up at him adoringly.

"The eyes of your dog," Oppenheimer mused. "The most unforgettable thing in the world."

He strolled off down the tiled path towards the executive building, the three boxers trotting sedately beside him.

"Mr. Marlowe?"

I turned to find that a tall sandy-haired man with a nose like a straphanger's elbow had sneaked up on me.

"I'm George Wilson. Glad to know you. I see you know Mr. Oppenheimer."

"Been talking to him. He told me how to run the picture business. Seems all it takes is fifteen hundred theaters."

"I've been working here five years. I've never even spoken to him."

"You just don't get pee'd on by the right dogs."

"You could be right. Just what can I do for you, Mr. Marlowe?"

"I want to see Mavis Weld."

"She's on the set. She's in a picture that's shooting."

"Could I see her on the set for a minute?"

He looked doubtful. "What kind of pass did they give you?"

"Just a pass, I guess." I held it out to him. He looked it over.

"Ballou sent you. He's her agent. I guess we can manage. Stage 12. Want to go over there now?"

"If you have time."

"I'm the unit publicity man. That's what my time is for." We walked along the tiled path towards the corners of two buildings. A concrete roadway went between them towards the back lot and the stages.

"You in Ballou's office?" Wilson asked.

"Just came from there."

"Quite an organization, I hear. I've thought of trying that business myself. There's nothing in this but a lot of grief."

We passed a couple of uniformed cops, then turned into a narrow alley between two stages. A red wigwag was swinging in the middle of the alley, a red light was on over a door marked 12, and a bell was ringing steadily above the red light. Wilson stopped beside the door. Another cop in a tilted-back chair nodded to him, and looked me over with that dead gray expression that grows on them like scum on a water tank.

The bell and the wigwag stopped and the red light went off. Wilson pulled a heavy door open and I went in past him. Inside was another door. Inside that what seemed after the sunlight to be pitch-darkness. Then I saw a concentration of lights in the far corner. The rest of the enormous sound stage seemed to be empty.

We went towards the lights. As we drew near the floor seemed to be covered with thick black cables. There were rows of folding chairs, a cluster of portable dressing rooms with names on the doors. We were wrong way on to the set and all I could see was the wooden backing and on either side a big screen. A couple of back-projection machines sizzled off to the side.

A voice shouted: "Roll 'em." A bell rang loudly. The two screens came alive with tossing waves. Another calmer voice said: "Watch your positions, please, we may have to end up matching this little vignette. All right, action."

Wilson stopped dead and touched my arm. The voices of the actors came out of nowhere, neither loud nor distinct, an unimportant murmur with no meaning.

One of the screens suddenly went blank. The smooth voice, without change of tone, said: "Cut."

The bell rang again and there was a general sound of movement. Wilson and I went on. He whispered in my ear: "If Ned Gammon doesn't get this take before lunch, he'll bust Torrance on the nose."

"Oh. Torrance in this?" Dick Torrance at the time was a ranking star of the second grade, a not uncommon type of Hollywood actor that nobody really wants but a lot of people in the end have to take for lack of better.

"Care to run over the scene again, Dick?" the calm voice asked, as we came around the corner of the set and saw what it was—the deck of a pleasure yacht near the stern. There were two girls and three men in the scene. One of the men was middle-aged, in sport clothes, lounging in a deck chair. One wore whites and had red hair and looked like the yacht's captain. The third was the amateur yachtsman, with the handsome cap, the blue jacket with gold buttons, the white shoes and slacks and the supercilious charm. This was Torrance. One of the girls was a dark beauty who had been younger; Susan Crawley. The other was Mavis Weld. She wore a wet white sharkskin swim suit, and had evidently just come aboard. A make-up man was spraying water on her face and arms and the edges of her blond hair.

Torrance hadn't answered. He turned suddenly and

stared at the camera. "You think I don't know my lines?"

A gray-haired man in gray clothes came forward into the light from the shadowy background. He had hot black eyes, but there was no heat in his voice.

"Unless you changed them intentionally," he said, his eyes steady on Torrance.

"It's just possible that I'm not used to playing in front of a back projection screen that has a habit of running out of film only in the middle of a take."

"That's a fair complaint," Ned Gammon said. "Trouble is he only has two hundred and twelve feet of film, and that's my fault. If you could take the scene just a little faster—"

"Huh." Torrance snorted. "If *I* could take it a little faster. Perhaps Miss Weld could be prevailed upon to climb aboard this yacht in rather less time than it would take to build the damn boat."

Mavis Weld gave him a quick, contemptuous look.

"Weld's timing is just right," Gammon said. "Her performance is just right too."

Susan Crawley shrugged elegantly. "I had the impression she could speed it up a trifle, Ned. It's good, but it *could* be better."

"If it was any better, darling," Mavis Weld told her smoothly, "somebody might call it acting. You wouldn't want anything like that to happen in *your* picture, would you."

Torrance laughed. Susan Crawley turned and glared at him. "What's funny, Mister Thirteen?"

Torrance's face settled into an icy mask. "The name again?" he almost hissed.

"Good heavens, you mean you didn't know," Susan Crawley said wonderingly. "They call you Mister Thirteen because any time you play a part it means twelve other guys have turned it down."

"I see," Torrance said coolly, then burst out laughing

again. He turned to Ned Gammon. "Okay, Ned. Now everybody's got the rat poison out of their system, maybe we can give it to you the way you want it."

Ned Gammon nodded. "Nothing like a little hamming to clear the air. All right here we go."

He went back beside the camera. The assistant shouted "roll 'em" and the scene went through without a hitch.

"Cut," Gammon said. "Print that one. Break for lunch everybody."

The actors came down a flight of rough wooden steps and nodded to Wilson. Mavis Weld came last, having stopped to put on a terry-cloth robe and a pair of beach sandals. She stopped dead when she saw me. Wilson stepped forward.

"Hello, George," Mavis Weld said, staring at me. "Want something from me?"

"Mr. Marlowe would like a few words with you. Okay?"

"Mr. Marlowe?"

Wilson gave me a quick sharp look. "From Ballou's office. I supposed you knew him."

"I may have seen him." She was still staring at me. "What is it?"

I didn't speak.

After a moment she said, "Thanks, George. Better come along to my dressing room, Mr. Marlowe."

She turned and walked off around the far side of the set. A green and white dressing room stood against the wall. The name on the door was Miss Weld. At the door she turned and looked around carefully. Then she fixed her lovely blue eyes on my face.

"And now, Mr. Marlowe?"

"You *do* remember me?"

"I believe so."

"Do we take up where we left off—or have a new deal with a clean deck?"

"Somebody let you in here. Who? Why? That takes explaining."

"I'm working for you. I've been paid a retainer and Ballou has the receipt."

"How very thoughtful. And suppose I don't want you to work for me? Whatever your work is."

"All right, be fancy," I said. I took the Dancers photo out of my pocket and held it out. She looked at me a long steady moment before she dropped her eyes. Then she looked at the snapshot of herself and Steelgrave in the booth. She looked at it gravely without movement. Then very slowly she reached up and touched the tendrils of damp hair at the side of her face. Ever so slightly she shivered. Her hand came out and she took the photograph. She stared at it. Her eyes came up again slowly, slowly.

"Well?" she asked.

"I have the negative and some other prints. You would have had them, if you had had more time and known where to look. Or if he had stayed alive to sell them to you."

"I'm a little chilly," she said. "And I have to eat some lunch." She held the photo out to me.

"You're a little chilly and you have to eat some lunch," I said.

I thought a pulse beat in her throat. But the light was not too good. She smiled very faintly. The bored-aristocrat touch.

"The significance of all this escapes me," she said.

"You're spending too much time on yachts. What you mean is I know you and I know Steelgrave, so what has this photo got that makes anybody give me a diamond dog collar?"

"All right," she said. "What?"

"I don't know," I said. "But if finding out is what it takes to shake you out of this duchess routine, I'll find out. And in the meantime you're still chilly and you still have to eat some lunch."

"And you've waited too long," she said quietly. "You haven't anything to sell. Except perhaps your life."

"I'd sell that cheap. For love of a pair of dark glasses and a delphinium-blue hat and a crack on the head from a high-heeled slipper."

Her mouth twitched as if she was going to laugh. But there was no laughter in her eyes.

"Not to mention three slaps in the face," she said. "Goodbye, Mr. Marlowe. You came too late. Much, much too late."

"For me—or for you?" She reached back and opened the door of the dressing room.

"I think for both of us." She went in quickly, leaving the door open.

"Come in and shut the door," her voice said from the dressing room.

I went in and shut the door. It was no fancy custom-built star's dressing room. Strictly utility only. There was a shabby couch, one easy chair, a small dressing table with mirror and two lights, a straight chair in front of it, a tray that had held coffee.

Mavis Weld reached down and plugged in a round electric heater. Then she grabbed up a towel and rubbed the damp edges of her hair. I sat down on the couch and waited.

"Give me a cigarette." She tossed the towel to one side. Her eyes came close to my face as I lit the cigarette for her. "How did you like that little scene we ad libbed on the yacht?"

"Bitchy."

"We're all bitches. Some smile more than others, that's all. Show business. There's something cheap about it. There always has been. There was a time when actors went in at the back door. Most of them still should. Great strain, great urgency, great hatred, and it comes out in nasty little scenes. They don't mean a thing."

"Cat talk," I said.

She reached up and pulled a fingertip down the side of my cheek. It burned like a hot iron. "How much money do you make, Marlowe?"

"Forty bucks a day and expenses. That's the asking price. I take twenty-five. I've taken less." I thought about Orfamay's worn twenty.

She did that with her finger again and I just didn't grab hold of her. She moved away from me and sat in the chair, drawing the robe close. The electric heater was making the little room warm.

"Twenty-five dollars a day," she said wonderingly.

"Little lonely dollars."

"Are they very lonely?"

"Lonely as lighthouses."

She crossed her legs and the pale glow of her skin in the light seemed to fill the room.

"So ask me the questions," she said, making no attempt to cover her thighs.

"Who's Steelgrave?"

"A man I've known for years. And liked. He owns things. A restaurant or two. Where he comes from—that I don't know."

"But you know him very well."

"Why don't you ask me if I sleep with him?"

"I don't ask that kind of questions."

She laughed and snapped ash from her cigarette. "Miss Gonzales would be glad to tell you."

"The hell with Miss Gonzales."

"She's dark and lovely and passionate. And very, very kind."

"And exclusive as a mailbox," I said. "The hell with her. About Steelgrave—has he ever been in trouble?"

"Who hasn't?"

"With the police."

Her eyes widened a little too innocently. Her laugh was a little too silvery. "Don't be ridiculous. The man is worth a couple of million dollars."

"How did he get it?"

"How would I know?"

"All right. You wouldn't. That cigarette's going to burn your fingers." I leaned across and took the stub out of her hand. Her hand lay open on her bare leg. I touched the palm with a fingertip. She drew away from me and tightened the hand into a fist.

"Don't do that," she said sharply.

"Why? I used to do that to girls when I was a kid."

"I know." She was breathing a little fast. "It makes me feel very young and innocent and kind of naughty. And I'm far from being young and innocent any more."

"Then you don't really know anything about Steelgrave."

"I wish you'd make up your mind whether you are giving me a third degree or making love to me."

"My mind has nothing to do with it," I said.

After a silence she said: "I really do have to eat something, Marlowe. I'm working this afternoon. You wouldn't want me to collapse on the set, would you?"

"Only stars do that." I stood up. "Okay, I'll leave. Don't forget I'm working for you. I wouldn't be if I thought you'd killed anybody. But you were there. You took a big chance. There was something you wanted very badly."

She reached the photo out from somewhere and stared at it, biting her lip. Her eyes came up without her head moving.

"It could hardly have been this."

"That was the one thing he had so well hidden that it was not found. But what good is it? You and a man called Steelgrave in a booth at The Dancers. Nothing in that."

"Nothing at all," she said.

"So it has to be something about Steelgrave—or something about the date."

Her eyes snapped down to the picture again. "There's nothing to tell the date," she said quickly. "Even if it meant something. Unless the cut-out piece—"

"Here." I gave her the cut-out piece. "But you'll need a magnifier. Show it to Steelgrave. Ask *him* if it means anything. Or ask Ballou."

I started towards the exit of the dressing room. "Don't kid yourself the date can't be fixed," I said over my shoulder. "Steelgrave won't."

"You're just building a sand castle, Marlowe."

"Really?" I looked back at her, not grinning. "You really think that? Oh no you don't. You went there. The man was murdered. You had a gun. He was a known crook. And I found something the police would love to have me hide from them. Because it must be as full of motive as the ocean is full of salt. As long as the cops don't find it I have a license. And as long as somebody else doesn't find it I don't have an ice pick in the back of my neck. Would you say I was in an overpaid profession?"

She just sat there and looked at me, one hand on her kneecap, squeezing it. The other moving restlessly, finger by finger, on the arm of the chair.

All I had to do was turn the knob and go on out. I don't know why it had to be so hard to do.

20

THERE WAS THE USUAL coming and going in the corridor outside my office and when I opened the door and walked into the musty silence of the little waiting room there was the usual feeling of having been dropped down a well dried up twenty years ago to which no one would come back ever. The smell of old dust hung in the air as flat and stale as a football interview.

I opened the inner door and inside there it was the same dead air, the same dust along the veneer, the same broken promise of a life of ease. I opened the windows and turned on the radio. It came up too loud and when I had it tuned down to normal the phone sounded as if it had been ringing for some time. I took my hat off it and lifted the receiver.

It was high time I heard from her again. Her cool compact voice said: "This time I really mean it."

"Go on."

"I lied before. I'm not lying now. I really have heard from Orrin."

"Go on."

"You're not believing me. I can tell by your voice."

"You can't tell anything by my voice. I'm a detective. Heard from him how?"

"By phone from Bay City."

"Wait a minute." I put the receiver down on the stained brown blotter and lit my pipe. No hurry. Lies are always patient. I took it up again.

"We've been through that routine," I said. "You're pretty forgetful for your age. I don't think Dr. Zugsmith would like it."

"Please don't tease me. This is very serious. He got my letter. He went to the post office and asked for his mail. He knew where I'd be staying. And about when I'd be here. So he called up. He's staying with a doctor he got to know down there. Doing some kind of work for him. I told you he had two years medical."

"Doctor have a name?"

"Yes. A funny name. Dr. Vincent Lagardie."

"Just a minute. There's somebody at the door."

I laid the phone down very carefully. It might be brittle. It might be made of spun glass. I got a handkerchief out and wiped the palm of my hand, the one that had been holding it. I got up and went to the built-in wardrobe and looked at my face in the flawed mirror. It was me all right. I had a strained look. I'd been living too fast.

Dr. Vincent Lagardie, 965 Wyoming Street. Catty-corners from The Garland Home of Peace. Frame house on the corner. Quiet. Nice neighborhood. Friend of the extinct Clausen. Maybe. Not according to him. But still maybe.

I went back to the telephone and squeezed the jerks out of my voice. "How would you spell that?" I asked.

She spelled it—with ease and precision. "Nothing to do then, is there?" I said. "All jake to the angels—or whatever they say in Manhattan, Kansas."

"Stop sneering at me. Orrin's in a lot of trouble.

Some——" her voice quivered a little and her breath came quickly, "some gangsters are after him."

"Don't be silly, Orfamay. They don't have gangsters in Bay City. They're all working in pictures. What's Dr. Lagardie's phone number?"

She gave it to me. It was right. I won't say the pieces were beginning to fall into place, but at least they were getting to look like parts of the same puzzle. Which is all I ever get or ask.

"Please go down there and see him and help him. He's afraid to leave the house. After all I did pay you."

"I gave it back."

"Well, I offered it to you again."

"You more or less offered me other things that are more than I'd care to take."

There was silence.

"All right," I said. "All right. If I can stay free that long. I'm in a lot of trouble myself."

"Why?"

"Telling lies and not telling the truth. It always catches up with me. I'm not as lucky as some people."

"But I'm not lying, Philip. I'm not lying. I'm frantic."

"Take a deep breath and get frantic so I can hear it."

"They might kill him," she said quietly.

"And what is Dr. Vincent Lagardie doing all this time?"

"He doesn't know, of course. Please, please go at once. I have the address here. Just a moment."

And the little bell rang, the one that rings far back at the end of the corridor, and is not loud, but you'd better hear it. No matter what other noises there are you'd better hear it.

"He'll be in the phone book," I said. "And by an odd coincidence I have a Bay City phone book. Call me around four. Or five. Better make it five."

I hung up quickly. I stood up and turned the radio off, not having heard a thing it said. I closed the windows again. I opened the drawer of my desk and took out the Luger and strapped it on. I fitted my hat on my head. On the way out I had another look at the face in the mirror.

I looked as if I had made up my mind to drive off a cliff.

21

THEY WERE JUST FINISHING a funeral service at The
Garland Home of Peace. A big gray hearse was waiting
at the side entrance. Cars were clotted along both sides
of the street, three black sedans in a row at the side of
Dr. Vincent Lagardie's establishment. People were coming sedately down the walk from the funeral chapel to the
corner and getting into their cars. I stopped a third of a
block away and waited. The cars didn't move. Then three
people came out with a woman heavily veiled and all in
black. They half carried her down to a big limousine. The
boss mortician fluttered around making elegant little gestures and body movements as graceful as a Chopin ending.
His composed gray face was long enough to wrap twice
around his neck.

The amateur pallbearers carried the coffin out the side
door and professionals eased the weight from them and
slid it into the back of the hearse as smoothly as if it
had no more weight than a pan of butter rolls. Flowers
began to grow into a mound over it. The glass doors were
closed and motors started all over the block.

A few moments later nothing was left but one sedan across the way and the boss mortician sniffing a tree-rose on his way back to count the take. With a beaming smile he faded into his neat colonial doorway and the world was still and empty again. The sedan that was left hadn't moved. I drove along and made a U-turn and came up behind it. The driver wore blue serge and a soft cap with a shiny peak. He was doing a crossword puzzle from the morning paper. I stuck a pair of those diaphanous mirror sunglasses on my nose and strolled past him toward Dr. Lagardie's place. He didn't look up. When I was a few yards ahead I took the glasses off and pretended to polish them on my handkerchief. I caught him in one of the mirror lenses. He still didn't look up. He was just a guy doing a crossword puzzle. I put the mirror glasses back on my nose, and went around to Dr. Lagardie's front door.

The sign over the door said: Ring and Enter. I rang, but the door wouldn't let me enter. I waited. I rang again. I waited again. There was silence inside. Then the door opened a crack very slowly, and the thin expressionless face over a white uniform looked out at me.

"I'm sorry. Doctor is not seeing any patients today." She blinked at the mirror glasses. She didn't like them. Her tongue moved restlessly inside her lips.

"I'm looking for a Mr. Quest. Orrin P. Quest."

"Who?" There was a dim reflection of shock behind her eyes.

"Quest. Q as in quintessential, U as in uninhibited, E as in Extrasensory, S as in Subliminal, T as in Toots. Put them all together and they spell Brother."

She looked at me as if I had just come up from the floor of the ocean with a drowned mermaid under my arm.

"I beg your pardon. Dr. Lagardie is not—"

She was pushed out of the way by invisible hands and a

thin dark haunted man stood in the half-open doorway.

"I am Dr. Lagardie. What is it, please?"

I gave him a card. He read it. He looked at me. He had the white pinched look of a man who is waiting for a disaster to happen.

"We talked over the phone," I said. "About a man named Clausen."

"Please come in," he said quickly. "I don't remember, but come in."

I went in. The room was dark, the blinds drawn, the windows closed. It was dark, and it was cold.

The nurse backed away and sat down behind a small desk. It was an ordinary living room with light painted woodwork which had once been dark, judging by the probable age of the house. A square arch divided the living room from the dining room. There were easy chairs and a center table with magazines. It looked like what it was—the reception room of a doctor practicing in what had been a private home.

The telephone rang on the desk in front of the nurse. She started and her hand went out and then stopped. She stared at the telephone. After a while it stopped ringing.

"What was the name you mentioned?" Dr. Lagardie asked me softly.

"Orrin Quest. His sister told me he was doing some kind of work for you, Doctor. I've been looking for him for days. Last night he called her up. From here, she said."

"There is no one of that name here," Dr. Lagardie said politely. "There hasn't been."

"You don't know him at all?"

"I have never heard of him."

"I can't figure why he would say that to his sister."

The nurse dabbed at her eyes furtively. The telephone on her desk burred and made her jump again. "Don't answer it," Dr. Lagardie said without turning his head.

We waited while it rang. Everybody waits while a telephone rings. After a while it stopped.

"Why don't you go home, Miss Watson? There's nothing for you to do here."

"Thank you, Doctor." She sat without moving, looking down at the desk. She squeezed her eyes shut and blinked them open. She shook her head hopelessly.

Dr. Lagardie turned back to me. "Shall we go into my office?"

We went across through another door leading to a hallway. I walked on eggs. The atmosphere of the house was charged with foreboding. He opened a door and ushered me into what must have once been a bedroom, but nothing suggested a bedroom. It was a small compact doctor's office. An open door showed a part of an examination room. A sterilizer was working in the corner. There were a lot of needles cooking in it.

"That's a lot of needles," I said, always quick with an idea.

"Sit down, Mr. Marlowe."

He went behind the desk and sat down and picked up a long thin letter-opening knife.

He looked at me levelly from his sorrowful eyes. "No, I don't know anyone named Orrin Quest, Mr. Marlowe. I can't imagine any reason in the world why a person of that name should say he was in my house."

"Hiding out," I said.

His eyebrows went up. "From what?"

"From some guys that might want to stick an ice pick in the back of his neck. On account of he is a little too quick with his little Leica. Taking people's photographs when they want to be private. Or it could be something else, like peddling reefers and he got wise. Am I talking in riddles?"

"It was you who sent the police here," he said coldly.

I didn't say anything.

"It was you who called up and reported Clausen's death."

I said the same as before.

"It was you who called me up and asked me if I knew Clausen. I said I did not."

"But it wasn't true."

"I was under no obligation to give you information, Mr. Marlowe."

I nodded and got a cigarette out and lit it. Dr. Lagardie glanced at his watch. He turned in his chair and switched off the sterilizer. I looked at the needles. A lot of needles. Once before I had had trouble in Bay City with a guy who cooked a lot of needles.

"What makes it?" I asked him. "The yacht harbor?"

He picked up the wicked-looking paper knife with a silver handle in the shape of a nude woman. He pricked the ball of his thumb. A pearl of dark blood showed on it. He put it to his mouth and licked it. "I like the taste of blood," he said softly.

There was a distant sound as of the front door opening and closing. We both listened to it carefully. We listened to retreating steps on the front steps of the house. We listened hard.

"Miss Watson has gone home," Dr. Lagardie said. "We are all alone in the house." He mulled that over and licked his thumb again. He laid the knife down carefully on the desk blotter. "Ah, the question of the yacht harbor," he added. "The proximity of Mexico you are thinking of, no doubt. The ease with which marihuana—"

"I wasn't thinking so much of marihuana any more." I stared again at the needles. He followed my stare. He shrugged.

I said: "Why so many of them?"

"Is it any of your business?"

"Nothing's any of my business."

"But you seem to expect your questions to be answered."

"I'm just talking," I said. "Waiting for something to happen. Something's going to happen in this house. It's leering at me from corners."

Dr. Lagardie licked another pearl of blood off his thumb.

I looked hard at him. It didn't buy me a way into his soul. He was quiet, dark and shuttered and all the misery of life was in his eyes. But he was still gentle.

"Let me tell you about the needles," I said.

"By all means." He picked the long thin knife up again.

"Don't do that," I said sharply. "It gives me the creeps. Like petting snakes."

He put the knife down again gently and smiled. "We do seem to talk in circles," he suggested.

"We'll get there. About the needles. A couple of years back I had a case that brought me down here and mixed me up with a doctor named Almore. Lived over on Altair Street. He had a funny practice. Went out nights with a big case of hypodermic needles—all ready to go. Loaded with the stuff. He had a peculiar practice. Drunks, rich junkies, of whom there are far more than people think, overstimulated people who had driven themselves beyond the possibility of relaxing. Insomniacs—all the neurotic types that can't take it cold. Have to have their little pills and little shots in the arm. Have to have help over the humps. It gets to be all humps after a while. Good business for the doctor. Almore was the doctor for them. It's all right to say it now. He died a year or so back. Of his own medicine."

"And you think I may have inherited his practice?"

"Somebody would. As long as there are the patients, there will be the doctor."

He looked even more exhausted than before. "I think you are an ass, my friend. I did not know Dr. Almore.

And I do not have the sort of practice you attribute to
him. As for the needles—just to get that trifle out of the
way—they are in somewhat constant use in the medical
profession today, often for such innocent medicaments as
vitamin injections. And needles get dull. And when they
are dull they are painful. Therefore in the course of the
day one may use a dozen or more. Without narcotics in a
single one."

He raised his head slowly and stared at me with a fixed
contempt.

"I can be wrong," I said. "Smelling that reefer smoke
over at Clausen's place yesterday, and having him call
your number on the telephone—and call you by your
first name—all this probably made me jump to wrong
conclusions."

"I have dealt with addicts," he said. "What doctor has
not? It is a complete waste of time."

"They get cured sometimes."

"They can be deprived of their drug. Eventually after
great suffering they can do without it. That is not curing
them, my friend. That is not remvoing the nervous or
emotional flaw which made them become addicts. It is
making them dull negative people who sit in the sun and
twirl their thumbs and die of sheer boredom and inani-
tion."

"That's a pretty raw theory, doctor."

"You raised the subject. I have disposed of it. I will
raise another subject. You may have noticed a certain
atmosphere and strain about this house. Even with those
silly mirror glasses on. Which you may now remove. They
don't make you look in the least like Cary Grant."

I took them off. I'd forgotten all about them.

"The police have been here, Mr. Marlowe. A certain
Lieutenant Maglashan, who is investigating Clausen's
death. He would be pleased to meet you. Shall I call him?
I'm sure he would come back."

"Go ahead, call him," I said. "I just stopped off here on my way to commit suicide."

His hand went towards the telephone but was pulled to one side by the magnetism of the paper knife. He picked it up again. Couldn't leave it alone, it seemed.

"You could kill a man with that," I said.

"Very easily," and he smiled a little.

"An inch and a half in the back of the neck, square in the center, just under the occipital bulge."

"An ice pick would be better," he said. "Especially a short one, filed down very sharp. It would not bend. If you miss the spinal cord, you do no great damage."

"Takes a bit of medical knowledge then?" I got out a poor old package of Camels and untangled one from the cellophane.

He just kept on smiling. Very faintly, rather sadly. It was not the smile of a man in fear. "That would help," he said softly. "But any reasonably dexterous person could acquire the technique in ten minutes."

"Orrin Quest had a couple of years medical," I said.

"I told you I did not know anybody of that name."

"Yeah, I know you did. I didn't quite believe you."

He shrugged his shoulders. But his eyes as always went to the knife in the end.

"We're a couple of sweethearts," I said. "We just sit here making with the old over-the-desk dialogue. As though we hadn't a care in the world. Because both of us are going to be in the clink by nightfall."

He raised his eyebrows again. I went on:

"You, because Clausen knew you by your first name. And you may have been the last man he talked to. Me, because I've been doing all the things a P.I. never gets away with. Hiding evidence, hiding information, finding bodies and not coming in with my hat in my hand to these lovely incorruptible Bay City cops. Oh, I'm through. Very much through. But there's a wild perfume in the air this afternoon. I don't seem to care. Or I'm in love. I just don't seem to care."

"You have been drinking," he said slowly.

"Only Chanel No. 5, and kisses, and the pale glow of lovely legs, and the mocking invitation in deep blue eyes. Innocent things like that."

He just looked sadder than ever. "Women can weaken a man terribly, can they not?" he said.

"Clausen."

"A hopeless alcoholic. You probably know how they are. They drink and drink and don't eat. And little by little the vitamin deficiency brings on the symptoms of delirium. There is only one thing to do for them." He turned and looked at the sterilizer. "Needles, and more needles. It makes me feel dirty. I am a graduate of the Sorbonne. But I practice among dirty little people in a dirty little town."

"Why?"

"Because of something that happened years ago—in another city. Don't ask me too much, Mr. Marlowe."

"He used your first name."

"It is a habit with people of a certain class. Onetime actors especially. And onetime crooks."

"Oh," I said. "That all there is to it?"

"All."

"Then the cops coming here doesn't bother you on account of Clausen. You're just afraid of this other thing that happened somewhere else long gone. Or it could even be love."

"Love?" He dropped the word slowly off the end of his tongue, tasting it to the last. A bitter little smile stayed after the word, like powder smell in the air after a gun is fired. He shrugged and pushed a desk cigarette box from behind a filing tray and over to my side of the desk.

"Not love then," I said. "I'm trying to read your mind. Here you are a guy with a Sorbonne degree and a cheap little practice in a cheap and nasty little town. I know it well. So what are you doing here? What are you doing with people like Clausen? What was the rap, Doctor? Narcotics, abortions, or were you by any chance a medic for the gang boys in some hot Eastern city?"

"As for instance?" he smiled thinly.

"As for instance Cleveland."

"A very wild suggestion, my friend." His voice was like ice now.

"Wild as all hell," I said. "But a fellow like me with very limited brains tends to try to fit the things he knows into a pattern. It's often wrong, but it's an occupational disease with me. It goes like this, if you want to listen."

"I am listening." He picked the knife up again and pricked lightly at the blotter on his desk.

"You knew Clausen. Clausen was killed very skillfully with an ice pick, killed while I was in the house, upstairs talking to a grifter named Hicks. Hicks moved out fast taking a page of the register with him, the page that had Orrin Quest's name on it. Later that afternoon Hicks was killed with an ice pick in L.A. His room had been searched. There was a woman there who had come to buy something from him. She didn't get it. I had more time to search. I did get it. Presumption A: Clausen and Hicks killed by same man, not necessarily for same reason. Hicks killed because he muscled in on another guy's racket and muscled the other guy out. Clausen killed because he was a babbling drunk and might know who would be likely to kill Hicks. Any good so far?"

"Not the slightest interest to me," Dr. Lagardie said.

"But you *are* listening. Sheer good manners, I suppose. Okay. Now what did I find? A photo of a movie queen and an ex-Cleveland gangster, maybe, now a Hollywood restaurant owner, etc., having lunch on a particular day. Day when this ex-Cleveland gangster was supposed to be in hock at the County Jail, also day when ex-Cleveland gangster's onetime sidekick was shot dead on Franklin Avenue in Los Angeles. Why was he in hock? Tip-off that he was who he was, and say what you like against the L.A. cops they do try to run back-East hot shots out of town. Who gave them the tip? The guy they pinched gave it to them himself, because his ex-partner was being troublesome and had to be rubbed out, and being in jail was a first-class alibi when it happened."

"All fantastic," Dr. Lagardie smiled wearily. "Utterly fantastic."

"Sure. It gets worse. Cops couldn't prove anything on ex-gangster. Cleveland police not interested. The L.A. cops turn him loose. But they wouldn't have turned him loose if they'd seen that photo. Photo therefore strong blackmail material, first against ex-Cleveland character, if he really is the guy; secondly against movie queen for being seen around with him in public. A good man could make a fortune out of that photo. Hicks not good enough. Paragraph. Presumption B: Orrin Quest, the boy I'm trying to find, took that photo. Taken with Contax or Leica, without flashbulb, without subjects knowing they were being photographed. Quest had a Leica and liked to do things like that. In this case of course he had a more commercial motive. Question, how did he get a chance to take photo? Answer, the movie queen was his sister. She would let him come up and speak to her. He was out of work, needed money. Likely enough she gave him some and made it a condition he stay away from her. She wants no part of her family. Is it still utterly fantastic, Doctor?"

He stared at me moodily. "I don't know," he said slowly. "It begins to have possibilities. But why are you telling this rather dangerous story to me?"

He reached a cigarette out of the box and tossed me one casually. I caught it and looked it over. Egyptian, oval and fat, a little rich for my blood. I didn't light it, just sat holding it between my fingers, watching his dark unhappy eyes. He lit his own cigarette and puffed nervously.

"I'll tie you in on it now," I said. "You knew Clausen. Professionally, you said. I showed him I was a dick. He tried at once to call you up: He was too drunk to talk to you. I caught the number and later told you he was dead. Why? If you were on the level, you would call the cops. You didn't. Why? You knew Clausen, you could have known some of his roomers. No proof either way. Paragraph. Presumption C: you knew Hicks or Orrin Quest or both. The L.A. cops couldn't or didn't establish identity of ex-Cleveland character—let's give him his new name, call him Steelgrave. But *somebody* had to be able to—if that photo was worth killing people over. Did you ever practice medicine in Cleveland, Doctor?"

"Certainly not." His voice seemed to come from far off. His eyes were remote too. His lips opened barely enough to admit his cigarette. He was very still.

I said: "They have a whole roomful of directories over at the telephone office. From all over the country. I checked you up."

"A suite in a downtown office building," I said. "And now this—an almost furtive practice in a little beach town. You'd have liked to change your name—but you couldn't and keep your license. Somebody had to mastermind this deal, Doctor. Clausen was a bum, Hicks a stupid lout, Orrin Quest a nasty-minded creep. But they could be used. You couldn't go up against Steelgrave directly. You wouldn't have stayed alive long enough to brush your teeth. You had to work through pawns—expendable pawns. Well—are we getting anywhere?"

He smiled faintly and leaned back in his chair with a sigh. "Presumption D, Mr. Marlowe," he almost whispered. "You are an unmitigated idiot."

I grinned and reached for a match to light his fat Egyptian cigarette.

"Added to all the rest," I said, "Orrin's sister calls me up and tells me he is in your house. There are a lot of weak arguments taken one at a time, I admit. But they do seem to sort of focus on you." I puffed peacefully on the cigarette.

He watched me. His face seemed to fluctuate and become vague, to move far off and come back. I felt a tightness in my chest. My mind had slowed to a turtle's gallop.

"What's going on here?" I heard myself mumble.

I put my hands on the arms of the chair and pushed myself up. "Been dumb, haven't I?" I said, with the cigarette still in my mouth and me still smoking it. Dumb was hardly the word. Have to coin a new word.

I was out of the chair and my feet were stuck in two barrels of cement. When I spoke my voice seemed to come through cottonwool.

I let go of the arms of the chair and reached for the cigarette. I missed it clean a couple of time, then got my hand around it. It didn't feel like a cigarette. It felt like the hind leg of an elephant. With sharp toenails. They stuck into my hand. I shook my hand and the elephant took his leg away.

A vague but enormously tall figure swung around in front of me and a mule kicked me in the chest. I sat down on the floor.

"A little potassium hydrocyanide," a voice said, over the transatlantic telephone. "Not fatal, not even dangerous. Merely relaxing. . . ."

I started to get up off the floor. You ought to try it sometime. But have somebody nail the floor down first. This one looped the loop. After a while it steadied a little. I settled for an angle of forty-five degrees. I took hold of myself and started to go somewhere. There was a thing that might have been Napoleon's tomb on the horizon. That was a good enough objective. I started that way. My heart beat fast and thick and I was having trouble opening my lungs. Like after being winded at football. You think your breath will never come back. Never, never, never.

Then it wasn't Napoleon's tomb any more. It was a raft on a swell. There was a man on it. I'd seen him somewhere. Nice fellow. We'd got on fine. I started towards him and hit a wall with my shoulder. That spun me around. I started clawing for something to hold on to. There was nothing but the carpet. How did I get down there? No use asking. It's a secret. Every time you ask a question they just push the floor in your face. Okay, I started to crawl along the carpet. I was on what formerly had been my hands and knees. No sensation proved it. I crawled towards a dark wooden wall. Or it could have been black marble. Napoleon's tomb again. What did I ever do to Napoleon? What for should he keep shoving his tomb at me?

"Need a drink of water," I said.

I listened for the echo. No echo. Nobody said anything. Maybe I didn't say it. Maybe it was just an idea I thought better of. Potassium cyanide. That's a couple of long words to be worrying about when you're crawling through tunnels. Nothing fatal, he said. Okay, this is just fun. What you might call semi-fatal. Philip Marlowe, 38, a private license operator of shady reputation, was apprehended by police last night while crawling through the Ballona Storm Drain with a grand piano on his back. Questioned at the University Heights Police station Marlowe declared he was taking the piano to the Maharajah of Coot-Berar. Asked why he was wearing spurs Marlowe declared that a client's confidence was sacred. Marlowe is being held for investigation. Chief Hornside said police were not yet ready to say more. Asked if the piano was in tune Chief Hornside declared that he had played the Minute Waltz on it in thirty-five seconds and so far as he could tell there were no strings in the piano. He intimated that something else was. A complete statement to the press will be made within twelve hours, Chief Hornside said abruptly. Speculation is rife that Marlowe was attempting to dispose of a body.

A face swam towards me out of the darkness. I changed direction and started for the face. But it was too late in the afternoon. The sun was setting. It was getting dark rapidly. There was no face. There was no wall, no desk. Then there was no floor. There was nothing at all.

I wasn't even there.

22

A BIG BLACK GORILLA with a big black paw had his big black paw over my face and was trying to push it through the back of my neck. I pushed back. Taking the weak side of an argument is my specialty. Then I realized that he was trying to keep me from opening my eyes.

I decided to open my eyes just the same. Others have done it, why not me? I gathered my strength and very slowly, keeping the back straight, flexing the thighs and knees, using the arms as ropes, I lifted the enormous weight of my eyelids.

I was looking at the ceiling, lying on my back on the floor, a position in which my calling has occasionally placed me. I rolled my head. My lungs felt stiff and my mouth felt dry. The room was just Dr. Lagardie's consulting room. Same chair, same desk, same walls and window. There was a shuttered silence hanging around.

I got up on my haunches and braced myself on the floor and shook my head. It went into a flat spin. It spun down about five thousand feet and then I dragged it out and leveled off. I blinked. Same floor, same desk, same walls. But no Dr. Lagardie.

I wet my lips and made some kind of a vague noise to which nobody paid any attention. I got up on my feet. I was as dizzy as a dervish, as weak as a worn-out washer, as low as a badger's belly, as timid as a titmouse, and as unlikely to succeed as a ballet dancer with a wooden leg.

I groped my way over behind the desk and slumped into Lagardie's chair and began to paw fitfully through his equipment for a likely-looking bottle of liquid fertilizer. Nothing doing. I got up again. I was as hard to lift as a dead elephant. I staggered around looking into cabinets of shining white enamel which contained everything somebody else was in a hurry for. Finally, after what seemed like four years on the road gang, my little hand closed around six ounces of ethyl alcohol. I got the top off the bottle and sniffed. Grain alcohol. Just what the label said. All I needed now was a glass and some water. A good man ought to be able to get that far. I started through the door to the examination room. The air still had the aromatic perfume of overripe peaches. I hit both sides of the doorway going through and paused to take a fresh sighting.

At that moment I was aware that steps were coming down the hall. I leaned against the wall wearily and listened.

Slow, dragging steps, with a long pause between each. At first they seemed furtive. Then they just seemed very, very tired. An old man trying to make it to his last armchair. That made two of us. And then I thought, for no reason at all, of Orfamay's father back there on the porch in Manhattan, Kansas, moving quietly along to his rocking chair with his cold pipe in his hand, to sit down and look out over the front lawn and have himself a nice economical smoke that required no matches and no tobacco and didn't mess up the living-room carpet. I arranged his chair

for him. In the shade at the end of the porch where the
bougainvillaea was thick I helped him sit down. He looked
up and thanked me with the good side of his face. His
fingernails scratched on the arms of the chair as he leaned
back.

The fingernails scratched, but it wasn't on the arm of
any chair. It was a real sound. It was close by, on the
outside of a closed door that led from the examination
room to the hallway. A thin feeble scratch, possibly a
young kitten wanting to be let in. Okay, Marlowe, you're
an old animal lover. Go over and let the kitten in. I
started. I made it with the help of the nice examination
couch with the rings on the end and the nice clean
towels. The scratching had stopped. Poor little kitten, outside and wanting in. A tear formed itself in my eye and
trickled down my furrowed cheek. I let go of the examination table and made a smooth four yards to the door.
The heart was bumping inside me. And the lungs still had
that feeling of having been in storage for a couple of years.
I took a deep breath and got hold of the doorknob and
opened it. Just at the last moment it occurred to me to
reach for a gun. It occurred to me but that's as far as I
got. I'm a fellow that likes to take an idea over by the
light and have a good look at it. I'd have had to let go of
the doorknob. It seemed like too big an operation. I just
twisted the knob and opened the door instead.

He was braced to the doorframe by four hooked fingers
made of white wax. He had eyes an eighth of an inch
deep, pale gray-blue, wide open. They looked at me but
they didn't see me. Our faces were inches apart. Our
breathing met in midair. Mine was quick and harsh, his
was the far-off whisper which has not yet begun to rattle.
Blood bubbled from his mouth and ran down his chin.
Something made me look down. Blood drained slowly
down the inside of his trouser leg and out on his shoe and

from his shoe it flowed without haste to the floor. It was already a small pool.

I couldn't see where he had been shot. His teeth clicked and I thought he was going to speak, or try to speak. But that was the only sound from him. He had stopped breathing. His jaw fell slack. Then the rattle started. It isn't a rattle at all, of course. It isn't anything like a rattle.

Rubber heels squeaked on the linoleum between the rug and the door sill. The white fingers slid away from the door frame. The man's body started to wind up on the legs. The legs refused to hold it. They scissored. His torso turned in midair, like a swimmer in a wave, and jumped at me.

In the same moment his other arm, the one that had been out of sight, came up and over in a galvanic sweep that seemed not to have any possible living impetus behind it. It fell across my left shoulder as I reached for him. A bee stung me between the shoulder blades. Something besides the bottle of alcohol I had been holding thumped to the floor and rattled against the bottom of the wall.

I clamped my teeth hard and spread my feet and caught him under the arms. He weighed like five men. I took a step back and tried to hold him up. It was like trying to lift one end of a fallen tree. I went down with him. His head bumped the floor. I couldn't help it. There wasn't enough of me working to stop it. I straightened him out a bit and got away from him. I climbed up on my knees, and bent down and listened. The rattle stopped. There was a long silence. Then there was a muted sigh, very quiet and indolent and without urgency. Another silence. Another still slower sigh, languid and peaceful as a summer breeze drifting past the nodding roses.

Something happened to his face and behind his face, the indefinable thing that happens in that always baffling and inscrutable moment, the smoothing out, the going back over the years to the age of innocence. The face now had a vague inner amusement, an almost roguish lift at the corners of the mouth. All of which was very silly, because I knew damn well, if I ever knew anything at all, that Orrin P. Quest had not been that kind of boy.

In the distance a siren wailed. I stayed kneeling and listened. It wailed and went away. I got to my feet and went over and looked out of the side window. In front of The Garland Home of Peace another funeral was forming up. The street was thick with cars again. People walked slowly up the path past the tree roses. Very slowly, the men with their hats in their hands long before they reached the little colonial porch.

I dropped the curtain and went over and picked up the bottle of ethyl alcohol and wiped it off with my handkerchief and laid it aside. I was no longer interested in alcohol. I bent down again and the bee-sting between my shoulder blades reminded me that there was something else to pick up. A thing with a round white wooden handle that lay against the baseboard. An ice pick with a filed-down blade not more than three inches long. I held it against the light and looked at the needle-sharp tip. There might or might not have been a faint stain of my blood on it. I pulled a finger gently beside the point. No blood. The point was very sharp.

I did some more work with my handkerchief and then bent down and put the ice pick on the palm of his right hand, white and waxy against the dull nap of the carpet. It looked too arranged. I shook his arm enough to make it roll off his hand to the floor. I thought about going through his pockets, but a more ruthless hand than mine would have done that already.

In a flash of sudden panic I went through mine instead. Nothing had been taken. Even the Luger under my arm had been left. I dragged it out and sniffed at it. It had not been fired, something I should have known without looking. You don't walk around much after being shot with a Luger.

I stepped over the dark red pool in the doorway and looked along the hall. The house was still silent and waiting. The blood trail led me back and across to a room furnished like a den. There was a studio couch and a desk, some books and medical journals, an ash tray with five fat oval stubs in it. A metallic glitter near the leg of the studio couch turned out to be a used shell from an automatic—.32 caliber. I found another under the desk. I put them in my pocket.

I went back out and up the stairs. There were two bedrooms both in use, one pretty thoroughly stripped of clothes. In an ash tray more of Dr. Lagardie's oval stubs. The other room contained Orrin Quest's meager wardrobe, his spare suit and overcoat neatly hung in the closet, his shirts and socks and underwear equally neat in the drawers of a chest. Under the shirts at the back I found a Leica with an F.2 lens.

I left all these things as they were and went back downstairs into the room where the dead man lay indifferent to these trifles. I wiped off a few more doorknobs out of sheer perverseness, hesitated over the phone in the front room, and left without touching it. The fact that I was still walking around was a pretty good indication that the good Dr. Lagardie hadn't killed anybody.

People were still crawling up the walk to the oddly undersized colonial porch of the funeral parlors across the street. An organ was moaning inside.

I went around the corner of the house and got into my car and left. I drove slowly and breathed deeply from the bottom of my lungs, but I still couldn't seem to get enough oxygen.

Bay City ends about four miles from the ocean. I stopped in front of the last drugstore. It was time for me to make one more of my anonymous phone calls. Come and pick up the body, fellows. Who am I? Just a lucky boy who keeps finding them for you. Modest too. Don't even want my name mentioned.

I looked at the drugstore and in through the plate-glass front. A girl with slanted cheaters was reading at a magazine. She looked something like Orfamay Quest. Something tightened up my throat.

I let the clutch in and drove on. She had a right to know first, law or no law. And I was far outside the law already.

23

I STOPPED at the office door with the key in my hand. Then I went noiselessly along to the other door, the one that was always unlocked, and stood there and listened. She might be in there already, waiting, with her eyes shining behind the slanted cheaters and the small moist mouth willing to be kissed. I would have to tell her a harder thing than she dreamed of, and then after a while she would go and I would never see her again.

I didn't hear anything. I went back and unlocked the other door and picked the mail up and carried it over and dumped it on the desk. Nothing in it made me feel any taller. I left it and crossed to turn the latch in the other door and after a long slow moment I opened it and looked out. Silence and emptiness. A folded piece of paper lay at my feet. It had been pushed under the door. I picked it up and unfolded it.

"Please call me at the apartment house. Most urgent. I must see you." It was signed D.

I dialed the number of the Chateau Bercy and asked

for Miss Gonzales. Who was calling, please? One moment please, Mr. Marlowe. Buzz, buzz. Buzz, buzz.

" 'Allo?"

"The accent's a bit thick this afternoon."

"Ah, it is you, amigo. I waited so long in your funny little office. Can you come over here and talk to me?"

"Impossible. I'm waiting for a call."

"Well, may I come there?"

"What's it all about?"

"Nothing I could discuss on the telephone, amigo."

"Come ahead."

I sat there and waited for the telephone to ring. It didn't ring. I looked out of the window. The crowd was seething on the boulevard, the kitchen of the coffee shop next door was pouring the smell of Blue Plate Specials out of its ventilator shaft. Time passed and I sat there hunched over the desk, my chin in a hand, staring at the mustard-yellow plaster of the end wall, seeing on it the vague figure of a dying man with a short ice pick in his hand, and feeling the sting of its point between my shoulder blades. Wonderful what Hollywood will do to a nobody. It will make a radiant glamour queen out of a drab little wench who ought to be ironing a truck driver's shirts, a he-man hero with shining eyes and brilliant smile reeking of sexual charm out of some overgrown kid who was meant to go to work with a lunchbox. Out of a Texas car hop with the literacy of a character in a comic strip it will make an international courtesan, married six times to six millionaires and so blasé and decadent at the end of it that her idea of a thrill is to seduce a furniture mover in a sweaty undershirt.

And by remote control it might even take a small-town prig like Orrin Quest and make an ice-pick murderer out of him in a matter of months, elevating his simple meanness into the classic sadism of the multiple killer.

It took her a little over ten minutes to get there. I heard

the door open and close and I went through to the waiting room and there she was, the All-American Gardenia. She hit me right between the eyes. Her own were deep and dark and unsmiling.

She was all in black, like the night before, but a tailor-made outfit this time, a wide black straw hat set at a rakish angle, the collar of a white silk shirt folded out over the collar of her jacket, and her throat brown and supple and her mouth as red as a new fire engine.

"I waited a long time," she said. "I have not had any lunch."

"I had mine," I said. "Cyanide. Very satisfying. I've only just stopped looking blue."

"I am not in an amusing mood this morning, amigo."

"You don't have to amuse me," I said. "I amuse myself. I do a brother act that has me rolling in the aisle. Let's go inside."

We went into my private thinking parlor and sat down.

"You always wear black?" I asked.

"But yes. It is more exciting when I take my clothes off."

"Do you have to talk like a whore?"

"You do not know much about whores, amigo. They are always most respectable. Except of course the very cheap ones."

"Yeah," I said. "Thanks for telling me. What is the urgent matter we have to talk about? Going to bed with you is not urgent. It can be done any day."

"You are in a nasty mood."

"Okay. I'm in a nasty mood."

She got one of her long brown cigarettes out of her bag and fitted it carefully into the golden tweezers. She waited for me to light it for her. I didn't so she lit it herself with a golden lighter.

She held this doohickey in a black gauntleted glove

and stared at me out of depthless black eyes that had no laughter in them now.

"Would you like to go to bed with me?"

"Most anyone would. But let's leave sex out of it for now."

"I do not draw a very sharp line between business and sex," she said evenly. "And you cannot humiliate me. Sex is a net with which I catch fools. Some of these fools are useful and generous. Occasionally one is dangerous."

She paused thoughtfully.

I said: "If you're waiting for me to say something that lets on I know who a certain party is—okay, I know who he is."

"Can you prove it?"

"Probably not. The cops couldn't."

"The cops," she said contemptuously, "do not always tell all they know. They do not always prove everything they could prove. I suppose you know he was in jail for ten days last February."

"Yes."

"Did it not occur to you as strange that he did not get bail?"

"I don't know what charge they had him on. If it was as a material witness—"

"Do you not think he could get the charge changed to something bailable—if he really wanted to?"

"I haven't thought much about it," I lied. "I don't know the man."

"You have never spoken to him?" she asked idly, a little too idly.

I didn't answer.

She laughed shortly. "Last night, amigo. Outside Mavis Weld's apartment. I was sitting in a car across the street."

"I may have bumped into him accidentally. Was that the guy?"

"You do not fool me at all."

"Okay. Miss Weld was pretty rough with me. I went away sore. Then I meet this ginzo with her doorkey in his hand. I yank it out of his hand and toss it behind some bushes. Then I apologize and go get it for him. He seemed like a nice little guy too."

"Ver-ry nice," she drawled. "He was *my* boy friend also."

I grunted.

"Strange as it may seem I'm not a hell of a lot interested in your love life, Miss Gonzales. I assume it covers a wide field—all the way from Stein to Steelgrave."

"Stein?" she asked softly. "Who is Stein?"

"A Cleveland hot shot that got himself gunned in front of your apartment house last February. He had an apartment there. I thought perhaps you might have met him."

She let out a silvery little laugh. "Amigo, there are men I do not know. Even at the Chateau Bercy."

"Reports say he was gunned two blocks away," I said. "I like it better that it happened right in front. And you were looking out of the window and saw it happen. And saw the killer run away and just under a street light he turned back and the light caught his face and darned if it wasn't old man Steelgrave. You recognized him by his rubber nose and the fact that he was wearing his tall hat with the pigeons on it."

She didn't laugh.

"You like it better that way," she purred.

"We could make more money that way."

"But Steelgrave was in jail," she smiled. "And even if he was not in jail—even if, for example, I happened to be friendly with a certain Dr. Chalmers who was county jail physician at the time and he told me, in an intimate moment, that he had given Steelgrave a pass to go to the dentist—with a guard of course, but the guard was a reasonable man—on the very day Stein was shot—even if this happened to be true, would it not be a very poor way to use the information by blackmailing Steelgrave?"

"I hate to talk big," I said, "but I'm not afraid of Steelgrave—or a dozen like him in one package."

"But I am, amigo. A witness to a gang murder is not in a very safe position in this country. No, we will not blackmail Steelgrave. And we will not say anything about Mr. Stein, whom I may or may not have known. It is enough that Mavis Weld is a close friend of a known gangster and is seen in public with him."

"We'd have to prove he was a known gangster," I said.

"Can we not do that?"

"How?"

She made a disappointed mouth. "But I felt sure that was what you had been doing these last couple of days."

"Why?"

"I have private reasons."

"They mean nothing to me while you keep them private."

She got rid of the brown cigarette stub in my ash tray. I leaned over and squashed it out with the stub of a pencil. She touched my hand lightly with a gauntleted finger. Her smile was the reverse of anesthetic. She leaned back and crossed her legs. The little lights began to dance in her eyes. It was a long time between passes—for her.

"Love is such a dull word," she mused. "It amazes me that the English language so rich in the poetry of love can accept such a feeble word for it. It has no life, no resonance. It suggests to me little girls in ruffled summer dresses, with little pink smiles, and little shy voices, and probably the most unbecoming underwear."

I said nothing. With an effortless change of pace she became businesslike again.

"Mavis will get $75,000 a picture from now on, and eventually $150,000. She has started to climb and nothing will stop her. Except possibly a bad scandal."

"Then somebody ought to tell her who Steelgrave is," I said. "Why don't you? And incidentally, suppose we did have all this proof, what's Steelgrave doing all the time we're putting the bite on Weld?"

"Does he have to know? I hardly think she would tell him. In fact, I hardly think she would go on having anything to do with him. But that would not matter to us—if we had our proof. And if she knew we had it."

Her black gauntleted hand moved towards her black bag, stopped, drummed lightly on the edge of the desk, and so got back to where she could drop it in her lap. She hadn't looked at the bag. I hadn't either.

I stood up. "I might happen to be under some obligation to Miss Weld. Ever think of that?"

She just smiled.

"And if that was so," I said, "don't you think it's about time you got the hell out of my office?"

She put her hands on the arms of her chair and started to get up, still smiling. I scooped the bag before she could change direction. Her eyes filled with glare. She made a spitting sound.

I opened the bag and went through and found a white envelope that looked a little familiar. Out of it I shook the photo at The Dancers, the two pieces fitted together and pasted on another piece of paper.

I closed the bag and tossed it across to her.

She was on her feet now, her lips drawn back over her teeth. She was very silent.

"Interesting," I said and snapped a digit at the glazed surface of the print. "If it's not a fake. Is that Steelgrave?"

The silvery laugh bubbled up again. "You are a ridiculous character, amigo. You really are. I did not know they made such people any more."

"Prewar stock," I said. "We're getting scarcer every day. Where did you get this?"

"From Mavis Weld's purse in Mavis Weld's dressing room. While she was on the set."

"She know?"

"She does not know."

"I wonder where she got it."

"From you."

"Nonsense." I raised my eyebrows a few inches. "Where would *I* get it?"

She reached the gauntleted hand across the desk. Her voice was cold. "Give it back to me, please."

"I'll give it back to Mavis Weld. And I hate to tell you this, Miss Gonzales, but I'd never get anywhere as a blackmailer. I just don't have the engaging personality."

"Give it back to me!" she said sharply. "If you do not—"

She cut herself off. I waited for her to finish. A look of contempt showed on her smooth features.

"Very well," she said. "It is my mistake. I thought you were smart, I can see that you are just another dumb private eye. This shabby little office," she waved a black gloved hand at it, "and the shabby little life that goes on here—they ought to tell me what sort of idiot you are."

"They do," I said.

She turned slowly and walked to the door. I got around the desk and she let me open it for her.

She went out slowly. The way she did it hadn't been learned at business college.

She went on down the hall without looking back. She had a beautiful walk.

The door bumped against the pneumatic doorcloser and very softly clicked shut. It seemed to take a long time to do that. I stood there watching it as if I had never seen it happen before. Then I turned and started back towards my desk and the phone rang.

I picked it up and answered it. It was Christy French. "Marlowe? We'd like to see you down at headquarters."

"Right away?"

"If not sooner," he said and hung up.

I slipped the pasted-together print from under the blotter and went over to put it in the safe with the others. I put my hat on and closed the window. There was nothing to wait for. I looked at the green tip on the sweep hand of my watch. It was a long time until five o'clock. The sweep hand went around and around the dial like a door-to-door salesman. The hands stood at four-ten. You'd think she'd have called up by now. I peeled my coat off and unstrapped the shoulder harness and locked it with the Luger in the desk drawer. The cops don't like you to be wearing a gun in their territory. Even if you have the right to wear one. They like you to come in properly humble, with your hat in your hand, and your voice low and polite, and your eyes full of nothing.

I looked at the watch again. I listened. The building seemed quiet this afternoon. After a while it would be silent and then the madonna of the dark-gray mop would come shuffling along the hall, trying doorknobs.

I put my coat back on and locked the communicating door and switched off the buzzer and let myself out into the hallway. And then the phone rang. I nearly took the door off its hinges getting back to it. It was her voice all right, but it had a tone I had never heard before. A cool balanced tone, not flat or empty or dead, or even childish. Just the voice of a girl I didn't know and yet did know. What was in that voice I knew before she said more than three words.

"I called you up because you told me to," she said. "But you don't have to tell me anything. I went down there."

I was holding the phone with both hands.

"You went down there," I said. "Yes. I heard that. So?"

"I—borrowed a car," she said. "I parked across the street. There were so many cars you would never have noticed me. There's a funeral home there. I wasn't following you. I tried to go after you when you came out but I don't know the streets down there at all. I lost you. So I went back."

"What did you go back for?"

"I don't really know. I thought you looked kind of funny when you came out of the house. Or maybe I just had a feeling. He being my brother and all. So I went back and rang the bell. And nobody answered the door. I thought that was funny too. Maybe I'm psychic or something. All of a sudden I seemed to have to get into that house. And I didn't know how to do it, but I had to."

"That's happened to me," I said, and it was my voice, but somebody had been using my tongue for sandpaper.

"I called the police and told them I had heard shots," she said. "They came and one of them got into the house through a window. And then he let the other one in. And after a while they let me in. And then they wouldn't let me go. I had to tell them all about it, who he was, and that I had lied about the shots, but I was afraid something had happened to Orrin. And I had to tell them about you too."

"That's all right," I said. "I'd have told them myself as soon as I could get a chance to tell *you*."

"It's kind of awkward for you, isn't it?"

"Yes."

"Will they arrest you or something?"

"They could."

"You left him lying there on the floor. Dead. You had to, I guess."

"I had my reasons," I said. "They won't sound too good, but I had them. It made no difference to him."

"Oh you'd have your reasons all right," she said. "You're very smart. You'd always have reasons for things.

Well, I guess you'll have to tell the police your reasons too."

"Not necessarily."

"Oh yes, you will," the voice said, and there was a ring of pleasure in it I couldn't account for. "You certainly will. They'll make you."

"We won't argue about that," I said. "In my business a fellow does what he can to protect a client. Sometimes he goes a little too far. That's what I did. I've put myself where they can hurt me. But not entirely for you."

"You left him lying on the floor, dead," she said. "And I don't care what they do to you. If they put you in prison, I think I would like that. I bet you'll be awfully brave about it."

"Sure," I said. "Always a gay smile. Do you see what he had in his hand?"

"He didn't have anything in his hand."

"Well, lying near his hand."

"There wasn't anything. There wasn't anything at all. What sort of thing?"

"That's fine," I said. "I'm glad of that. Well, goodbye. I'm going down to headquarters now. They want to see me. Good luck, if I don't see you again."

"You'd better keep your good luck," she said. "You might need it. And I wouldn't want it."

"I did my best for you," I said. "Perhaps if you'd given me a little more information in the beginning—"

She hung up while I was saying it.

I put the phone down in its cradle as gently as if it was a baby. I got out a handkerchief and wiped the palms of my hands. I went over to the washbasin and washed my hands and face. I sloshed cold water on my face and dried off hard with the towel and looked at it in the mirror.

"You drove off a cliff all right," I said to the face.

24

IN THE CENTER of the room was a long yellow oak table. Its edges were unevenly grooved with cigarette burns. Behind it was a window with wire over the stippled glass. Also behind it with a mess of papers spread out untidily in front of him was Detective-Lieutenant Fred Beifus. At the end of the table leaning back on two legs of an armchair was a big burly man whose face had for me the vague familiarity of a face previously seen in a halftone on newsprint. He had a jaw like a park bench. He had the butt end of a carpenter's pencil between his teeth. He seemed to be awake and breathing, but apart from that he just sat.

There were two rolltop desks at the other side of the table and there was another window. One of the rolltop desks was backed to the window. A woman with orange-colored hair was typing out a report on a typewriter stand beside the desk. At the other desk, which was endways to the window, Christy French sat in a tilted-back swivel chair with his feet on the corner of the desk. He was looking out of the window, which was open and afforded a magnificent view of the police parking lot and the back of a billboard.

"Sit down there," Beifus said, pointing.

I sat down across from him in a straight oak chair without arms. It was far from new and when new had not been beautiful.

"This is Lieutenant Moses Maglashan of the Bay City police," Beifus said. "He don't like you any better than we do."

Lieutenant Moses Maglashan took the carpenter's pencil out of his mouth and looked at the teeth marks in the fat octagonal pencil butt. Then he looked at me. His eyes went over me slowly exploring me, noting me, cataloguing me. He said nothing. He put the pencil back in his mouth.

Beifus said: "Maybe I'm a queer, but for me you don't have no more sex appeal than a turtle." He half turned to the typing woman in the corner. "Millie."

She swung around from the typewriter to a shorthand notebook. "Name's Philip Marlowe," Beifus said. "With an 'e' on the end, if you're fussy. License number?"

He looked back at me. I told him. The orange queen wrote without looking up. To say she had a face that would have stopped a clock would have been to insult her. It would have stopped a runaway horse.

"Now if you're in the mood," Beifus told me, "you could start in at the beginning and give us all the stuff you left out yesterday. Don't try to sort it out. Just let it flow natural. We got enough stuff to check you as you go along."

"You want me to make a statement?"

"A very full statement," Beifus said. "Fun, huh?"

"This statement is to be voluntary and without coercion?"

"Yeah. They all are." Beifus grinned.

Maglashan looked at me steadily for a moment. The

orange queen turned back to her typing. Nothing for her yet. Thirty years of it had perfected her timing.

Maglashan took a heavy worn pigskin glove out of his pocket and put it on his right hand and flexed his fingers.

"What's that for?" Beifus asked him.

"I bite my nails times," Maglashan said. "Funny. Only bite 'em on my right hand." He raised his slow eyes to stare at me. "Some guys are more voluntary than others," he said idly. "Something to do with the kidneys, they tell me. I've known guys of the not so voluntary type that had to go to the can every fifteen minutes for weeks after they got voluntary. Couldn't seem to hold water."

"Just think of that," Beifus said wonderingly.

"Then there's the guys can't talk above a husky whisper," Maglashan went on. "Like punch-drunk fighters that have stopped too many with their necks."

Maglashan looked at me. It seemed to be my turn.

"Then there's the type that won't go to the can at all," I said. "They try too hard. Sit in a chair like this for thirty hours straight. Then they fall down and rupture a spleen or burst a bladder. They overco-operate. And after sunrise court, when the tank is empty, you find them dead in a dark corner. Maybe they ought to have seen a doctor, but you can't figure everything, can you, Lieutenant?"

"We figure pretty close down in Bay City," he said. "When we got anything to figure with."

There were hard lumps of muscle at the corners of his jaws. His eyes had a reddish glare behind them.

"I could do lovely business with you," he said staring at me. "Just lovely."

"I'm sure you could, Lieutenant. I've always had a swell time in Bay City—while I stayed conscious."

"I'd keep you conscious a long long time, baby. I'd make a point of it. I'd give it my personal attention."

Christy French turned his head slowly and yawned.

"What makes you Bay City cops so tough?" he asked. "You pickle your nuts in salt water or something?"

Beifus put his tongue out so that the tip showed and ran it along his lips.

"We've always been tough," Maglashan said, not looking at him. "We like to be tough. Jokers like this character here keep us tuned up." He turned back to me. "So you're the sweetheart that phoned in about Clausen. You're right handy with a pay phone, ain't you, sweetheart?"

I didn't say anything.

"I'm talking to you, sweetheart," Maglashan said. "I asked you a question, sweetheart. When I ask a question I get answered. Get that, sweetheart?"

"Keep on talking and you'll answer yourself," Christy French said. "And maybe you won't like the answer, and maybe you'll be so damn tough you'll have to knock yourself out with that glove. Just to prove it."

Maglashan straightened up. Red spots the size of half-dollars glowed dully on his cheeks.

"I come up here to get co-operation," he told French slowly. "The big razzoo I can get to home. From my wife. Here I don't expect the wise numbers to work out on me."

"You'll get co-operation," French said. "Just don't try to steal the picture with that nineteen-thirty dialogue." He swung his chair around and looked at me. "Let's take out a clean sheet of paper and play like we're just starting this investigation. I know all your arguments. I'm no judge of them. The point is do you want to talk or get booked as a material witness?"

"Ask the questions," I said. "If you don't like the answers, you can book me. If you book me, I get to make a phone call."

"Correct," French said, *"if* we book you. But we don't have to. We can ride the circuit with you. It might take days."

"And canned cornbeef hash to eat," Beifus put in cheerfully.

"Strictly speaking, it wouldn't be legal," French said. "But we do it all the time. Like you do a few things which you hadn't ought to do maybe. Would you say you were legal in this picture?"

"No."

Maglashan let out a deep throated, "Ha!"

I looked across at the orange queen who was back to her notebook, silent and indifferent.

"You got a client to protect," French said.

"Maybe."

"You mean you did have a client. She ratted on you."

I said nothing.

"Name's Orfamay Quest," French said, watching me.

"Ask your questions," I said.

"What happened down there on Idaho Street?"

"I went there looking for her brother. He'd moved away, she said, and she'd come out here to see him. She was worried. The manager, Clausen, was too drunk to talk sense. I looked at the register and saw another man had moved into Quest's room. I talked to this man. He told me nothing that helped."

French reached around and picked a pencil off the desk and tapped it against his teeth. "Ever see this man again?"

"Yes. I told him who I was. When I went back downstairs Clausen was dead. And somebody had torn a page out of the register. The page with Quest's name on it. I called the police."

"But you didn't stick around?"

"I had no information about Clausen's death."

"But you didn't stick around," French repeated. Maglashan made a savage noise in his throat and threw the carpenter's pencil clear across the room. I watched it bounce against the wall and floor and come to a stop.

"That's correct," I said.

"In Bay City," Maglashan said, "we could murder you for that."

"In Bay City you could murder me for wearing a blue tie," I said.

He started to get up. Beifus looked sideways at him and said: "Leave Christy handle it. There's always a second show."

"We could break you for that," French said to me without inflexion.

"Consider me broke," I said. "I never liked the business anyway."

"So you came back to your office. What then?"

"I reported to the client. Then a guy called me up and asked me over to the Van Nuys Hotel. He was the same guy I had talked to down on Idaho Street, but with a different name."

"You could have told us that, couldn't you?"

"If I had, I'd have had to tell you everything. That would have violated the conditions of my employment."

French nodded and tapped his pencil. He said slowly: "A murder wipes out agreements like that. Two murders ought to do it double. And two murders by the same method, treble. You don't look good, Marlowe. You don't look good at all."

"I don't even look good to the client," I said, "after today."

"What happened today?"

"She told me her brother had called her up from this doctor's house. Dr. Lagardie. The brother was in danger. I was to hurry on down and take care of him. I hurried on down. Dr. Lagardie and his nurse had the office closed. They acted scared. The police had been there." I looked at Maglashan.

"Another of his phone calls," Maglashan snarled.

"Not me this time," I said.

"All right. Go on," French said, after a pause.

"Lagardie denied knowing anything about Orrin Quest. He sent his nurse home. Then he slipped me a doped cigarette and I went away from there for a while. When I came to I was alone in the house. Then I wasn't. Orrin Quest, or what was left of him, was scratching at the door. He fell through it and died as I opened it. With his last ounce of strength he tried to stick me with an ice pick." I moved my shoulders. The place between them was a little stiff and sore, nothing more.

French looked hard at Maglashan. Maglashan shook his head, but French kept on looking at him. Beifus began to whistle under his breath. I couldn't make out the tune at first, and then I could. It was "Old Man Mose is Dead."

French turned his head and said slowly: "No ice pick was found by the body."

"I left it where it fell," I said.

Maglashan said: "Looks like I ought to be putting on my glove again." He stretched it between his fingers. "Somebody's a goddam liar and it ain't me."

"All right," French said. "All right. Let's not be theatrical. Suppose the kid did have an ice pick in his hand, that doesn't prove he was born holding one."

"Filed down," I said. "Short. Three inches from the handle to the tip of the point. That's not the way they come from the hardware store."

"Why would he want to stick you?" Beifus asked with his derisive grin. "You were his pal. You were down there to keep him safe for his sister."

"I was just something between him and the light," I said. "Something that moved and could have been a man and could have been the man that hurt him. He was dying on his feet. I'd never seen him before. If he ever saw me, I didn't know it."

"It could have been a beautiful friendship," Beifus said with a sigh. "Except for the ice pick, of course."

"And the fact that he had it in his hand and tried to stick me with it could mean something."

"For instance what?"

"A man in his condition acts from instinct. He doesn't invent new techniques. He got me between the shoulder blades, a sting, the feeble last effort of a dying man. Maybe it would have been a different place and a much deeper penetration if he had had his health."

Maglashan said: "How much longer we have to barber round with this monkey? You talk to him like he was human. Leave me talk to him my way."

"The captain doesn't like it," French said casually.

"Hell with the captain."

"The captain doesn't like small-town cops saying the hell with him," French said.

Maglashan clamped his teeth tight and the line of his jaw showed white. His eyes narrowed and glistened. He took a deep breath through his nose.

"Thanks for the co-operation," he said and stood up. "I'll be on my way." He rounded the corner of the table and stopped beside me. He put his left hand out and tilted my chin up again.

"See you again, sweetheart. In *my* town."

He lashed me across the face twice with the wrist end of the glove. The buttons stung sharply. I put my hand up and rubbed my lower lip.

French said: "For Chrissake, Maglashan, sit down and let the guy speak his piece. And keep your hands off him."

Maglashan looked back at him and said: "Think you can make me?"

French just shrugged. After a moment Maglashan rubbed his big hand across his mouth and strolled back to his chair. French said:

"Let's have your ideas about all this, Marlowe."

"Among other things Clausen was probably pushing

reefers," I said. "I sniffed marihuana smoke in his apartment. A tough little guy was counting money in the kitchen when I got there. He had a gun and a sharpened rat-tail file, both of which he tried to use on me. I took them away from him and he left. He would be the runner. But Clausen was liquored to a point where you wouldn't want to trust him any more. They don't go for that in the organizations. The runner thought I was a dick. Those people wouldn't want Clausen picked up. He would be too easy to milk. The minute they smelled dick around the house Clausen would be missing."

French looked at Maglashan. "That make any sense to you?"

"It could happen," Maglashan said grudgingly.

French said: "Suppose it was so, what's it got to do with this Orrin Quest?"

"Anybody can smoke reefers," I said. "If you're dull and lonely and depressed and out of a job, they might be very attractive. But when you smoke them you get warped ideas and calloused emotions. And marihuana affects different people different ways. Some it makes very tough and some it just makes never-no-mind. Suppose Quest tried to put the bite on somebody and threatened to go to the police. Quite possibly all three murders are connected with the reefer gang."

"That don't jibe with Quest having a filed-down ice pick," Beifus said.

I said: "According to the lieutenant here he didn't have one. So I must have imagined that. Anyhow, he might just have picked it up. They might be standard equipment around Dr. Lagardie's house. Get anything on him?"

He shook his head. "Not so far."

"He didn't kill me, probably he didn't kill anybody," I said. "Quest told his sister—according to her—that he was working for Dr. Lagardie, but that some gangsters were after him."

"This Lagardie," French said, prodding at his blotter with a pen point, "what do you make of him?"

"He used to practise in Cleveland. Downtown in a large way. He must have had his reasons for hiding out in Bay City."

"Cleveland, huh?" French drawled and looked at a corner of the ceiling. Beifus looked down at his papers. Maglashan said:

"Probably an abortionist. I've had my eye on him for some time."

"Which eye?" Beifus asked him mildly.

Maglashan flushed.

French said: "Probably the one he didn't have on Idaho Street."

Maglashan stood up violently. "You boys think you're so goddam smart it might interest you to know that we're just a small town police force. We got to double in brass once in a while. Just the same I like that reefer angle. It might cut down my work considerable. I'm looking into it right now."

He marched solidly to the door and left. French looked after him. Beifus did the same. When the door closed they looked at each other.

"I betcha they pull that raid again tonight," Beifus said.

French nodded.

Beifus said: "In a flat over a laundry. They'll go down on the beach and pull in three or four vagrants and stash them in the flat and then they'll line them up for the camera boys after they pull the raid."

French said: "You're talking too much, Fred."

Beifus grinned and was silent. French said to me: "If you were guessing, what would you guess they were looking for in that room at the Van Nuys?"

"A claim check for a suitcase full of weed."

"Not bad," French said. "And still guessing where would it have been?"

"I thought about that. When I talked to Hicks down at Bay City he wasn't wearing his muff. A man doesn't around the house. But he was wearing it on the bed at the Van Nuys. Maybe he didn't put it on himself."

French said: "So?"

I said: "Wouldn't be a bad place to stash a claim check."

French said: "You could pin it down with a piece of scotch tape. Quite an idea."

There was a silence. The orange queen went back to her typing. I looked at my nails. They weren't as clean as they might be. After the pause French said slowly:

"Don't think for a minute you're in the clear, Marlowe. Still guessing, how come Dr. Lagardie to mention Cleveland to you?"

"I took the trouble to look him up. A doctor can't change his name if he wants to go on practicing. The ice pick made you think of Weepy Moyer. Weepy Moyer operated in Cleveland. Sunny Moe Stein operated in Cleveland. It's true the ice-pick technique was different, but it was an ice pick. You said yourself the boys might have learned. And always with these gangs there's a doctor somewhere in the background."

"Pretty wild," French said. "Pretty loose connection."

"Would I do myself any good if I tightened it up?"

"Can you?"

"I can try."

French sighed. "The little Quest girl is okay," he said. "I talked to her mother back in Kansas. She really did come out here to look for her brother. And she really did hire you to do it. She gives you a good write-up. Up to a point. She really did suspect her brother was mixed up in something wrong. You make any money on the deal?"

"Not much," I said. "I gave her back the fee. She didn't have much."

"That way you don't have to pay income tax on it," Beifus said.

French said, "Let's break this off. The next move is up to the D.A. And if I know Endicott, it will be a week from Tuesday before he decides how to play it." He made a gesture towards the door.

I stood up. "Will it be all right if I don't leave town?" I asked.

They didn't bother to answer that one.

I just stood there and looked at them. The ice-pick wound between my shoulders had a dry sting, and the flesh around the place was stiff. The side of my face and mouth smarted where Maglashan had sideswiped me with his well-used pigskin glove. I was in the deep water. It was dark and unclear and the taste of the salt was in my mouth.

They just sat there and looked back at me. The orange queen was clacking her typewriter. Cop talk was no more treat to her than legs to a dance director. They had the calm weathered faces of healthy men in hard condition. They had the eyes they always have, cloudy and gray like freezing water. The firm set mouth, the hard little wrinkles at the corners of the eyes, the hard hollow meaningless stare, not quite cruel and a thousand miles from kind. The dull ready-made clothes, worn without style, with a sort of contempt; the look of men who are poor and yet proud of their power, watching always for ways to make it felt, to shove it into you and twist it and grin and watch you squirm, ruthless without malice, cruel and yet not always unkind. What would you expect them to be? Civilization had no meaning for them. All they saw of it was the failures, the dirt, the dregs, the aberrations and the disgust.

"What you standing there for?" Beifus asked sharply. "You want us to give you a great big spitty kiss? No snappy comeback, huh? Too bad." His voice fell away into a dull drone. He frowned and reached a pencil off the desk. With a quick motion of his fingers he snapped it in half and held the two halves out on his palm.

"We're giving you that much break," he said thinly, the smile all gone. "Go on out and square things up. What the hell you think we're turning you loose for? Maglashan bought you a rain check. Use it."

I put my hand up and rubbed my lip. My mouth had too many teeth in it.

Beifus lowered his eyes to the table, picked up a paper and began to read it. Christy French swung around in his chair and put his feet on the desk and stared out of the open window at the parking lot. The orange queen stopped typing. The room was suddenly full of heavy silence, like a fallen cake.

I went on out, parting the silence as if I was pushing my way through water.

25

THE OFFICE was empty again. No leggy brunettes, no little girls with slanted glasses, no neat dark men with gangster's eyes.

I sat down at the desk and watched the light fade. The going-home sounds had died away. Outside the neon signs began to glare at one another across the boulevard. There was something to be done, but I didn't know what. Whatever it was it would be useless. I tidied up my desk, listening to the scrape of a bucket on the tiling of the corridor. I put my papers away in the drawer, straightened the pen stand, got out a duster and wiped off the glass and then the telephone. It was dark and sleek in the fading light. It wouldn't ring tonight. Nobody would call me again. Not now, not this time. Perhaps not ever.

I put the duster away folded with the dust in it, leaned back and just sat, not smoking, not even thinking. I was a blank man. I had no face, no meaning, no personality, hardly a name. I didn't want to eat. I didn't even want a drink. I was the page from yesterday's calendar crumpled at the bottom of the waste basket.

So I pulled the phone towards me and dialed Mavis Weld's number. It rang and rang and rang. Nine times. That's a lot of ringing, Marlowe. I guess there's nobody home. Nobody home to you. I hung up. Who would you like to call now? You got a friend somewhere that might like to hear your voice? No. Nobody.

Let the telephone ring, please. Let there be somebody to call up and plug me into the human race again. Even a cop. Even a Maglashan. Nobody has to like me. I just want to get off this frozen star.

The telephone rang.

"Amigo," her voice said. "There is trouble. Bad trouble. She wants to see you. She likes you. She thinks you are an honest man."

"Where?" I asked. It wasn't really a question, just a sound I made. I sucked on a cold pipe and leaned my head on my hand, brooding at the telephone. It was a voice to talk to anyway.

"You will come?"

"I'd sit up with a sick parrot tonight. Where do I go?"

"I will come for you. I will be before your building in fifteen minutes. It is not easy to get where we go."

"How is it coming back," I asked, "or don't we care?"

But she had already hung up.

Down at the drugstore lunch counter I had time to inhale two cups of coffee and a melted-cheese sandwich with two slivers of ersatz bacon imbedded in it, like dead fish in the silt at the bottom of a drained pool.

I was crazy. I liked it.

26

IT WAS a black Mercury convertible with a light top. The top was up. When I leaned in at the door Dolores Gonzales slid over towards me along the leather seat.

"You drive please, amigo. I do not really ever like to drive."

The light from the drugstore caught her face. She had changed her clothes again, but it was still all black, save for a flame-colored shirt. Slacks and a kind of loose coat like a man's leisure jacket.

I leaned on the door of the car. "Why didn't she call me?"

"She couldn't. She did not have the number and she had very little time."

"Why?"

"It seemed to be while someone was out of the room for just a moment."

"And where is this place she called from?"

"I do not know the name of the street. But I can find the house. That is why I come. Please get into the car and let us hurry."

"Maybe," I said. "And again maybe I am not getting into the car. Old age and arthritis have made me cautious."

"Always the wisecrack," she said. "It is a very strange man."

"Always the wisecrack where possible," I said, "and it is a very ordinary guy with only one head—which has been rather harshly used at times. The times usually started out like this."

"Will you make love to me tonight?" she asked softly.

"That again is an open question. Probably not."

"You would not waste your time. I am not one of these synthetic blondes with a skin you could strike matches on. These ex-laundresses with large bony hands and sharp knees and unsuccessful breasts."

"Just for half an hour," I said, "let's leave the sex to one side. It's great stuff, like chocolate sundaes. But there comes a time you would rather cut your throat. I guess maybe I'd better cut mine."

I went around the car and slid under the wheel and started the motor.

"We go west," she said, "through the Beverly Hills and then farther on."

I let the clutch in and drifted around the corner to go south to Sunset. Dolores got one of her long brown cigarettes out.

"Did you bring a gun?" she asked.

"No. What would I want a gun for?" The inside of my left arm pressed against the Luger in the shoulder harness.

"It is better not perhaps." She fitted the cigarette into the little golden tweezer thing and lit it with the golden lighter. The light flaring in her face seemed to be swallowed up by her depthless black eyes.

I turned west on Sunset and swallowed myself up in three lanes of race-track drivers who were pushing their mounts hard to get nowhere and do nothing.

"What kind of trouble is Miss Weld in?"

"I do not know. She just said that it was trouble and she was much afraid and she needed you."

"You ought to be able to think up a better story than that."

She didn't answer. I stopped for a traffic signal and turned to look at her. She was crying softly in the dark.

"I would not hurt a hair of Mavis Weld's head," she said. "I do not quite expect that you would believe me."

"On the other hand," I said, "maybe the fact that you don't have a story helps."

She started to slide along the seat towards me.

"Keep to your own side of the car," I said. "I've got to drive this heap."

"You do not want my head on your shoulder?"

"Not in this traffic."

I stopped at Fairfax with the green light to let a man make a left turn. Horns blew violently behind. When I started again the car that had been right behind swung out and pulled level and a fat guy in a sweatshirt yelled:

"Aw go get yourself a hammock!"

He went on, cutting in so hard that I had to brake.

"I used to like this town," I said, just to be saying something and not to be thinking too hard. "A long time ago. There were trees along Wilshire Boulevard. Beverly Hills was a country town. Westwood was bare hills and lots offering at eleven hundred dollars and no takers. Hollywood was a bunch of frame houses on the interurban line. Los Angeles was just a big dry sunny place with ugly homes and no style, but goodhearted and peaceful. It had the climate they just yap about now. People used to sleep out on porches. Little groups who thought they were intellectual used to call it the Athens of America. It wasn't that, but it wasn't a neon-lighted slum either."

We crossed La Cienega and went into the curve of the Strip. The Dancers was a blaze of light. The terrace was packed. The parking lot was like ants on a piece of over-ripe fruit.

"Now we get characters like this Steelgrave owning restaurants. We get guys like that fat boy that bawled me out back there. We've got the big money, the sharp shooters, the percentage workers, the fast-dollar boys, the hoodlums out of New York and Chicago and Detroit—and Cleveland. We've got the flash restaurants and night clubs they run, and the hotels and apartment houses they own, and the grifters and con men and female bandits that live in them. The luxury trades, the pansy decorators, the Lesbian dress designers, the riffraff of a big hard-boiled city with no more personality than a paper cup. Out in the fancy suburbs dear old Dad is reading the sports page in front of a picture window, with his shoes off, thinking he is high class because he has a three-car garage. Mom is in front of her princess dresser trying to paint the suitcases out from under her eyes. And Junior is clamped onto the telephone calling up a succession of high school girls that talk pigeon English and carry contraceptives in their make-up kit."

"It is the same in all big cities, amigo."

"Real cities have something else, some individual bony structure under the muck. Los Angeles has Hollywood—and hates it. It ought to consider itself damn lucky. Without Hollywood it would be a mail-order city. Everything in the catalogue you could get better somewhere else."

"You are bitter tonight, amigo."

"I've got a few troubles. The only reason I'm driving this car with you beside me is that I've got so much trouble a little more will seem like icing."

"You have done something wrong?" she asked and came close to me along the seat.

"Well, just collecting a few bodies," I said. "Depends on the point of view. The cops don't like the work done by us amateurs. They have their own service."

"What will they do to you?"

"They might run me out of town and I couldn't care less. Don't push me so hard. I need this arm to shift gears with."

She pulled away in a huff. "I think you are very nasty to get along with," she said. "Turn right at the Lost Canyon Road."

After a while we passed the University. All the lights of the city were on now, a vast carpet of them stretching down the slope to the south and on into the almost infinite distance. A plane droned overhead losing altitude, its two signal lights winking on and off alternately. At Lost Canyon I swung right skirting the big gates that led into Bel-Air. The road began to twist and climb. There were too many cars; the headlights glared angrily down the twisting white concrete. A little breeze blew down over the pass. There was the odor of wild sage, the acrid tang of eucalyptus, and the quiet smell of dust. Windows glowed on the hillside. We passed a big white two storied Monterey house that must have cost $70,000 and had a cut-out illuminated sign in front: "Cairn Terriers."

"The next to the right," Dolores said.

I made the turn. The road got steeper and narrower. There were houses behind walls and masses of shrubbery but you couldn't see anything. Then we came to the fork and there was a police car with a red spotlight parked at it and across the right side of the fork two cars parked at right angles. A torch waved up and down. I slowed the car and stopped level with the police car. Two cops sat in it smoking. They didn't move.

"What goes on?"

"Amigo, I have no idea at all." Her voice had a hushed withdrawn sound. She might have been a little scared. I didn't know what of.

A tall man, the one with the torch, came around the side of the car and poked the flash at me, then lowered it.

"We're not using this road tonight," he said. "Going anywhere in particular?"

I set the brake, reached for a flash which Dolores got out of the glove compartment. I snapped the light on to the tall man. He wore expensive-looking slacks, a sport shirt with initials on the pocket and a polka-dot scarf knotted around his neck. He had horn-rimmed glasses and glossy wavy black hair. He looked as Hollywood as all hell.

I said: "Any explanation—or are you just making law?"

"The law is over there, if you want to talk to them." His voice held a tone of contempt. "We are merely private citizens. We live around here. This is a residential neighborhood. We mean to keep it that way."

A man with a sporting gun came out of the shadows and stood beside the tall man. He held the gun in the crook of his left arm, pointed muzzle down. But he didn't look as if he just had it for ballast.

"That's jake with me," I said. "I didn't have any other plans. We just want to go to a place."

"What place?" the tall man asked coolly.

I turned to Dolores. "What place?"

"It is a white house on the hill, high up," she said.

"And what did you plan to do up there?" the tall man asked.

"The man who lives there is my friend," she said tartly.

He shone the flash in her face for a moment. "You look swell," he said. "But we don't like your friend. We don't like characters that try to run gambling joints in this kind of neighborhood."

"I know nothing about a gambling joint," Dolores told him sharply.

"Neither do the cops," the tall man said. "They don't

even want to find out. What's your friend's name, darling?"

"That is not of your business," Dolores spit at him.

"Go on home and knit socks, darling," the tall man said. He turned to me.

"The road's not in use tonight," he said. "Now you know why."

"Think you can make it stick?" I asked him.

"It will take more than you to change our plans. You ought to see our tax assessments. And those monkeys in the prowl car—and a lot more like them down at the City Hall—just sit on their hands when we ask for the law to be enforced."

I unlatched the car door and swung it open. He stepped back and let me get out. I walked over to the prowl car. The two cops in it were leaning back lazily. Their loudspeaker was turned low, just audibly muttering. One of them was chewing gum rhythmically.

"How's to break up this road block and let the citizens through?" I asked him.

"No orders, buddy. We're just here to keep the peace. Anybody starts anything, we finish it."

"They say there's a gambling house up the line."

"They say," the cop said.

"You don't believe them?"

"I don't even try, buddy," he said, and spat past my shoulder.

"Suppose I have urgent business up there."

He looked at me without expression and yawned.

"Thanks a lot, buddy," I said.

I went back to the Mercury, got my wallet out and handed the tall man a card. He put his flash on it, and said: "Well?"

He snapped the flash off and stood silent. His face began to take form palely in the darkness.

"I'm on business. To me it's important business. Let

me through and perhaps you won't need this block tomorrow."

"You talk large, friend."

"Would I have the kind of money it takes to patronize a private gambling club?"

"*She* might," he flicked an eye at Dolores. "She might have brought you along for protection."

He turned to the shotgun man. "What do you think?"

"Chance it. Just two of them and both sober."

The tall one snapped his flash on again and made a side-sweep with it back and forth. A car motor started. One of the block cars backed around on to the shoulder. I got in and started the Mercury, went on through the gap and watched the block car in the mirror as it took up position again, then cut its high beam lights.

"Is this the only way in and out of here?"

"They think it is, amigo. There is another way, but it is a private road through an estate. We would have had to go around by the valley side."

"We nearly didn't get through," I told her. "This can't be very bad trouble anybody is in."

"I knew you would find a way, amigo."

"Something stinks," I said nastily. "And it isn't wild lilac."

"Such a suspicious man. Do you not even want to kiss me?"

"You ought to have used a little of that back at the road block. That tall guy looked lonely. You could have taken him off in the bushes."

She hit me across the mouth with the back of her hand. "You son of a bitch," she said casually. "The next drive-way on the left, if you please."

We topped a rise and the road ended suddenly in a wide black circle edged with whitewashed stones. Directly ahead was a wire fence with a wide gate in it, and a sign on the gate: Private Road. No Trespassing. The gate was open and a padlock hung from one end of a loose chain on the posts. I turned the car around a white oleander bush and was in the motor yard of a long low white house with a tile roof and a four-car garage in the corner, under a walled balcony. Both the wide garage doors were closed. There was no light in the house. A high moon made a bluish radiance on the white stucco walls. Some of the lower windows were shuttered. Four packing cases full of trash stood in a row at the foot of the steps. There was a big garbage can upended and empty. There were two steel drums with papers in them.

There was no sound from the house, no sign of life. I stopped the Mercury, cut the lights and the motor, and just sat. Dolores moved in the corner. The seat seemed to be shaking. I reached across and touched her. She was shivering.

"What's the matter?"

"Get—get out, please," she said as if her teeth chattered.

"How about you?"

She opened the door on her side and jumped out. I got out my side and left the door hanging open, the keys in the lock. She came around the back of the car and as she got close to me I could almost feel her shaking before she touched me. Then she leaned up against me hard thigh to thigh and breast to breast. Her arms went around my neck.

"I am being very foolish," she said softly. "He will kill me for this—just as he killed Stein. Kiss me."

I kissed her. Her lips were hot and dry. "Is he in there?"

"Yes."

"Who else?"

"Nobody else—except Mavis. He will kill her too."

"Listen—"

"Kiss me again. I have not very long to live, amigo.

When you are the finger for a man like that—you die young."

I pushed her away from me, but gently.

She stepped back and lifted her right hand quickly. There was a gun in it now.

I looked at the gun. There was a dull shine on it from the high moon. She held it level and her hand wasn't shaking now.

"What a friend I would make if I pulled this trigger," she said.

"They'd hear the shot down the road."

She shook her head. "No, there is a little hill between. I do not think they would hear, amigo."

I thought the gun would jump when she pulled the trigger. If I dropped just at the right moment—

I wasn't that good. I didn't say anything. My tongue felt large in my mouth.

She went on slowly, in a soft tired voice: "With Stein it did not matter. I would have killed him myself, gladly. That filth. To die is not much, to kill is not much. But to entice people to their deaths—" She broke off with what might have been a sob. "Amigo, I liked you for some strange reason. I should be far beyond such nonsense. Mavis took him away from me, but I did not want him to kill her. The world is full of men who have enough money."

"He seems like a nice little guy," I said, still watching the hand that held the gun. Not a quiver in it now.

She laughed contemptuously. "Of course he does. That is why he is what he is. You think you are tough, amigo. You are a very soft peach compared with Steelgrave." She lowered the gun and now it was my time to jump. I still wasn't good enough.

"He has killed a dozen men," she said. "With a smile for each one. I have known him for a long time. I knew him in Cleveland."

"With ice picks?" I asked.

"If I give you the gun, will you kill him for me?"

"Would you believe me if I promised?"

"Yes." Somewhere down the hill there was the sound of a car. But it seemed as remote as Mars, as meaningless as the chattering of monkeys in the Brazilian jungle. It had nothing to do with me.

"I'd kill him if I had to," I said licking along my lips.

I was leaning a little, knees bent, all set for a jump again.

"Good night, amigo. I wear black because I am beautiful and wicked—and lost."

She held the gun out to me. I took it. I just stood there holding it. For another silent moment neither of us moved. Then she smiled and tossed her head and jumped into the car. She started the motor and slammed the door shut. She idled the motor down and sat looking out at me. There was a smile on her face now.

"I was pretty good in there, no?" she said softly.

Then the car backed violently with a harsh tearing of the tires on the asphalt paving. The lights jumped on. The car curved away and was gone past the oleander bush. The lights turned left, into the private road. The lights drifted off among trees and the sound faded into the long-drawn whee of tree frogs. Then that stopped and for a moment there was no sound at all. And no light except the tired old moon.

I broke the magazine from the gun. It had seven shells in it. There was another in the breach. Two less than a full load. I sniffed at the muzzle. It had been fired since it was cleaned. Fired twice, perhaps.

I pushed the magazine into place again and held the gun on the flat of my hand. It had a white bone grip. .32 caliber.

Orrin Quest had been shot twice. The two exploded

shells I picked up on the floor of the room were .32 caliber.

And yesterday afternoon, in Room 332 of the Hotel Van Nuys, a blonde girl with a towel in front of her face had pointed a .32-caliber automatic with a white bone grip at me.

You can get too fancy about these things. You can also not get fancy enough.

27

I WALKED on rubber heels across to the garage and tried to open one of the two wide doors. There were no handles, so it must have been operated by a switch. I played a tiny pencil flash on the frame, but no switch looked at me.

I left that and prowled over to the trash barrels. Wooden steps went up to a service entrance. I didn't think the door would be unlocked for my convenience. Under the porch was another door. This was unlocked and gave on darkness and the smell of corded eucalyptus wood. I closed the door behind me and put the little flash on again. In the corner there was another staircase, with a thing like a dumb-waiter beside it. It wasn't dumb enough to let me work it. I started up the steps.

Somewhere remotely something buzzed. I stopped. The buzzing stopped. I started again. The buzzing didn't. I went on up to a door with no knob, set flush. Another gadget.

But I found the switch to this one. It was an oblong movable plate set into the door frame. Too many dusty hands had touched it. I pressed it and the door clicked and fell back off the latch. I pushed it open, with the tenderness of a young intern delivering his first baby.

Inside was a hallway. Through shuttered windows moonlight caught the white corner of a stove and the chromed griddle on top of it. The kitchen was big enough for a dancing class. An open arch led to a butler's pantry tiled to the ceiling. A sink, a huge icebox set into the wall, a lot of electrical stuff for making drinks without trying. You pick your poison, press a button, and four days later you wake up on the rubbing table in a reconditioning parlor.

Beyond the butler's pantry a swing door. Beyond the swing door a dark dining room with an open end to a glassed-in lounge into which the moonlight poured like water through the floodgates of a dam.

A carpeted hall led off somewhere. From another flat arch a flying buttress of a staircase went up into more darkness, but shimmered as it went in what might have been glass brick and stainless steel.

At last I came to what should be the living room. It was curtained and quite dark, but it had the feel of great size. The darkness was heavy in it and my nose twitched at a lingering odor that said somebody had been there not too long ago. I stopped breathing and listened. Tigers could be in the darkness watching me. Or guys with large guns, standing flat-footed, breathing softly with their mouths open. Or nothing and nobody and too much imagination in the wrong place.

I edged back to the wall and felt around for a light switch. There's always a light switch. Everybody has light switches. Usually on the right side as you go in. You go into a dark room and you want light. Okay, you have a light switch in a natural place at a natural height. This room hadn't. This was a different kind of house. They had odd ways of handling doors and lights. The gadget this time might be something fancy like having to sing A above high C, or stepping on a flat button under the carpet, or maybe you just spoke and said: "Let there be light," and a mike picked it up and turned the voice vibration into a low-power electrical impulse and a transformer built that up to enough voltage to throw a silent mercury switch.

I was psychic that night. I was a fellow who wanted company in a dark place and was willing to pay a high price for it. The Luger under my arm and the .32 in my hand made me tough. Two-gun Marlowe, the kid from Cyanide Gulch.

I took the wrinkles out of my lips and said aloud:

"Hello again. Anybody here needing a detective?"

Nothing answered me, not even a stand-in for an echo. The sound of my voice fell on silence like a tired head on a swansdown pillow.

And then amber light began to grow high up behind the cornice that circumnavigated the huge room. It brightened very slowly, as if controlled by a rheostat panel in a theater. Heavy apricot-colored curtains covered the windows.

The walls were apricot too. At the far end was a bar off to one side, a little catty-corner, reaching back into the space by the butler's pantry. There was an alcove with small tables and padded seats. There were floor lamps and soft chairs and love seats and the usual paraphernalia of a living room, and there were long shrouded tables in the middle of the floor space.

The boys back at the road block had something after all. But the joint was dead. The room was empty of life. It was almost empty. Not quite empty.

A blonde in a pale cocoa fur coat stood leaning against the side of a grandfather's chair. Her hands were in the pockets of the coat. Her hair was fluffed out carelessly and her face was not chalk-white because the light was not white.

"Hello again yourself," she said in a dead voice. "I still think you came too late."

"Too late for what?"

I walked towards her, a movement which was always a pleasure. Even then, even in that too silent house.

"You're kind of cute," she said. "I didn't think you were cute. You found a way in. You—" Her voice clicked off and strangled itself in her throat.

"I need a drink," she said after a thick pause. "Or maybe I'll fall down."

"That's a lovely coat," I said. I was up to her now. I reached out and touched it. She didn't move. Her mouth moved in and out, trembling.

"Stone marten," she whispered. "Forty thousand dollars. Rented. For the picture."

"Is this part of the picture?" I gestured around the room.

"This is the picture to end all pictures—for me. I—I do need that drink. If I try to walk—" the clear voice whispered away into nothing. Her eyelids fluttered up and down.

"Go ahead and faint," I said. "I'll catch you on the first bounce."

A smile struggled to arrange her face for smiling. She pressed her lips together, fighting hard to stay on her feet.

"Why did I come too late?" I asked. "Too late for what?"

"Too late to be shot."

"Shucks, I've been looking forward to it all evening. Miss Gonzales brought me."

"I know."

I reached out and touched the fur again. Forty thousand dollars is nice to touch, even rented.

"Dolores will be disappointed as hell," she said, her mouth edged with white.

"No."

"She put you on the spot—just as she did Stein."

"She may have started out to. But she changed her mind."

She laughed. It was a silly pooped-out little laugh like a child trying to be supercilious at a playroom tea party.

"What a way you have with the girls," she whispered. "How the hell do you do it, wonderful? With doped cigarettes? It can't be your clothes or your money or your personality. You don't have any. You're not too young, nor too beautiful. You've seen your best days and—"

Her voice had been coming faster and faster, like a motor with a broken governor. At the end she was chattering. When she stopped a spent sigh drifted along the silence and she caved at the knees and fell straight forward into my arms.

If it was an act it worked perfectly. I might have had guns in all nine pockets and they would have been as much use to me as nine little pink candles on a birthday cake.

But nothing happened. No hard characters peeked at me with automatics in their hands. No Steelgrave smiled at me with the faint dry remote killer's smile. No stealthy footsteps crept up behind me.

She hung in my arms as limp as a wet tea towel and not as heavy as Orrin Quest, being less dead, but heavy enough to make the tendons in my knee joints ache. Her eyes were closed when I pushed her head away from my chest. Her breath was inaudible and she had that bluish look on the parted lips.

I got my right hand under her knees and carried her over to a gold couch and spread her out on it. I straightened up and went along to the bar. There was a telephone on the corner of it but I couldn't find the way through to the bottles. So I had to swing over the top. I got a likely-looking bottle with a blue and silver label and five stars on it. The cork had been loosened. I poured dark and pungent brandy into the wrong kind of glass and went back over the bar top, taking the bottle with me.

She was lying as I had left her, but her eyes were open.

"Can you hold a glass?"

She could, with a little help. She drank the brandy and pressed the edge of the glass hard against her lips as if she wanted to hold them still. I watched her breathe into the glass and cloud it. A slow smile formed itself on her mouth.

"It's cold tonight," she said.

She swung her legs over the edge of the couch and put her feet on the floor.

"More," she said, holding the glass out. I poured into it. "Where's yours?"

"Not drinking. My emotions are being worked on enough without that."

The second drink made her shudder. But the blue look had gone away from her mouth and her lips didn't glare like stop lights and the little etched lines at the corners of her eyes were not in relief any more.

"Who's working on your emotions?"

"Oh, a lot of women that keep throwing their arms around my neck and fainting on me and getting kissed and so forth. Quite a full couple of days for a beat-up gumshoe with no yacht."

"No yacht," she said. "I'd hate that. I was brought up rich."

"Yeah," I said. "You were born with a Cadillac in your mouth. And I could guess where."

Her eyes narrowed. "Could you?"

"Didn't think it was a very tight secret, did you?"

"I—I—" She broke off and made a helpless gesture. "I can't think of any lines tonight."

"It's the technicolor dialogue," I said. "It freezes up on you."

"Aren't we talking like a couple of nuts?"

"We could get sensible. Where's Steelgrave?"

She just looked at me. She held the empty glass out and I took it and put it somewhere or other without taking my eyes off her. Nor she hers off me. It seemed as if a long long minute went by.

"He was here," she said at last, as slowly as if she had to invent the words one at a time. "May I have a cigarette?"

"The old cigarette stall," I said. I got a couple out and put them in my mouth and lit them. I leaned across and tucked one between her ruby lips.

"Nothing's cornier than that," she said. "Except maybe butterfly kisses."

"Sex is a wonderful thing," I said. "When you don't want to answer questions."

She puffed loosely and blinked, then put her hand up to adjust the cigarette. After all these years I can never put a cigarette in a girl's mouth where she wants it.

She gave her head a toss and swung the soft loose hair around her cheeks and watched me to see how hard that hit me. All the whiteness had gone now. Her cheeks were a little flushed. But behind her eyes things watched and waited.

"You're rather nice," she said, when I didn't do anything sensational. "For the kind of guy you are."

I stood that well too.

"But I don't really know what kind of guy you are, do I?" She laughed suddenly and a tear came from nowhere and slid down her cheek. "For all I know you might be nice for any kind of guy." She snatched the cigarette loose and put her hand to her mouth and bit on it. "What's the matter with me? Am I drunk?"

"You're stalling for time," I said. "But I can't make up my mind whether it's to give someone time to get here—or to give somebody time to get far away from here. And again it could just be brandy on top of shock. You're a little girl and you want to cry into your mother's apron."

"Not my mother," she said. "I could get as far crying into a rain barrel."

"Dealt and passed. So where is Steelgrave?"

"You ought to be glad wherever he is. He had to kill you. Or thought he had."

"You wanted me here, didn't you? Were you that fond of him?"

She blew cigarette ash off the back of her hand. A flake of it went into my eye and made me blink.

"I must have been," she said, "once." She put a hand down on her knee and spread the fingers out, studying the nails. She brought her eyes up slowly without moving her head. "It seems like about a thousand years ago I met a nice quiet little guy who knew how to behave in public and didn't shoot his charm around every bistro in town. Yes, I liked him. I liked him a lot."

She put her hand up to her mouth and bit a knuckle. Then she put the same hand into the pocket of the fur coat and brought out a white-handled automatic, the brother of the one I had myself.

"And in the end I liked him with this," she said.

I went over and took it out of her hand. I sniffed the muzzle. Yes. That made two of them fired around.

"Aren't you going to wrap it up in a handkerchief, the way they do in the movies?"

I just dropped it into my other pocket, where it could pick up a few interesting crumbs of tobacco and some seeds that grow only on the southeast slope of the Beverly Hills City Hall. It might amuse a police chemist for a while.

28

I WATCHED HER for a minute, biting at the end of my lip. She watched me. I saw no change of expression. Then I started prowling the room with my eyes. I lifted up the dust cover on one of the long tables. Under it was a roulette layout but no wheel. Under the table was nothing.

"Try that chair with the magnolias on it," she said.

She didn't look towards it so I had to find it myself. Surprising how long it took me. It was a high-backed wing chair, covered in flowered chintz, the kind of chair that a long time ago was intended to keep the draft off while you sat crouched over a fire of cannel coal.

It was turned away from me. I went over there walking softly, in low gear. It almost faced the wall. Even at that it seemed ridiculous that I hadn't spotted him on my way back from the bar. He leaned in the corner of the chair with his head tilted back. His carnation was red and white and looked as fresh as though the flower girl had just pinned it into his lapel. His eyes were half open as such eyes usually are. They stared at a point in the corner of the ceiling. The bullet had gone through the outside pocket of his double-breasted jacket. It had been fired by someone who knew where the heart was.

I touched his cheek and it was still warm. I lifted his hand and let it fall. It was quite limp. It felt like the back of somebody's hand. I reached for the big artery in his neck. No blood moved in him and very little had stained his jacket. I wiped my hands off on my handkerchief and stood for a little longer looking down at his quiet little face. Everything I had done or not done, everything wrong and everything right—all wasted.

I went back and sat down near her and squeezed my kneecaps.

"What did you expect me to do?" she asked. "He killed my brother."

"Your brother was no angel."

"He didn't have to kill him."

"Somebody had to—and quick."

Her eyes widened suddenly.

I said: "Didn't you ever wonder why Steelgrave never went after me and why he let you go to the Van Nuys yesterday instead of going himself? Didn't you ever wonder why a fellow with his resources and experience never tried to get hold of those photographs, no matter what he had to do to get them?"

She didn't answer.

"How long have you known the photographs existed?" I asked.

"Weeks, nearly two months. I got one in the mail a couple of days after—after that time we had lunch together."

"After Stein was killed."

"Yes, of course."

"Did you think Steelgrave had killed Stein?"

"No. Why should I? Until tonight, that is."

"What happened after you got the photo?"

"My brother Orrin called me up and said he had lost his job and was broke. He wanted money. He didn't say anything about the photo. He didn't have to. There was only one time it could have been taken."

"How did he get your number?"

"Telephone? How did you?"

"Bought it."

"Well—" She made a vague movement with her hand. "Why not call the police and get it over with."

"Wait a minute. Then what? More prints of the photo?"

"One every week. I showed them to *him*." She gestured toward the chintzy chair. "He didn't like it. I didn't tell him about Orrin."

"He must have known. His kind find things out."

"I suppose so."

"But not where Orrin was hiding out," I said. "Or he wouldn't have waited this long. *When* did you tell Steelgrave?"

She looked away from me. Her fingers kneaded her arm. "Today," she said in a distant voice.

"Why today?"

Her breath caught in her throat. "Please," she said. "Don't ask me a lot of useless questions. Don't torment me. There's nothing you can do. I thought there was— when I called Dolores. There isn't now."

I said: "All right. There's something you don't seem to understand. Steelgrave knew that whoever was behind that photograph wanted money—a lot of money. He knew that sooner or later the blackmailer would have to show himself. That was what Steelgrave was waiting for. He didn't care anything about the photo itself, except for your sake."

"He certainly proved that," she said wearily.

"In his own way," I said.

Her voice came to me with glacial calm. "He killed my

brother. He told me so himself. The gangster showed through then all right. Funny people you meet in Hollywood, don't you—including me."

"You were fond of him once," I said brutally.

Red spots flared on her cheeks.

"I'm not fond of anybody," she said. "I'm all through being fond of people." She glanced briefly towards the highbacked chair. "I stopped being fond of him last night. He asked me about you, who you were and so on. I told him. I told him that I would have to admit that I was at the Van Nuys Hotel when that man was lying there dead."

"You were going to tell the police that?"

"I was going to tell Julius Oppenheimer. He would know how to handle it."

"If he didn't one of his dogs would," I said.

She didn't smile. I didn't either.

"If Oppenheimer couldn't handle it, I'd be through in pictures," she added without interest. "Now I'm through everywhere else as well."

I got a cigarette out and lit it. I offered her one. She didn't want one. I wasn't in any hurry. Time seemed to have lost its grip on me. And almost everything else. I was flat out.

"You're going too fast for me," I said, after a moment. "You didn't know when you went to the Van Nuys that Steelgrave was Weepy Moyer."

"No."

"Then what did you go there for?"

"To buy back those photographs."

"That doesn't check. The photographs didn't mean anything to you then. They were just you and him having lunch."

She stared at me and winked her eyes tight, then opened them wide. "I'm not going to cry," she said. "I said I didn't *know*. But when he was in jail that time, I had to know there was something about him that he didn't care to have known. I knew he had been in some kind of racket, I guess. But not killing people."

I said: "Uh-huh." I got up and walked around the highbacked chair again. Her eyes traveled slowly to watch me. I leaned over the dead Steelgrave and felt under his arm on the left side. There was a gun there in the holster. I didn't touch it. I went back and sat down opposite her again.

"It's going to cost a lot of money to fix this," I said.

For the first time she smiled. It was a very small smile, but it was a smile. "I don't have a lot of money," she said. "So that's out."

"Oppenheimer has. You're worth millions to him by now."

"He wouldn't chance it. Too many people have their knives into the picture business these days. He'll take his loss and forget it in six months."

"You said you'd go to him."

"I said if I got into a jam and hadn't really done anything, I'd go to him. But I have done something now."

"How about Ballou? You're worth a lot to him too."

"I'm not worth a plugged nickel to anybody. Forget it, Marlowe. You mean well, but I know these people."

"That puts it up to me," I said. "That would be why you sent for me."

"Wonderful," she said. "You fix it, darling. For free." Her voice was brittle and shallow again.

I went and sat beside her on the davenport. I took hold of her arm and pulled her hand out of the fur pocket and took hold of that. It was almost ice cold, in spite of the fur.

She turned her head and looked at me squarely. She shook her head a little. "Believe me, darling, I'm not worth it—even to sleep with."

I turned the hand over and opened the fingers out.

They were stiff and resisted. I opened them out one by one. I smoothed the palm of her hand.

"Tell me why you had the gun with you."

"The gun?"

"Don't take time to think. Just tell me. Did you mean to kill him?"

"Why not, darling? I thought I meant something to him. I guess I'm a little vain. He fooled me. Nobody means anything to the Steelgraves of this world. And nobody means anything to the Mavis Welds of this world any more."

She pulled away from me and smiled thinly. "I oughtn't to have given you that gun. If I killed you I might get clear yet."

I took it out and held it towards her. She took it and stood up quickly. The gun pointed at me. The small tired smile moved her lips again. Her finger was very firm on the trigger.

"Shoot high," I said. "I'm wearing my bullet-proof underwear."

She dropped the gun to her side and for a moment she just stood staring at me. Then she tossed the gun down on the davenport.

"I guess I don't like the script," she said. "I don't like the lines. It just isn't me, if you know what I mean."

She laughed and looked down at the floor. The point of her shoe moved back and forth on the carpeting. "We've had a nice chat, darling. The phone's over there at the end of the bar."

"Thanks, do you remember Dolores's number?"

"Why Dolores?"

When I didn't answer she told me. I went along the room to the corner of the bar and dialed. The same routine as before. Good evening, the Chateau Bercy, who is calling Miss Gonzales please. One moment, please, buzz, buzz, and then a sultry voice saying: "Hello?"

"This is Marlowe. Did you really mean to put me on a spot?"

I could almost hear her breath catch. Not quite. You can't really hear it over the phone. Sometimes you think you can.

"Amigo, but I am glad to hear your voice," she said, "I am so very very glad."

"Did you or didn't you?"

"I—I don't know. I am very sad to think that I might have. I like you very much."

"I'm in a little trouble here."

"Is he—" Long pause. Apartment house phone. Careful. "Is he there?"

"Well—in a way. He is and yet he isn't."

I really did hear her breath this time. A long indrawn sigh that was almost a whistle.

"Who else is there?"

"Nobody. Just me and my homework. I want to ask you something. It is deadly important. Tell me the truth. Where did you get that thing you gave me tonight?"

"Why, from him. He gave it to me."

"When?"

"Early this evening. Why?"

"How early?"

"About six o'clock, I think."

"*Why* did he give it to you?"

"He asked me to keep it. He always carried one."

"Asked you to keep it why?"

"He did not say, amigo. He was a man that did things like that. He did not often explain himself."

"Notice anything unusual about it? About what he gave you?"

"Why—no, I did not."

"Yes, you did. You noticed that it had been fired and that it smelled of burned powder."

"But I did not—"

"Yes, you did. Just like that. You wondered about it. You didn't like to keep it. You didn't keep it. You gave it back to him. You don't like them around anyhow."

There was a long silence. She said at last, "But of course. But why did he want me to have it? I mean, if that was what happened."

"He didn't tell you why. He just tried to ditch a gun on you and you weren't having any. Remember?"

"That is something I have to tell?"

"Sí."

"Will it be safe for me to do that?"

"When did you ever try to be safe?"

She laughed softly. "Amigo, you understand me very well."

"Goodnight," I said.

"One moment, you have not told me what happened."

"I haven't even telephoned you."

I hung up and turned.

Mavis Weld was standing in the middle of the floor watching me.

"You have your car here?" I asked.

"Yes."

"Get going."

"And do what?"

"Just go home. That's all."

"You can't get away with it," she said softly.

"You're my client."

"I can't let you. I killed him. Why should you be dragged into it?"

"Don't stall. And when you leave go the back way. Not the way Dolores brought me."

She stared me straight in the eyes and repeated in a tense voice, "But I killed him."

"I can't hear a word you say."

Her teeth took hold of her lower lip and held it cruelly. She seemed hardly to breathe. She stood rigid. I went

over close to her and touched her cheek with a fingertip.
I pressed it hard and watched the white spot turn red.

"If you want to know my motive," I said, "it has nothing to do with you. I owe it to the johns. I haven't played
clean cards in this game. They know. I know. I'm just
giving them a chance to use the loud pedal."

"As if anyone ever had to give them that," she said,
and turned abruptly and walked away. I watched her
to the arch and waited for her to look back. She went
on through without turning. After a long time I heard a
whirring noise. Then the bump of something heavy—
the garage door going up. A car started a long way off.
It idled down and after another pause the whirring noise
again.

When that stopped the motor faded off into the distance. I heard nothing now. The silence of the house hung
around me in thick loose folds like that fur coat around
the shoulders of Mavis Weld.

I carried the glass and bottle of brandy over to the
bar and climbed over it. I rinsed the glass in a little sink
and set the bottle back on the shelf. I found the trick
catch this time and swung the door open at the end
opposite the telephone. I went back to Steelgrave.

I took out the gun Dolores had given me and wiped
it off and put his small limp hand around the butt, held
it there and let go. The gun thudded to the carpet. The
position looked natural. I wasn't thinking about fingerprints. He would have learned long ago not to leave them
on any gun.

That left me with three guns. The weapon in his holster I took out and went and put it on the bar shelf under
the counter, wrapped in a towel. The Luger I didn't
touch. The other white-handled automatic was left. I
tried to decide about how far away from him it had
been fired. Beyond scorching distance, but probably very
close beyond. I stood about three feet from him and

fired two shots past him. They nicked peacefully into the wall. I dragged the chair around until it faced into the room. I laid the small automatic down on the dust cover of one of the roulette tables. I touched the big muscle in the side of his neck, usually the first to harden. I couldn't tell whether it had begun to set or not. But his skin was colder than it had been.

There was not a hell of a lot of time to play around with.

I went to the telephone and dialed the number of the Los Angeles Police Department. I asked the police operator for Christy French. A voice from homicide came on, said he had gone home and what was it. I said it was a personal call he was expecting. They gave me his phone number at home, reluctantly, not because they cared, but because they hate to give anybody anything any time.

I dialed and a woman answered and screamed his name. He sounded rested and calm.

"This is Marlowe. What were you doing?"

"Reading the funnies to my kid. He ought to be in bed. What's doing?"

"Remember over at the Van Nuys yesterday you said a man could make a friend if he got you something on Weepy Moyer?"

"Yeah."

"I need a friend."

He didn't sound very interested. "What you got on him?"

"I'm assuming it's the same guy. Steelgrave."

"Too much assuming, kid. We had him in the fish-bowl because we thought the same. It didn't pan any gold."

"You got a tip. He set that tip up himself. So the night Stein was squibbed off he would be where you knew."

"You just making this up—or got evidence?" He sounded a little less relaxed.

"If a man got out of jail on a pass from the jail doctor, could you prove that?"

There was a silence. I heard a child's voice complaining and a woman's voice speaking to the child.

"It's happened," French said heavily. "I dunno. That's a tough order to fill. They'd send him under guard. Did he get to the guard?"

"That's my theory."

"Better sleep on it. Anything else?"

"I'm out at Stillwood Heights. In a big house where they were setting up for gambling and the local residents didn't like it."

"Read about it. Steelgrave there?"

"He's here. I'm here alone with him."

Another silence. The kid yelled and I thought I heard a slap. The kid yelled louder. French yelled at somebody.

"Put him on the phone," French said at last.

"You're not bright tonight, Christy. Why would I call *you?*"

"Yeah," he said. "Stupid of me. What's the address there?"

"I don't know. But it's up at the end of Tower Road in Stillwood Heights and the phone number is Halldale 9-5033. I'll be waiting for you."

He repeated the number and said slowly: "This time you wait, huh?"

"It had to come sometime."

The phone clicked and I hung up.

I went back through the house putting on lights as I found them and came out at the back door at the top of the stairs. There was a floodlight for the motor yard. I put that on. I went down the steps and walked along to the oleander bush. The private gate stood open as before. I swung it shut, hooked up the chain and clicked the padlock. I went back, walking slowly, looking up at the moon, sniffing the night air, listening to the tree frogs and the crickets. I went into the house and found the front door and put the light on over that. There was a big parking space in front and a circular lawn with roses. But you had to slide back around the house to the rear to get away.

The place was a dead end except for the driveway through the neighboring grounds. I wondered who lived there. A long way off through trees I could see the lights of a big house. Some Hollywood big shot, probably, some wizard of the slobbery kiss, and the pornographic dissolve.

I went back in and felt the gun I had just fired. It was cold enough. And Mr. Steelgrave was beginning to look as if he meant to stay dead.

No siren. But the sound of a car coming up the hill at last. I went out to meet it, me and my beautiful dream.

29

THEY CAME IN as they should, big, tough and quiet, their eyes flickering with watchfulness and cautious with disbelief.

"Nice place," French said. "Where's the customer?"

"In there," Beifus said, without waiting for me to answer.

They went along the room without haste and stood in front of him looking down solemnly.

"Dead, wouldn't you say?" Beifus remarked, opening up the act.

French leaned down and took the gun that lay on the floor with thumb and finger on the trigger guard. His eyes flicked sideways and he jerked his chin. Beifus took the other white-handled gun by sliding a pencil into the end of the barrel.

"Fingerprints all in the right places, I hope," Beifus said. He sniffed. "Oh yeah, this baby's been working. How's yours, Christy?"

"Fired," French said. He sniffed again. "But not recently." He took a clip flash from his pocket and shone it into the barrel of the black gun. "Hours ago."

"Down at Bay City, in a house on Wyoming Street," I said.

Their heads swung around to me in unison.

"Guessing?" French asked slowly.

"Yes."

He walked over to the covered table and laid the gun down some distance from the other. "Better tag them right away, Fred. They're twins. We'll both sign the tags."

Beifus nodded and rooted around in his pockets. He came up with a couple of tie-on tags. The things cops carry around with them.

French moved back to me. "Let's stop guessing and get to the part you know."

"A girl I know called me this evening and said a client of mine was in danger up here—from him." I pointed with my chin at the dead man in the chair. "This girl rode me up here. We passed the road block. A number of people saw us both. She left me in back of the house and went home."

"Somebody with a name?" French asked.

"Dolores Gonzales, Chateau Bercy Apartments. On Franklin. She's in pictures."

"Oh-ho," Beifus said and rolled his eyes.

"Who's your client? Same one?" French asked.

"No. This is another party altogether."

"She have a name?"

"Not yet."

They stared at me with hard bright faces. French's jaw moved almost with a jerk. Knots of muscles showed at the sides of his jaw bone.

"New rules, huh?" he said softly.

I said, "There has to be some agreement about publicity. The D.A. ought to be willing."

Beifus said, "You don't know the D.A. good, Marlowe. He eats publicity like I eat tender young garden peas."

French said, "We don't give you any undertaking whatsoever."

"She hasn't any name," I said.

"There's a dozen ways we can find out, kid," Beifus said. "Why go into this routine that makes it tough for all of us?"

"No publicity," I said, "unless charges are actually filed."

"You can't get away with it, Marlowe."

"God damn it," I said, "this man killed Orrin Quest. You take that gun downtown and check it against the bullets in Quest. Give me that much at least, before you force me into an impossible position."

"I wouldn't give you the dirty end of a burnt match," French said.

I didn't say anything. He stared at me with cold hate in his eyes. His lips moved slowly and his voice was thick saying, "You here when he got it?"

"No."

"Who was?"

"He was," I said looking across at the dead Steelgrave.

"Who else?"

"I won't lie to you," I said. "And I won't tell you anything I don't want to tell—except on the terms I stated. I don't know who was here when he got it."

"Who was here when you got here?"

I didn't answer. He turned his head slowly and said to Beifus: "Put the cuffs on him. Behind."

Beifus hesitated. Then he took a pair of steel handcuffs out of his left hip pocket and came over to me. "Put your hands behind you," he said in an uncomfortable voice.

I did. He clicked the cuffs on. French walked over slowly and stood in front of me. His eyes were half closed. The skin around them was grayish with fatigue.

"I'm going to make a little speech," he said. "You're not going to like it."

I didn't say anything.

French said: "It's like this with us, baby. We're coppers and everybody hates our guts. And as if we didn't have enough trouble, we have to have you. As if we didn't get pushed around enough by the guys in the corner offices, the City Hall gang, the day chief, the night chief, the Chamber of Commerce, His Honor the Mayor in his paneled office four times as big as the three lousy rooms the whole homicide staff has to work out of. As if we didn't have to handle one hundred and fourteen homicides last year out of three rooms that don't have enough chairs for the whole duty squad to sit down in at once. We spend our lives turning over dirty underwear and sniffing rotten teeth. We go up dark stairways to get a gun punk with a skinful of hop and sometimes we don't get all the way up, and our wives wait dinner that night and all the other nights. We don't come home any more. And nights we do come home, we come home so goddam tired we can't eat or sleep or even read the lies the papers print about us. So we lie awake in the dark in a cheap house on a cheap street and listen to the drunks down the block having fun. And just about the time we drop off the phone rings and we get up and start all over again. Nothing we do is right, not ever. Not once. If we get a confession, we beat it out of the guy, they say, and some shyster calls us Gestapo in court and sneers at us when we muddle our grammar. If we make a mistake they put us back in uniform on Skid Row and we spend the nice cool summer evenings picking drunks out of the gutter and being yelled at by whores and taking knives away from greaseballs in zoot suits. But all that ain't enough to make us entirely happy. We got to have you."

He stopped and drew in his breath. His face glistened a little as if with sweat. He leaned forward from his hips.

"We got to have you," he repeated. "We got to have sharpers with private licenses hiding information and dodging around corners and stirring up dust for us to breathe in. We got to have you suppressing evidence and framing set-ups that wouldn't fool a sick baby. You wouldn't mind me calling you a goddam cheap double-crossing keyhole peeper, would you, baby?"

"You want me to mind?" I asked him.

He straightened up. "I'd love it," he said. "In spades redoubled."

"Some of what you say is true," I said. "Not all. Any private eye wants to play ball with the police. Sometimes it's a little hard to find out who's making the rules of the ball game. Sometimes he doesn't trust the police, and with cause. Sometimes he just gets in a jam without meaning to and has to play his hand out the way it's dealt. He'd usually rather have a new deal. He'd like to keep on earning a living."

"Your license is dead," French said. "As of now. That problem won't bother you any more."

"It's dead when the commission that gave it to me says so. Not before."

Beifus said quietly, "Let's get on with it, Christy. This could wait."

"I'm getting on with it," French said. "My way. This bird hasn't cracked wise yet. I'm waiting for him to crack wise. The bright repartee. Don't tell me you're all out of the quick stuff, Marlowe."

"Just what is it you want me to say?" I asked him.

"Guess," he said.

"You're a man eater tonight," I said. "You want to break me in half. But you want an excuse. And you want me to give it to you?"

"That might help," he said between his teeth.

"What would you have done in my place?" I asked him.

"I couldn't imagine myself getting that low."

He licked at the point of his upper lip. His right hand was hanging loose at his side. He was clenching and unclenching the fingers without knowing it.

"Take it easy, Christy," Beifus said. "Lay off."

French didn't move. Beifus came over and stepped between us. French said, "Get out of there, Fred."

"No."

French doubled his fist and slugged him hard on the point of the jaw. Beifus stumbled back and knocked me out of the way. His knees wobbled. He bent forward and coughed. He shook his head slowly in a bent-over position. After a while he straightened up with a grunt. He turned and looked at me. He grinned.

"It's a new kind of third degree," he said. "The cops beat hell out of each other and the suspect cracks up from the agony of watching."

His hand went up and felt the angle of his jaw. It already showed swelling. His mouth grinned but his eyes were still a little vague. French stood rooted and silent.

Beifus got out a pack of cigarettes and shook one loose and held the pack out to French. French looked at the cigarette, looked at Beifus.

"Seventeen years of it," he said. "Even my wife hates me."

He lifted his open hand and slapped Beifus across the cheek with it lightly. Beifus kept on grinning.

French said: "Was it you I hit, Fred?"

Beifus said: "Nobody hit me, Christy. Nobody that I can remember."

French said: "Take the cuffs off him and take him out to the car. He's under arrest. Cuff him to the rail if you think it's necessary."

"Okay." Beifus went around behind me. The cuffs came loose. "Come along, baby," Beifus said.

I stared hard at French. He looked at me as if I was the wallpaper. His eyes didn't seem to see me at all.

I went out under the archway and out of the house.

30

I NEVER KNEW his name, but he was rather short and thin for a cop, which was what he must have been, partly because he was there, and partly because when he leaned across the table to reach a card I could see the leather underarm holster and the butt end of a police .38.

He didn't speak much, but when he did he had a nice voice, a soft-water voice. And he had a smile that warmed the whole room.

"Wonderful casting," I said, looking at him across the cards.

We were playing double Canfield. Or he was. I was just there, watching him, watching his small and very neat and very clean hands go out across the table and touch a card and lift it delicately and put it somewhere else. When he did this he pursed his lips a little and whistled without tune, a low soft whistle, like a very young engine that is not yet sure of itself.

He smiled and put a red nine on a black ten.

"What do you do in your spare time?" I asked him.

"I play the piano a good deal," he said. "I have a

seven-foot Steinway. Mozart and Bach mostly. I'm a bit
old-fashioned. Most people find it dull stuff. I don't."

"Perfect casting," I said, and put a card somewhere.

"You'd be surprised how difficult some of that Mozart
is," he said. "It sounds so simple when you hear it played
well."

"Who can play it well?" I asked.

"Schnabel."

"Rubinstein?"

He shook his head. "Too heavy. Too emotional. Mozart is just music. No comment needed from the per-
former."

"I bet you get a lot of them in the confession mood,"
I said. "Like the job?"

He moved another card and flexed his fingers lightly.
His nails were bright but short. You could see he was a
man who loved to move his hands, to make little neat in-
conspicuous motions with them, motions without any special meaning, but smooth and flowing and light as swansdown. They gave him a feel of delicate things delicately
done, but not weak. Mozart, all right. I could see that.

It was about five-thirty, and the sky behind the screened
window was getting light. The rolltop desk in the corner
was rolled shut. The room was the same room I had been
in the afternoon before. Down at the end of the table the
square carpenter's pencil was lying where somebody had
picked it up and put it back after Lieutenant Maglashan
of Bay City threw it against the wall. The flat desk at
which Christy French had sat was littered with ash. An
old cigar butt clung to the extreme edge of a glass ash
tray. A moth circled around the overhead light on a drop
cord that had one of those green and white glass
shades they still have in country hotels.

"Tired?" he asked.

"Pooped."

"You oughtn't to get yourself involved in these elaborate messes. No point in it that I can see."

"No point in shooting a man?"

He smiled the warm smile. "You never shot anybody."

"What makes you say that?"

"Common sense—and a lot of experience sitting here with people."

"I guess you do like the job," I said.

"It's night work. Gives me the days to practice. I've had it for twelve years now. Seen a lot of funny ones come and go."

He got another ace out, just in time. We were almost blocked.

"Get many confessions?"

"I don't take confessions," he said. "I just establish a mood."

"Why give it all away?"

He leaned back and tapped lightly with the edge of a card on the edge of the table. The smile came again. "I'm not giving anything away. We got you figured long ago."

"Then what are they holding me for?"

He wouldn't answer that. He looked around at the clock on the wall. "I think we could get some food now." He got up and went to the door. He half opened it and spoke softly to someone outside. Then he came back and sat down again and looked at what we had in the way of cards.

"No use," he said. "Three more up and we're blocked. Okay with you to start over?"

"Okay with me if we never started at all. I don't play cards. Chess."

He looked up at me quickly. "Why didn't you say so? I'd rather have played chess too."

"I'd rather drink some hot black coffee as bitter as sin."

"Any minute now. But I won't promise the coffee's what you're used to."

"Hell, I eat anywhere. . . . Well, if I didn't shoot him, who did?"

"Guess that's what is annoying them."

"They ought to be glad to have him shot."

"They probably are," he said. "But they don't like the way it was done."

"Personally I thought it was as neat a job as you could find."

He looked at me in silence. He had the cards between his hands, all in a lump. He smoothed them out and flicked them over on their faces and dealt them rapidly into the two decks. The cards seemed to pour from his hands in a stream, in a blur.

"If you were that fast with a gun," I began.

The stream of cards stopped. Without apparent motion a gun took their place. He held it lightly in his right hand pointed at a distant corner of the room. It went away and the cards started flowing again.

"You're wasted in here," I said. "You ought to be in Las Vegas."

He picked up one of the packs and shuffled it slightly and quickly, cut it, and dealt me a king high flush in spades.

"I'm safer with a Steinway," he said.

The door opened and a uniformed man came in with a tray.

We ate canned cornbeef hash and drank hot but weak coffee. By that time it was full morning.

At eight-fifteen Christy French came in and stood with his hat on the back of his head and dark smudges under his eyes.

I looked from him to the little man across the table. But he wasn't there any more. The cards weren't there either. Nothing was there but a chair pushed in neatly to the table and the dishes we had eaten off gathered on a tray. For a moment I had that creepy feeling.

Then Christy French walked around the table and jerked the chair out and sat down and leaned his chin on his hand. He took his hat off and rumpled his hair. He stared at me with hard morose eyes. I was back in coptown again.

31

"The d.a. wants to see you at nine o'clock," he said. "After that I guess you can go on home. That is, if he doesn't hang a pinch on you. I'm sorry you had to sit up in that chair all night."

"It's all right," I said. "I needed the exercise."

"Yeah, back in the groove again," he said. He stared moodily at the dishes on the tray.

"Got Lagardie?" I asked him.

"No. He's a doctor all right, though." His eyes moved to mine. "He practiced in Cleveland."

I said: "I hate it to be that tidy."

"How do you mean?"

"Young Quest wants to put the bite on Steelgrave. So he just by pure accident runs into the one guy in Bay City that could prove who Steelgrave was. *That's* too tidy."

"Aren't you forgetting something?"

"I'm tired enough to forget my name. What?"

"Me too," French said. *"Somebody* had to tell him who Steelgrave was. When that photo was taken Moe

Stein hadn't been squibbed off. So what good was the photo unless somebody knew who Steelgrave was?"

"I guess Miss Weld knew," I said. "And Quest was her brother."

"You're not making much sense, chum." He grinned a tired grin. "Would she help her brother put the bite on her boy friend and on her too?"

"I give up. Maybe the photo was just a fluke. His other sister—my client that was—said he liked to take candid camera shots. The candider the better. If he'd lived long enough you'd have had him up for mopery."

"For murder," French said indifferently.

"Oh?"

"Maglashan found that ice pick all right. He just wouldn't give out to you."

"There'd have to be more than that."

"There is, but it's a dead issue. Clausen and Mileaway Marston both had records. The kid's dead. His family's respectable. He had an off streak in him and he got in with the wrong people. No point in smearing his family just to prove the police can solve a case."

"That's white of you. How about Steelgrave?"

"That's out of my hands." He started to get up. "When a gangster gets his how long does the investigation last?"

"Just as long as it's front-page stuff," I said. "But there's a question of identity involved here."

"No."

I stared at him. "How do you mean, no?"

"Just no. We're sure." He was on his feet now. He combed his hair with his fingers and rearranged his tie and hat. Out of the corner of his mouth he said in a low voice: "Off the record—we were always sure. We just didn't have a thing on him."

"Thanks," I said, "I'll keep it to myself. How about the guns?"

He stopped and stared down at the table. His eyes

came up to mine rather slowly. "They both belonged to Steelgrave. What's more he had a permit to carry a gun. From the sheriff's office in another county. Don't ask me why. One of them—" he paused and looked up at the wall over my head—"one of them killed Quest. . . . The same gun killed Stein."

"Which one?"

He smiled faintly. "It would be hell if the ballistics man got them mixed up and we didn't know," he said.

He waited for me to say something. I didn't have anything to say. He made a gesture with his hand.

"Well, so long. Nothing personal you know, but I hope the D.A. takes your hide off—in long thin strips."

He turned and went out.

I could have done the same, but I just sat there and stared across the table at the wall, as if I had forgotten how to get up. After a while the door opened and the orange queen came in. She unlocked her rolltop desk and took her hat off of her impossible hair and hung her jacket on a bare hook in the bare wall. She opened the window near her and uncovered her typewriter and put paper in it. Then she looked across at me. "Waiting for somebody?"

"I room here," I said. "Been here all night."

She looked at me steadily for a moment. "You were here yesterday afternoon. I remember."

She turned to her typewriter and her fingers began to fly. From the open window behind her came the growl of cars filling up the parking lot. The sky had a white glare and there was not much smog. It was going to be a hot day.

The telephone rang on the orange queen's desk. She talked into it inaudibly, and hung up. She looked across at me again.

"Mr. Endicott's in his office," she said. "Know the way?"

"I worked there once. Not for him, though. I got fired."

She looked at me with that City Hall look they have. A voice that seemed to come from anywhere but her mouth said:

"Hit him in the face with a wet glove."

I went over near her and stood looking down at the orange hair. There was plenty of gray at the roots.

"Who said that?"

"It's the wall," she said. "It talks. The voices of the dead men who have passed through on the way to hell."

I went out of the room walking softly and shut the door against the closer so that it wouldn't make any noise.

32

YOU GO IN through double swing doors. Inside the double doors there is a combination PBX and information desk at which sits one of those ageless women you see around municipal offices everywhere in the world. They were never young and will never be old. They have no beauty, no charm, no style. They don't have to please anybody. They are safe. They are civil without ever quite being polite and intelligent and knowledgeable without any real interest in anything. They are what human beings turn into when they trade life for existence and ambition for security.

Beyond this desk there is a row of glassed-in cubicles stretching along one side of a very long room. On the other side is the waiting room, a row of hard chairs all facing one way, towards the cubicles.

About half of the chairs were filled with people waiting and the look of long waiting on their faces and the expectation of still longer waiting to come. Most of them were shabby. One was from the jail, in denim, with a guard. A white-faced kid built like a tackle, with sick, empty eyes.

At the back of the line of cubicles a door was lettered SEWELL ENDICOTT DISTRICT ATTORNEY. I knocked and went on into a big airy corner room. A nice enough room, old-fashioned with padded black leather chairs and pictures of former D.A.'s and governors on the walls. Breeze fluttered the net curtains at four windows. A fan on a high shelf purred and swung slowly in a languid arc.

Sewell Endicott sat behind a flat dark desk and watched me come. He pointed to a chair across from him. I sat down. He was tall, thin and dark with loose black hair and long delicate fingers.

"You're Marlowe?" he said in a voice that had a touch of the soft South.

I didn't think he really needed an answer to that. I just waited.

"You're in a bad spot, Marlowe. You don't look good at all. You've been caught suppressing evidence helpful to the solution of a murder. That is obstructing justice. You could go up for it."

"Suppressing what evidence?" I asked.

He picked a photo off his desk and frowned at it. I looked across at the other two people in the room. They sat in chairs side by side. One of them was Mavis Weld. She wore the dark glasses with the wide white bows. I couldn't see her eyes, but I thought she was looking at me. She didn't smile. She sat very still.

By her side sat a man in an angelic pale-gray flannel suit with a carnation the size of a dahlia in his lapel. He was smoking a monogrammed cigarette and flicking the ashes on the floor, ignoring the smoking stand at his elbow. I knew him by pictures I had seen in the papers. Lee Farrell, one of the hottest trouble-shooting lawyers in the country. His hair was white but his eyes were bright and young. He had a deep outdoor tan. He looked as if it would cost a thousand dollars to shake hands with him.

Endicott leaned back and tapped the arm of his chair with his long fingers. He turned with polite deference to Mavis Weld.

"And how well did you know Steelgrave, Miss Weld?"

"Intimately. He was very charming in some ways. I can hardly believe—" She broke off and shrugged.

"And you are prepared to take the stand and swear as to the time and place when this photograph was taken?" He turned the photograph over and showed it to her.

Farrell said indifferently, "Just a moment. Is that the evidence Mr. Marlowe is supposed to have suppressed?"

"I ask the questions," Endicott said sharply.

Farrell smiled. "Well, in case the answer is yes, that photo isn't evidence of anything."

Endicott said softly: "Will you answer my question, Miss Weld?"

She said quietly and easily: "No, Mr. Endicott, I couldn't swear when that picture was taken or where. I didn't know it was being taken."

"All you have to do is look at it," Endicott suggested.

"And all I know is what I get from looking at it," she told him.

I grinned. Farrell looked at me with a twinkle. Endicott caught the grin out of the corner of his eye. "Something you find amusing?" he snapped at me.

"I've been up all night. My face keeps slipping," I said.

He gave me a stern look and turned to Mavis Weld again.

"Will you amplify that, Miss Weld?"

"I've had a lot of photos taken of me, Mr. Endicott. In a lot of different places and with a lot of different people. I have had lunch and dinner at The Dancers with Mr. Steelgrave and with various other men. I don't know what you want me to say."

Farrell put in smoothly, "If I understand your point, you would like Miss Weld to be your witness to connect this photo up. In what kind of proceeding?"

"That's my business," Endicott said shortly. "Somebody shot Steelgrave to death last night. It could have been a woman. It could even have been Miss Weld. I'm sorry to say that, but it seems to be in the cards."

Mavis Weld looked down at her hands. She twisted a white glove between her fingers.

"Well, let's assume a proceeding," Farrell said. "One in which that photo is part of your evidence—if you can get it in. But you can't get it in. Miss Weld won't get it in for you. All she knows about the photo is what she sees by looking at it. What anybody can see. You'd have to connect it up with a witness who could swear as to when, how and where it was taken. Otherwise I'd object—if I happened to be on the other side. I could even introduce experts to swear the photo was faked."

"I'm sure you could," Endicott said dryly. "The only man who could connect it up for you is the man who took it," Farrell went on without haste or heat. "I understand he's dead. I suspect that was why he was killed."

Endicott said: "This photo is clear evidence of itself that at a certain time and place Steelgrave was not in jail and therefore had no alibi for the killing of Stein."

Farrell said: "It's evidence when and if you get it introduced in evidence, Endicott. For Pete's sake, I'm not trying to tell you the law. You know it. Forget that picture. It proves nothing whatsoever. No paper would dare print it. No judge would admit it in evidence, because no competent witness can connect it up. And if that's the evidence Marlowe suppressed, then he didn't in a legal sense suppress evidence at all."

"I wasn't thinking of trying Steelgrave for murder,"

Endicott said dryly. "But I *am* a little interested in who killed him. The police department, fantastically enough, also has an interest in that. I hope our interest doesn't offend you."

Farrell said: "Nothing offends me. That's why I'm where I am. Are you sure Steelgrave was murdered?"

Endicott just stared at him. Farrell said easily: "I understand two guns were found, both the property of Steelgrave."

"Who told you?" Endicott asked sharply. He leaned forward frowning.

Farrell dropped his cigarette into the smoking stand and shrugged. "Hell, these things come out. One of these guns had killed Quest and also Stein. The other had killed Steelgrave. Fired at close quarters too. I admit those boys don't as a rule take that way out. But it could happen."

Endicott said gravely: "No doubt. Thanks for the suggestion. It happens to be wrong."

Farrell smiled a little and was silent. Endicott turned slowly to Mavis Weld.

"Miss Weld, this office—or the present incumbent of it at least—doesn't believe in seeking publicity at the expense of people to whom a certain kind of publicity might be fatal. It is my duty to determine whether anyone should be brought to trial for any of these murders, and to prosecute them, if the evidence warrants it. It is not my duty to ruin your career by exploiting the fact that you had the bad luck or bad judgment to be the friend of a man who, although never convicted or even indicted for any crime, was undoubtedly a member of a criminal mob at one time. I don't think you have been quite candid with me about this photograph, but I won't press the matter now. There is not much point in my asking you whether you shot Steelgrave. But I do ask you whether you have any knowledge that would point to who may have or might have killed him."

Farrell said quickly: "Knowledge, Miss Weld—not mere suspicion."

She faced Endicott squarely. "No."

He stood up and bowed. "That will be all for now then. Thanks for coming in."

Farrell and Mavis Weld stood up. I didn't move. Farrell said: "Are you calling a press conference?"

"I think I'll leave that to you, Mr. Farrell. You have always been very skillful in handling the press."

Farrell nodded and went to open the door. They went out. She didn't seem to look at me when she went out, but something touched the back of my neck lightly. Probably accidental. Her sleeve.

Endicott watched the door close. He looked across the desk at me. "Is Farrell representing you? I forgot to ask him."

"I can't afford him. So I'm vulnerable."

He smiled thinly. "I let them take all the tricks and then salve my dignity by working out on you, eh?"

"I couldn't stop you."

"You're not exactly proud of the way you have handled things, are you, Marlowe?"

"I got off on the wrong foot. After that I just had to take my lumps."

"Don't you think you owe a certain obligation to the law?"

"I would—if the law was like you."

He ran his long pale fingers through his tousled black hair.

"I could make a lot of answers to that," he said. They'd all sound about the same. The citizen is the law. In this country we haven't got around to understanding that. We think of the law as an enemy. We're a nation of cop-haters."

"It'll take a lot to change that," I said. "On both sides."

He leaned forward and pressed a buzzer. "Yes," he said quietly. "It will. But somebody has to make a beginning. Thanks for coming in."

As I went out a secretary came in at another door with a fat file in her hand.

33

A SHAVE AND a second breakfast made me feel a little less like the box of shavings the cat had had kittens in. I went up to the office and unlocked the door and sniffed in the twice-breathed air and the smell of dust. I opened a window and inhaled the fry-cook smell from the coffee shop next door. I sat down at my desk and felt the grit on it with my fingertips. I filled a pipe and lit it and leaned back and looked around.

"Hello," I said.

I was just talking to the office equipment, the three green filing cases, the threadbare piece of carpet, the customer's chair across from me, and the light fixture in the ceiling with three dead moths in it that had been there for at least six months. I was talking to the pebbled glass panel and the grimy woodwork and the pen set on the desk and the tired, tired telephone. I was talking to the scales on an alligator, the name of the alligator being Marlowe, a private detective in our thriving little community. Not the brainiest guy in the world, but cheap. He started out cheap and he ended cheaper still.

I reached down and put the bottle of Old Forester up on the desk. It was about a third full. Old Forester. Now who gave you that, pal? That's green-label stuff. Out of your class entirely. Must have been a client. I had a client once.

And that got me thinking about her, and maybe I have stronger thoughts than I know. The telephone rang, and the funny little precise voice sounded just as it had the first time she called me up.

"I'm in that telephone booth," she said. "If you're alone, I'm coming up."

"Uh-huh."

"I suppose you're mad at me," she said.

"I'm not mad at anybody. Just tired."

"Oh yes you are," her tight little voice said. "But I'm coming up anyway. I don't care if you *are* mad at me."

She hung up. I took the cork out of the bottle of Old Forester and gave a sniff at it. I shuddered. That settled it. Any time I couldn't smell whiskey without shuddering I was through.

I put the bottle away and got up to unlock the communicating door. Then I heard her tripping along the hall. I'd know those tight little footsteps anywhere. I opened the door and she came up to me and looked at me shyly.

It was all gone. The slanted cheaters, and the new hair-do and the smart little hat and the perfume and the prettied-up touch. The costume jewelry, the rouge, the everything. All gone. She was right back where she started that first morning. Same brown tailor-made, same square bag, same rimless glasses, same prim little narrow-minded smile.

"It's me," she said. "I'm going home."

She followed me into my private thinking parlor and

sat down primly and I sat down just any old way and stared at her.

"Back to Manhattan," I said. "I'm surprised they let you."

"I may have to come back."

"Can you afford it?"

She gave a quick little half-embarrassed laugh. "It won't cost me anything," she said. She reached up and touched the rimless glasses. "These feel all wrong now," she said. "I liked the others. But Dr. Zugsmith wouldn't like them at all." She put her bag on the desk and drew a line along the desk with her fingertip. That was just like the first time too.

"I can't remember whether I gave you back your twenty dollars or not," I said. "We kept passing it back and forth until I lost count."

"Oh, you gave it to me," she said. "Thank you."

"Sure?"

"I never make mistakes about money. Are you all right? Did they hurt you?"

"The police? No. And it was as tough a job as they ever didn't do."

She looked innocently surprised. Then her eyes glowed. "You must be awfully brave," she said.

"Just luck," I said. I picked up a pencil and felt the point. It was a good sharp point, if anybody wanted to write anything. I didn't. I reached across and slipped the pencil through the strap of her bag and pulled it towards me.

"Don't touch my bag," she said quickly and reached for it.

I grinned and drew it out of her reach. "All right. But it's such a cute little bag. It's so like you."

She leaned back. There was a vague worry behind her eyes, but she smiled. "You think I'm cute—Philip? I'm so ordinary."

"I wouldn't say so."

"You wouldn't?"

"Hell no, I think you're one of the most unusual girls I ever met." I swung the bag by its strap and set it down on the corner of the desk. Her eyes fastened on it quickly, but she licked her lip and kept on smiling at me.

"And I bet you've known an awful lot of girls," she said. "Why—" she looked down and did that with her fingertip on the desk again—"why didn't you ever get married?"

I thought of all the ways you answer that. I thought of all the women I had liked that much. No, not all. But some of them.

"I suppose I know the answer," I said. "But it would just sound corny. The ones I'd maybe like to marry— well, I haven't what they need. The others you don't have to marry. You just seduce them—if they don't beat you to it."

She flushed to the roots of her mousy hair.

"You're horrid when you talk like that."

"That goes for some of the nice ones too," I said. "Not what you said. What I said. You wouldn't have been so hard to take yourself."

"Don't talk like that, please!"

"Well, would you?"

She looked down at the desk. "I wish you'd tell me," she said slowly, "what happened to Orrin. I'm all confused."

"I told you he probably went off the rails. The first time you came in. Remember?"

She nodded slowly, still blushing.

"Abnormal sort of home life," I said. "Very inhibited sort of guy and with a very highly developed sense of his own importance. It looked at you out of the picture you gave me. I don't want to go psychological on you, but I

figure he was just the type to go very completely haywire, if he went haywire at all. Then there's that awful
money hunger that runs in your family—all except one."

She smiled at me now. If she thought I meant her,
that was jake with me.

"There's one question I want to ask you," I said. "Was
your father married before?"

She nodded, yes.

"That helps. Leila had another mother. That suits me
fine. Tell me some more. After all I did a lot of work
for you, for a very low fee of no dollars net."

"You got paid," she said sharply. "Well paid. By
Leila. And don't expect me to call her Mavis Weld. I
won't do it."

"You didn't know I was going to get paid."

"Well—" there was a long pause, during which her eyes
went to her bag again—"you did get paid."

"Okay, pass that. Why wouldn't you tell me who she
was?"

"I was ashamed. Mother and I were both ashamed."

"Orrin wasn't. He loved it."

"Orrin?" There was a tidy little silence while she looked
at her bag again. I was beginning to get curious about
that bag. "But he had been out here and I suppose he'd
got used to it."

"Being in pictures isn't that bad, surely."

"It wasn't just that," she said swiftly, and her tooth
came down on the outer edge of her lower lip and something flared in her eyes and very slowly died away. I
just put another match to my pipe. I was too tired to
show emotions, even if I felt any.

"I know. Or anyway I kind of guessed. How did Orrin
find out something about Steelgrave that the cops didn't
know?"

"I—I don't know," she said slowly, picking her way

among her words like a cat on a fence. "Could it have been that doctor?"

"Oh sure," I said, with a big warm smile. "He and Orrin got to be friends somehow. A common interest in sharp tools maybe."

She leaned back in her chair. Her little face was thin and angular now. Her eyes had a watchful look.

"Now you're just being nasty," she said. "Every so often you have to be that way."

"Such a pity," I said. "I'd be a lovable character if I'd let myself alone. Nice bag." I reached for it and pulled it in front of me and snapped it open.

She came up out of her chair and lunged.

"You let my bag alone!"

I looked her straight in the rimless glasses. "You want to go home to Manhattan, Kansas, don't you? Today? You got your ticket and everything?"

She worked her lips and slowly sat down again.

"Okay," I said. "I'm not stopping you. I just wondered how much dough you squeezed out of the deal."

She began to cry. I opened the bag and went through it. Nothing until I came to the zipper pocket at the back. I unzipped and reached in. There was a flat packet of new bills in there. I took them out and riffled them. Ten centuries. All new. All nice. An even thousand dollars. Nice traveling money.

I leaned back and tapped the edge of the packet on my desk. She sat silent now, staring at me with wet eyes. I got a handkerchief out of her bag and tossed it across to her. She dabbed at her eyes. She watched me around the handkerchief. Once in a while she made a nice little appealing sob in her throat.

"Leila gave the money to me," she said softly.

"What size chisel did you use?"

She just opened her mouth and a tear ran down her cheek into it.

"Skip it," I said. I dropped the pack of money back into the bag, snapped the bag shut and pushed it across the desk to her. "I guess you and Orrin belong to that class of people that can convince themselves that everything they do is right. He can blackmail his sister and then when a couple of small-time crooks get wise to his racket and take it away from him, he can sneak up on them and knock them off with an ice pick in the back of the neck. Probably didn't even keep him awake that night. You can do much the same. Leila didn't give you that money. Steelgrave gave it to you. For what?"

"You're filthy," she said. "You're vile. How dare you say such things to me?"

"Who tipped off the law that Dr. Lagardie knew Clausen? Lagardie thought I did. I didn't. So you did. Why? To smoke out your brother who was not cutting you in—because right then he had lost his deck of cards and was hiding out. I'd like to see some of those letters he wrote home. I bet they're meaty. I can see him working at it, watching his sister, trying to get her lined up for his Leica, with the good Doctor Lagardie waiting quietly in the background for his share of the take. What did you hire me for?"

"I didn't know," she said evenly. She wiped her eyes again and put the handkerchief away in the bag and got herself all collected and ready to leave. "Orrin never mentioned any names. I didn't even know Orrin had lost his pictures. But I knew he had taken them and that they were very valuable. I came out to make sure."

"Sure of what?"

"That Orrin treated me right. He could be awfully mean sometimes. He might have kept all the money himself."

"Why did he call you up night before last?"

"He was scared. Dr. Lagardie wasn't pleased with him any more. He didn't have the pictures. Somebody else had them. Orrin didn't know who. But he was scared."

"I had them. I still have," I said. "They're in that safe."

She turned her head very slowly to look at the safe. She ran a fingertip questioningly along her lip. She turned back.

"I don't believe you," she said, and her eyes watched me like a cat watching a mousehole.

"How's to split that grand with me. You get the pictures."

She thought about it. "I could hardly give you all that money for something that doesn't belong to you," she said, and smiled. "Please give them to me. Please, Philip. Leila ought to have them back."

"For how much dough?"

She frowned and looked hurt.

"She's my client now," I said. "But double-crossing her wouldn't be bad business—at the right price."

"I don't believe you have them."

"Okay." I got up and went to the safe. In a moment I was back with the envelope. I poured the prints and the negative out on the desk—my side of the desk. She looked down at them and started to reach.

I picked them up and shuffled them together and held one so that she could look at it. When she reached for it I moved it back.

"But I can't see it so far away," she complained.

"It costs money to get closer."

"I never thought you were a crook," she said with dignity.

I didn't say anything. I relit my pipe.

"I could make you give them to the police," she said.

"You could try."

Suddenly she spoke rapidly. "I couldn't give you this money I have, really I couldn't. We—well mother and

I owe money still on account of father and the house isn't clear and—"

"What did you sell Steelgrave for the grand?"

Her mouth fell open and she looked ugly. She closed her lips and pressed them together. It was a tight hard little face that I was looking at.

"You had one thing to sell," I said. "You knew where Orrin was. To Steelgrave that information was worth a grand. Easy. It's a question of connecting up evidence. You wouldn't understand. Steelgrave went down there and killed him. He paid you the money for the address."

"Leila told him," she said in a faraway voice.

"Leila told me she told him," I said. "If necessary Leila would tell the world she told him. Just as she would tell the world she killed Steelgrave—if that was the only way out. Leila is a sort of free-and-easy Hollywood babe that doesn't have very good morals. But when it comes to bedrock guts—she has what it takes. She's not the ice-pick type. And she's not the blood-money type."

The color flowed away from her face and left her as pale as ice. Her mouth quivered, then tightened up hard into a little knot. She pushed her chair back and leaned forward to get up.

"Blood money," I said quietly. "Your own brother. And you set him up so they could kill him. A thousand dollars blood money. I hope you'll be happy with it."

She stood away from the chair and took a couple of steps backward. Then suddenly she giggled.

"Who could prove it?" she half squealed. "Who's alive to prove it? You? Who are you? A cheap shyster, a nobody." She went off into a shrill peal of laughter. "Why even twenty dollars buys you."

I was still holding the packet of photos. I struck a match and dropped the negative into the ash tray and watched it flare up.

She stopped dead, frozen in a kind of horror. I started to tear the pictures up into strips. I grinned at her.

"A cheap shyster," I said. "Well, what would you expect. I don't have any brothers or sisters to sell out. So I sell out my clients."

She stood rigid and glaring. I finished my tearing-up job and lit the scraps of paper in the tray.

"One thing I regret," I said. "Not seeing your meeting back in Manhattan, Kansas, with dear old Mom. Not seeing the fight over how to split that grand. I bet that would be something to watch."

I poked at the paper with a pencil to keep it burning. She came slowly, step by step, to the desk and her eyes were fixed on the little smoldering heap of torn prints.

"I could tell the police," she whispered. "I could tell them a lot of things. They'd believe me."

"I could tell them who shot Steelgrave," I said. "Because I know who didn't. They might believe *me*."

The small head jerked up. The light glinted on the glasses. There were no eyes behind them.

"Don't worry," I said. "I'm not going to. It wouldn't cost me enough. And it would cost somebody else too much."

The telephone rang and she jumped a foot. I turned and reached for it and put my face against it and said, "Hello."

"Amigo, are you all right?"

There was a sound in the background. I swung around and saw the door click shut. I was alone in the room.

"Are you all right, amigo?"

"I'm tired. I've been up all night. Apart from——"

"Has the little one called you up?"

"The little sister? She was just in here. She's on her way back to Manhattan with the swag."

"The swag?"

"The pocket money she got from Steelgrave for fingering her brother."

There was a silence, then she said gravely, "You cannot know that, amigo."

"Like I know I'm sitting leaning on this desk holding on to this telephone. Like I know I hear your voice. And not quite so certainly, but certainly enough like I know who shot Steelgrave."

"You are somewhat foolish to say that to me, amigo. I am not above reproach. You should not trust me too much."

"I make mistakes, but this won't be one. I've burned all the photographs. I tried to sell them to Orfamay. She wouldn't bid high enough."

"Surely you are making fun, amigo."

"Am I? Who of?"

She tinkled her laugh over the wire. "Would you like to take me to lunch?"

"I might. Are you home?"

"Sí."

"I'll come over in a little while."

"But I shall be delighted."

I hung up.

The play was over. I was sitting in the empty theater. The curtain was down and projected on it dimly I could see the action. But already some of the actors were getting vague and unreal. The little sister above all. In a couple of days I would forget what she looked like. Because in a way she *was* so unreal. I thought of her tripping back to Manhattan, Kansas, and dear old Mom, with that fat little new little thousand dollars in her purse. A few people had been killed so she could get it, but I didn't think that would bother her for long. I thought of her getting down to the office in the morning—what was the man's name? Oh yes. Dr. Zugsmith—and dusting off

his desk before he arrived and arranging the magazines
in the waiting room. She'd have her rimless cheaters on
and a plain dress and her face would be without make-up
and her manners to the patients would be most correct.

"Dr. Zugsmith will see you now, Mrs. Whoosis."

She would hold the door open with a little smile and
Mrs. Whoosis would go in past her and Dr. Zugsmith
would be sitting behind his desk as professional as hell
with a white coat on and his stethoscope hanging around
his neck. A case file would be in front of him and his
note pad and prescription pad would be neatly squared
off. Nothing that Dr. Zugsmith didn't know. You couldn't
fool him. He had it all at his fingertips. When he looked
at a patient he knew the answers to all the questions he
was going to ask just as a matter of form.

When he looked at his receptionist, Miss Orfamay
Quest, he saw a nice quiet young lady, properly dressed
for a doctor's office, no red nails, no loud make-up, nothing to offend the old-fashioned type of customer. An
ideal receptionist, Miss Quest.

Dr. Zugsmith, when he thought about her at all thought
of her with self-satisfaction. He had made her what she
was. She was just what the doctor ordered.

Most probably he hadn't made a pass at her yet. Maybe they don't in those small towns. Ha, ha! I grew up in
one.

I changed position and looked at my watch and got
that bottle of Old Forester up out of the drawer after all.
I sniffed it. It smelled good. I poured myself a good stiff
jolt and held it up against the light.

"Well, Dr. Zugsmith," I said out loud, just as if he was
sitting there on the other side of the desk with a drink in
his hand, "I don't know you very well and you don't
know me at all. Ordinarily I don't believe in giving advice
to strangers, but I've had a short intensive course of Miss
Orfamay Quest and I'm breaking my rule. If ever that

little girl wants anything from you, give it to her quick. Don't stall around or gobble about your income tax and your overhead. Just wrap yourself in a smile and shell out. Don't get involved in any discussions about what belongs to who. Keep the little girl happy, that's the main thing. Good luck to you, Doctor, and don't leave any harpoons lying around the office."

I drank off half of my drink and waited for it to warm me up. When it did that I drank the rest and put the bottle away.

I knocked the cold ashes out of my pipe and refilled it from the leather humidor an admirer had given me for Christmas, the admirer by an odd coincidence having the same name as mine.

When I had the pipe filled I lit it carefully, without haste, and went on out and down the hall, as breezy as a Britisher coming in from a tiger hunt.

34

THE CHATEAU BERCY was old but made over. It had the sort of lobby that asks for plush and india-rubber plants, but gets glass brick, cornice lighting, three-cornered glass tables, and a general air of having been redecorated by a parolee from a nut hatch. Its color scheme was bile green, linseed-poultice brown, sidewalk gray and monkey-bottom blue. It was as restful as a split lip.

The small desk was empty but the mirror behind it could be diaphanous, so I didn't try to sneak up the stairs. I rang a bell and a large soft man oozed out from behind a wall and smiled at me with moist soft lips and bluish-white teeth and unnaturally bright eyes.

"Miss Gonzales," I said. "Name's Marlowe. She's expecting me."

"Why, yes of course," he said, fluttering his hands. "Yes, of course. I'll telephone up at once." He had a voice that fluttered too.

He picked up the telephone and gurgled into it and put it down.

"Yes, Mr. Marlowe. Miss Gonzales says to come right

up. Apartment 412." He giggled. "But I suppose you know."

"I know now," I said. "By the way were you here last February?"

"Last February? Last February? Oh yes, I was here last February." He pronounced it exactly as spelled.

"Remember the night Stein got chilled out front?"

The smile went away from the fat face in a hurry. "Are you a police officer?" His voice was now thin and reedy.

"No. But your pants are unzipped, if you care."

He looked down with horror and zipped them up with hands that almost trembled.

"Why thank you," he said. "Thank you." He leaned across the low desk. "It was not exactly out front," he said. "That is not exactly. It was almost to the next corner."

"Living here, wasn't he?"

"I'd really rather not talk about it. Really I'd rather not talk about it." He paused and ran his pinkie along his lower lip. "Why do you ask?"

"Just to keep you talking. You want to be more careful, bud. I can smell it on your breath."

The pink flowed all over him right down to his neck. "If you suggest I have been drinking—"

"Only tea," I said. "And not from a cup."

I turned away. He was silent. As I reached the elevator I looked back. He stood with his hands flat on the desk and his head strained around to watch me. Even from a distance he seemed to be trembling.

The elevator was self-service. The fourth floor was cool gray, the carpet thick. There was a small bell push beside Apartment 412. It chimed softly inside. The door was swung open instantly. The beautiful deep dark eyes looked at me and the red red mouth smiled at me. Black slacks and the flame-colored shirt, just like last night.

"Amigo," she said softly. She put her arms out. I took

hold of her wrists and brought them together and made her palms touch. I played patacake with her for a moment. The expression in her eyes was languorous and fiery at the same time.

I let go of her wrists, closed the door with my elbow and slid past her. It was like the first time.

"You ought to carry insurance on those," I said touching one. It was real enough. The nipple was as hard as a ruby.

She went into her joyous laugh. I went on in and looked the place over. It was French gray and dusty blue. Not her colors, but very nice. There was a false fireplace with gas logs, and enough chairs and tables and lamps, but not too many. There was a neat little cellarette in the corner.

"You like my little apartment, amigo?"

"Don't say little apartment. That sounds like a whore too."

I didn't look at her. I didn't want to look at her. I sat down on a davenport and rubbed a hand across my forehead.

"Four hours sleep and a couple of drinks," I said. "And I'd be able to talk nonsense to you again. Right now I've barely strength to talk sense. But I've got to."

She came to sit close to me. I shook my head. "Over there. I really do have to talk sense."

She sat down opposite and looked at me with grave dark eyes. "But yes, amigo, whatever you wish. I am your girl—at least I would gladly be your girl."

"Where did you live in Cleveland?"

"In Cleveland?" Her voice was very soft, almost cooing. "Did I say I had lived in Cleveland?"

"You said you knew him there."

She thought back and then nodded. "I was married then, amigo. What is the matter?"

"You did live in Cleveland then?"

"Yes," she said softly.

"You got to know Steelgrave how?"

"It was just that in those days it was fun to know a gangster. A form of inverted snobbery, I suppose. One went to the places where they were said to go and if one was lucky, perhaps some evening—"

"You let him pick you up."

She nodded brightly. "Let us say *I* picked *him* up. He was a very nice little man. Really, he was."

"What about the husband? *Your* husband. Or don't you remember?"

She smiled. "The streets of the world are paved with discarded husbands," she said.

"Isn't it the truth? You find them everywhere. Even in Bay City."

That bought me nothing. She shrugged politely. "I would not doubt it."

"Might even be a graduate of the Sorbonne. Might even be mooning away in a measly small-town practice. Waiting and hoping. That's one coincidence I'd like to eat. It has a touch of poetry."

The polite smile stayed in place on her lovely face.

"We've slipped far apart," I said. "Ever so far. And we got to be pretty clubby there for a while."

I looked down at my fingers. My head ached. I wasn't even forty per cent of what I ought to be. She reached me a crystal cigarette box and I took one. She fitted one for herself into the golden tweezers. She took it from a different box.

"I'd like to try one of yours," I said.

"But Mexican tobacco is so harsh to most people."

"As long as it's tobacco," I said, watching her. I made up my mind. "No, you're right. I wouldn't like it."

"What," she asked carefully, "is the meaning of this by-play?"

"Desk clerk's a muggle-smoker."

She nodded slowly. "I have warned him," she said. "Several times."

"Amigo," I said.

"What?"

"You don't use much Spanish do you? Perhaps you don't know much Spanish. Amigo gets worn to shreds."

"We are not going to be like yesterday afternoon, I hope," she said slowly.

"We're not. The only thing Mexican about you is a few words and a careful way of talking that's supposed to give the impression of a person speaking a language they had to learn. Like saying 'do not' instead of 'don't.' That sort of thing."

She didn't answer. She puffed gently on her cigarette and smiled.

"I'm in bad trouble downtown," I went on. "Apparently Miss Weld had the good sense to tell it to her boss—Julius Oppenheimer—and he came through. Got Lee Farrell for her. I don't think they think she shot Steelgrave. But they think I know who did, and they don't love me any more."

"And do you know, amigo?"

"Told you over the phone I did."

She looked at me steadily for a longish moment. "I was there." Her voice had a dry serious sound for once.

"It was very curious, really. The little girl wanted to see the gambling house. She had never seen anything like that and there had been in the papers—"

"She was staying here—with you?"

"Not in my apartment, amigo. In a room I got for her here."

"No wonder she wouldn't tell me," I said. "But I guess you didn't have time to teach her the business."

She frowned very slightly and made a motion in the air

with the brown cigarette. I watched its smoke write something unreadable in the still air.

"Please. As I was saying she wanted to go to that house. So I called him up and he said to come along. When we got there he was drunk. I have never seen him drunk before. He laughed and put his arm around little Orfamay and told her she had earned her money well. He said he had something for her, then he took from his pocket a billfold wrapped in a cloth of some kind and gave it to her. When she unwrapped it there was a hole in the middle of it and the hole was stained with blood."

"That wasn't nice," I said. "I wouldn't even call it characteristic."

"You did not know him very well."

"True. Go on."

"Little Orfamay took the billfold and stared at it and then stared at him and her white little face was very still. Then she thanked him and opened her bag to put the billfold in it, as I thought—it was all very curious—"

"A scream," I said. "It would have had me gasping on the floor."

"—but instead she took a gun out of her bag. It was a gun he had given Mavis, I think. It was like the one—"

"I know exactly what it was like," I said. "I played with it some."

"She turned around and shot him dead with one shot. It was very dramatic."

She put the brown cigarette back in her mouth and smiled at me. A curious, rather distant smile, as if she was thinking of something far away.

"You made her confess to Mavis Weld," I said.

She nodded.

"Mavis wouldn't have believed *you,* I guess."

"I did not care to risk it."

"It wasn't you gave Orfamay the thousand bucks, was

it, darling? To make her tell? She's a little girl who would go a long way for a thousand bucks."

"I do not care to answer that," she said with dignity.

"No. So last night when you rushed me out there, you already knew he was dead and there wasn't anything to be afraid of and all that act with the gun was just an act."

"I do not like to play God," she said softly. "There was a situation and I knew that somehow or other you would get Mavis out of it. There was no one else who would. Mavis was determined to take the blame."

"I better have a drink," I said. "I'm sunk."

She jumped up and went to the little cellarette. She came back with a couple of huge glasses of Scotch and water. She handed me one and watched me over her glass as I tried it out. It was wonderful. I drank some more. She sank down into her chair again, and reached for the golden tweezers.

"I chased her out," I said, finally. "Mavis, I'm talking about. She told me she had shot him. She had the gun. The twin of the one you gave me. You didn't probably notice that yours had been fired."

"I know very little about guns," she said softly.

"Sure. I counted the shells in it, and assuming it had been full to start with, two had been fired. Quest was killed with two shots from a .32 automatic. Same caliber. I picked up the empty shells in the den down there."

"Down where, amigo?"

It was beginning to grate. Too much amigo, far too much.

"Of course I couldn't know it was the same gun, but it seemed worth trying out. Only confuse things up a little anyhow, and give Mavis that much break. So I switched guns on him, and put his behind the bar. His was a black .38. More like what he would carry, if he carried one at all. Even with a checked grip you can leave prints, but with an ivory grip you're apt to leave a fair set of finger marks on the left side. Steelgrave wouldn't carry that kind of gun."

Her eyes were round and empty and puzzled. "I am afraid I am not following you too well."

"And if he killed a man he would kill him dead, and be sure of it. This guy got up and walked a bit."

A flash of something showed in her eyes and was gone.

"I'd like to say he talked a bit," I went on. "But he didn't. His lungs were full of blood. He died at my feet. Down there."

"But down where? You have not told me where it was that this—"

"Do I have to?"

She sipped from her glass. She smiled. She put the glass down. I said:

"You were present when little Orfamay told him where to go."

"Oh yes, of course." Nice recovery. Fast and clean. But her smile looked a little more tired.

"Only he didn't go," I said.

Her cigarette stopped in midair. That was all. Nothing else. It went on slowly to her lips. She puffed elegantly.

"That's what's been the matter all along," I said. "I just wouldn't buy what was staring me in the face. Steelgrave is Weepy Moyer. That's solid, isn't it?"

"Most certainly. And it can be proved."

"Steelgrave is a reformed character and doing fine. Then this Stein comes out bothering him, wanting to cut in. I'm guessing, but that's about how it would happen. Okay, Stein has to go. Steelgrave doesn't want to kill anybody—and he has never been accused of killing anybody. The Cleveland cops wouldn't come out and get him. No charges pending. No mystery—except that he had been connected with a mob in some capacity. But he has to get rid of Stein. So he gets himself pinched. And then he gets out of jail by bribing the jail doctor, and he kills Stein and goes back into jail at once. When the killing shows up whoever let him out of jail is going to run like hell and destroy any records there might be of his going out. Because the cops will come over and ask questions."

"Very naturally, amigo."

I looked her over for cracks, but there weren't any yet.

"So far so good. But we've got to give this lad credit for a few brains. Why did he let them hold him in jail for ten days? Answer One, to make himself an alibi. Answer Two, because he knew that sooner or later this question of him being Moyer was going to get aired, so why not give them the time and get it over with? That way any time a racket boy gets blown down around here they're not going to keep pulling Steelgrave in and trying to hang the rap on him."

"You like that idea, amigo?"

"Yes. Look at it this way. Why would he have lunch in a public place the very day he was out of the cooler to knock Stein off? And if he did, why would young Quest happen around to snap that picture? Stein hadn't been killed, so the picture wasn't evidence of anything. I like people to be lucky, but that's *too* lucky. Again, even if Steelgrave didn't know his picture had been taken, he knew who Quest was. Must have. Quest had been tapping his sister for eating money since he lost his job, maybe before. Steelgrave had a key to her apartment. He must have known something about this brother of hers. Which simply adds up to the result, that *that* night of all nights Steelgrave would *not* have shot Stein—even if he had planned to."

"It is now for me to ask you who did," she said politely.

"Somebody who knew Stein and could get close to him. Somebody who already knew that photo had been taken, knew who Steelgrave was, knew that Mavis Weld was on the edge of becoming a big star, knew that her association with Steelgrave was dangerous, but would be a thousand times more dangerous if Steelgrave could be framed for the murder of Stein. Knew Quest, because he had been to Mavis Weld's apartment, and had met him there and given him the works, and he was a boy that could be knocked clean out of his mind by that sort of treatment. Knew that those bone-handled .32's were registered to Steelgrave, although he had only bought them to give to a couple of girls, and if he carried a gun himself, it would be one that was not registered and could not be traced to him. Knew—"

"Stop!" Her voice was a sharp stab of sound, but neither frightened nor even angry. "You will stop at once, please! I will not tolerate this another minute. You will now go!"

I stood up. She leaned back and a pulse beat in her throat. She was exquisite, she was dark, she was deadly. And nothing would ever touch her, not even the law.

"Why did you kill Quest?" I asked her.

She stood up and came close to me, smiling again. "For two reasons, amigo. He was more than a little crazy and in the end he would have killed me. And the other reason is that none of this—absolutely none of it—was for money. It was for love."

I started to laugh in her face. I didn't. She was dead serious. It was out of this world.

"No matter how many lovers a woman may have," she said softly, "there is always one she cannot bear to lose to another woman. Steelgrave was the one."

I just stared into her lovely dark eyes. "I believe you," I said at last.

"Kiss me, amigo."

"Good God!"

"I must have men, amigo. But the man I loved is dead. I killed him. That man I would not share."

"You waited a long time."

"I can be patient—as long as there is hope."

"Oh, nuts."

She smiled a free, beautiful and perfectly natural smile. "And you cannot do a damn thing about all this, darling, unless you destroy Mavis Weld utterly and finally."

"Last night she proved she was willing to destroy herself."

"If she was not acting." She looked at me sharply and laughed. "That hurt, did it not? You are in love with her."

I said slowly, "That would be kind of silly. I could sit in the dark with her and hold hands, but for how long? In a little while she will drift off into a haze of glamour and expensive clothes and froth and unreality and muted sex. She won't be a real person any more. Just a voice from a sound track, a face on a screen. I'd want more than that."

I moved towards the door without putting my back to her. I didn't really expect a slug. I thought she liked better having me the way I was—and not being able to do a damn thing about any of it.

I looked back as I opened the door. Slim, dark and lovely and smiling. Reeking with sex. Utterly beyond the moral laws of this or any world I could imagine.

She was one for the book all right. I went out quietly. Very softly her voice came to me as I closed the door.

"Querido—I have liked you very much. It is too bad."

I shut the door.

35

As the elevator opened at the lobby a man stood there waiting for it. He was tall and thin and his hat was pulled low over his eyes. It was a warm day but he wore a thin topcoat with the collar up. He kept his chin low.

"Dr. Lagardie," I said softly.

He glanced at me with no trace of recognition. He moved into the elevator. It started up.

I went across to the desk and banged the bell. The large fat soft man came out and stood with a pained smile on his loose mouth. His eyes were not quite so bright.

"Give me the phone."

He reached down and put it on the desk. I dialed Madison 7911. The voice said: "Police." This was the Emergency Board.

"Chateau Bercy Apartments, Franklin and Girard in Hollywood. A man named Dr. Vincent Lagardie wanted for questioning by homicide, Lieutenants French and Beifus, has just gone up to Apartment 412. This is Philip Marlowe, a private detective."

"Franklin and Girard. Wait there please. Are you armed?"

"Yes."

"Hold him if he tries to leave."

I hung up and wiped my mouth off. The fat softy was leaning against the counter, white around the eyes.

They came fast—but not fast enough. Perhaps I ought to have stopped him. Perhaps I had a hunch what he would do, and deliberately let him do it. Sometimes when I'm low I try to reason it out. But it gets too complicated. The whole damn case was that way. There was never a point where I could do the natural obvious thing without stopping to rack my head dizzy with figuring how it would affect somebody I owed something to.

When they cracked the door he was sitting on the couch holding her pressed against his heart. His eyes were blind and there was bloody foam on his lips. He had bitten through his tongue.

Under her left breast and tight against the flame-colored shirt lay the silver handle of a knife I had seen before. The handle was in the shape of a naked woman. The eyes of Miss Dolores Gonzales were half open and on her lips there was the dim ghost of a provocative smile.

"The Hippocrates smile," the ambulance intern said, and sighed. "On her it looks good."

He glanced across at Dr. Lagardie who saw nothing and heard nothing, if you could judge by his face.

"I guess somebody lost a dream," the intern said. He bent over and closed her eyes.

THE END

About the Author

RAYMOND CHANDLER was born in Chicago, Illinois, on July 23, 1888, but spent most of his boyhood and youth in England, where he attended Dulwich College and later worked as a free-lance journalist for *The Westminster Gazette* and *The Spectator*. During World War I, he served in France with the First Division of the Canadian Expeditionary Force, transferring later to the Royal Flying Corps (R.A.F.). In 1919 he returned to the United States, settling in California, where he eventually became director of a number of independent oil companies. The Depression put an end to his business career, and in 1933, at the age of forty-five, he turned to writing, publishing his first stories in *Black Mask*. His first novel, *The Big Sleep,* was published in 1939. Never a prolific writer, he published only one collection of stories and seven novels in his lifetime. In the last year of his life he was elected president of the Mystery Writers of America. He died in La Jolla, California, on March 26, 1959.